American Angels Tag Up

Jim E. Johnson

DEDICATION

For Wilma, Mellisa, Mom, Dad, and all of those who support my writing eff orts. I would also like to dedicate this novel to the sports entertainers who inspired the characters of Santana Garvin and Tori Blanton; WWE NXT Superstar Santana Garrett, and Impact Wrestling Superstar Tessa Blanchard.

ACKNOWLEDGEMENTS

Local law enforcement inspires us to all be better at what we do. Without their courage and tenacity, none of us who write such works, would not give voice to such events. And I would like to further acknowledge the National Novel Writing Month Contest for your encouragement in giving writers the venue to fi nd and display their voices in literature.

FORWARD

There are times when telling a story through the voice of a character, brings a whole new perspective on life or a certain organization. Authors experiment which is better; then take off and sometimes write an entire series of novels. I experimented with Jason Vaughn in three different series; and with private eye Joseph Hampton.

Now I bring a new voice; that of full time federal agent and part time pro wrestler Victoria Blanton, or Tori for short. Only twenty-one years old, Tori grew up fast in light of the death of her mother Charlene Tolliver Wayne, her step-father Terry, and her twin younger siblings who are never named to protect Tori's well-being.

Not only did she survive this horrific tragedy but endures the harassment of her older siblings connected to the Dixie Mafia: Thaddeus or Tad, Theodore Junior, and sister Tessa. Added to the fact she's estranged from her father, Theodore Blanton Senior; Tori's formidable years met with conflict the moment she entered the Federal Law Enforcement Training Center in Glynco, Georgia.

However, a year passed, and she finds herself allied with the federal task force in Corpus Christi under the command of NCIS SAC Jason Andrew Vaughn. So Tori…take it away!

ONE

Task Force Corpus Christi; the only NCIS-led federal task force in the world…and I'm here. Not bad for a twenty-one-year-old federal agent and part-time professional wrestler. Graduating college in three years was no small task either. But given I'm in a unique situation, you'd try to get through college as quickly as possible too.

I'm Tori Blanton, and I just completed my first year as newly-minted agent for the Naval Criminal Investigative Service or NCIS for short. My long brown hair, brown eyes sort of complement what my mother used to call my button nose. Then again, my five-foot-five build gave me a petite, but muscular look for someone who carried a billed weight of one-hundred twenty-five pounds. But due to lack of bookings and no tryouts for major wrestling brands, I decided to put my energies into making the world safe from criminals, terrorists and not-so-intelligent Marines and sailors.

Oh, that situation I mentioned earlier; I sort of have a less-than-savory reputation for having had a cop for a step-father and a mob-boss for a biological father. Sort of like Fred Dryer's character from the *Hunter* TV series; you know…the mob doesn't trust the guy because he was a cop. And the reverse; the cops not trusting him because of his family ties to the L.A. Mob? There you have it: my life in a nutshell. However, in my case, my father, 'Tough' Teddy Blanton, stayed connected to the Dixie Mafia. He ran illegal gambling and massage parlors for the affluent in the mid-south area between the Carolinas. No wonder the FBI wanted to recruit me for their academy in Quantico. But, like some kids who discovered their parents' connection to organized crime, I did my best to distance myself the moment I found out.

However, when I decided on a fall back career of law enforcement, my two brothers Tad and Junior; as well as my older sister Tessa, decided I didn't need a stable father figure in step-dad Terry Wayne or my mother Charlene. I couldn't ever prove my siblings killed them, but it forever changed our family dynamic. No more holidays with the Blanton family; I looked into changing my name permanently after that.

After I received my parking permit for NAS Corpus Christi, I drove my navy Ford Fusion sedan over to the NCIS Regional Agency Office on the station. I must remember to properly thank Lance Corporal Daniel Motts before I leave today. *Such a hunky-looking Marine.* Some men in uniform always caught my attention, especially when they sport sky-blue eyes. Oh my lord was he ever handsome.

I parked outside the building connected to a boat launch and walked inside. The lobby had a gift shop as well as a coffee bar for hungry or less than alive agents. As I push the button next to the silver metallic elevator doors, an older and more distinguished agent appeared next to me. I noticed his dark gray pin-stripe suit with the light pink dress shirt and wine-colored tie. He definitely wore summer tones well. He was three inches taller and had a nice medium muscular build.

"First day?" The question hit me like a blast of cold air.

I turned slightly, "Yes, it is."

When he turned to face me, I became lost in his green eyes. Unfortunately, I recovered quickly due to the gold wedding band on his left hand. He smiled and chuckled a little. "You'll do for a newbie. I can't really call you a 'probie' since that's only reserved for agents who've been on the job a year or less. You definitely carry yourself well for someone under the age of twenty-five."

Wait, how did this guy know I was under the age of twenty-five? "Do I give off some…youthful, inexperienced vibe Agent…?"

"Vaughn, Jason Vaughn; I'm pleased to be acquainted with you Agent Blanton." He stuck out his hand and I shook it on instinct. *Oh my god, oh my god, oh my god…he's my BOSS!* "Is it okay if I call you Tori when you're not seated in the squad room?"

"Of course sir." *Oh lord, I sounded like a cheerleader with a crush on the quarterback!* "What I mean is sir; it's perfectly fine to call me by my first name away from the usual crowds around here."

"Good to know; it'll help as far as you getting settled around here. We usually try to keep it light and humorous for the most part." I felt him distance himself in thought and speech for a moment. "Sorry Tori, most of my key agents are married to someone in local law enforcement or serving as a liaison from another agency. Both NCIS Agent Coltrane and FBI Liaison Coltrane retired two months ago and I've attempted to fill those positions. Also, I've asked my wife over at Corpus Christi PD to recommend a liaison from her department."

"As in Corpus Christi Police Chief Jennifer Vaughn?" He gave me one of those *well-done* looks of surprise. Usually, I never impress a new boss like that.

"You've done your homework Agent Blanton; why so surprised to meet me here?"

"Sir, your file photo was deleted from the NCIS server in Naples."

He nodded. "Asst. Dir. Vale my old friend; you hid me from my new agent...rascal!" Apparently, NCIS Assistant Director Leo Vale was an older friend of my new boss than a boss with NCIS. "Vale's worried due to our growing reputation for getting things done, he felt the less conspicuous his top leaders under him were, the safer our teams and families would be at this point. Then again, ever since our last case in Chicago, he's been a little fidgety."

"Is that normal for Asst. Dir. Vale sir?" Again with the sir. Why can't I relax around this guy? But I remember: my training agent was an old, crotchety cuss named Jerry Garner. I'd call him sir and he'd yell, "*I work for a living Blanton; don't sir me!*" However, I heard Vaughn was a naval officer prior to joining NCIS.

"Not normally; I believe Leo's thinking retirement. I've been contemplating it myself. But I promise until you get your sea legs under you here, I'm not going anywhere." I admire confidence in a boss; except for Garner. He was the epitome of a pain in the ass. "Tori, how are you considering how your last case went in Malta?"

Ouch, he had to lead the conversation with...that. The Interpol task-force I worked with almost lost every single agent, me included. The Sicilian Mafia brats who almost killed me received confirmation from a source within the FBI. We were on our way to make arrests in a smuggling ring. Our location; the Isle of Malta. My partner from the DEA, Santana

Garvin, learned an FBI agent named Rhonda Bass, let our arrival time slip to protect one of her other cases. If I ever come across that hussy, she and I will have words! "I'm better. Still dealing with nightmares of those guys beating me like a piñata, but I'm getting better."

"No sexual assault?"

"They tried, but the SEAL team arrived just as they tried to rip my bra and panties off. The big bruisers realized I was quite handy with a field knife."

Vaughn gave an appropriate *Ah* as he looked at me with a sly grin. "The bloody rose tattoos you left on each of the hoods as they slowly died of asphyxiation. Cracks in the C-3, C-4 vertebrae?"

"Yes, not full enough to cause instant death, but enough to torture the brain stem into thinking you'll remain alive…until you suddenly aren't." And old Marine neighbor of my stepdad's taught me that maneuver. The mistake the Sicilian hoods made; they didn't tie me up. Those morons held me in place trying to rape and kill me.

When SEAL Team Two landed, the distraction allowed me to quickly break each of the three necks and since I was in a dungeon of sorts, I took a sadistic pleasure in carving a bloody rose over each of their hearts. The mob would come to call me *Rosa del Diavolo*–the Devil's Rose. I did something no woman had ever done; scared the holy hell out of the Sicilian Mafia. Vaughn resumed our discussion, "It's an effective tool, but I'd prefer you shoot your targets rather than get into a hand-to-hand situation, Blanton. You start to get a bloodthirsty, savage rep and NCIS wouldn't keep you. Hell, they're still trying to get me to retire or move off!"

"Just because of a little fourteen-day vacation in the desert with a Republican Guard colonel and lots of torture and a final desire to return to action?" Again with the pleasant surprise on Vaughn's face. Yes, anyone who has heard of Jason Vaughn's exploits as a Navy SEAL knows of his fourteen-day ordeal and the manner of his escape. Those events helped shape his career as a federal agent.

"I haven't even known you what, five minutes? And I already like you, Blanton." I just hope my casework impressed him as much as my homework. "When we exit the elevator, stay on my six and I'll deal with Boop." Boop referred to NCIS SSA Cheryl "Betty Boop" Garcia; a lady known for being especially tough on new agents to the office.

We exit the elevator and immediately, were pounced upon, not literally of course, by a dark curly-haired woman almost my height with a white dress blouse and navy cotton slacks with red peep-toe shoes. Her blue eyes frantic with worry as I've met the animated Boop Garcia. "Boss, tell me Vale talked to you already concerning that new agent named Blanton?"

"Full briefing." Vaughn's eyes danced with mischief as he nodded my way. Garcia realized she spoke out of school and she smiled some kind of sinister grin I only saw on Garner's face a time or two. "And I'm assuming based on your lack of good manners Agent Garcia, you spoke with Jerry Garner prior to meeting her just now."

"Unfortunately, sir." Garcia's not shy about her apparent disdain for my appearance here in Corpus Christi. So my unsavory rep precedes me; not a surprise. "He…suggested she work on files at her desk until she can be… calm enough for fieldwork."

"Really?" I've sensed that tone before. My ex-boss Garner always made assumptions that his word carries the weight of our entire agency behind his position; until the Director sat him down one day and set him straight. Hence after my six months of training with that jerk, I chose an Agent-Afloat assignment aboard the *Ronald Reagan*. "And does Jerry Garner's word overrule mine in this office?"

"No, but there are the usual political considerations."

"And the other shoe drops," Vaughn smiled.

Garcia continued. "John Cole from the FBI is up in your office…along with two potential candidates for Cass's position: former NCIS Agent Daniel Court and current offering…Rhonda Bass!" Without realizing it, my fists balled up and my knuckles cracked. Both Vaughn and Garcia looked to me. "I take it based on your balled up fists; you have an issue with Agent Bass?" She had no clue how much I had an issue with Rhonda Bass!

"Well Boop, if I was Agent Blanton and I heard the FBI agent who blew my op on a distant Mediterranean island, was present, I'd be less than enthusiastic about her sharing an office with me. Then again, I speak from personal experience on that front. So Agent Blanton," now he addressed me with that *I'm in charge* voice, "If I have you sit outside my office and keep my assistant, Polly company, will you promise me to not attack or otherwise assault Agent Bass?"

Although I was sorely tempted to tear Bass limb from haughty limb, I knew my career expectancy would be nil if I let Bass get under my skin now. "I can keep calm while she's in your office. I can keep calm when she exits your office and goes downstairs. She parks at a desk here in the squad room; that's pushing it, sir."

I watched as Garcia give Vaughn an *I'm not sure about her* look. I was being honest about my feelings as my attempt to remain professional about the opportunistic fibby Bass. Clearly, Garcia knew both Bass and Court, but something told me I partially won Garcia over when she nodded her head from side to side. "My personal feelings for Blanton aside, due to a lack of a thorough look at her file, I can conclude Bass would be a liability for TFCC Jace."

"I have to agree with your assessment Boop." Maybe I didn't win her over after all. I started over to my desk. "Agent Blanton?"

I looked back and just shook my head. "It never changes; they discover my family lineage and the judgments begin." I gathered up my desk box. "Maybe I should just get out and go try out with one of the Indie promotions in Houston.

I appreciate the opportunity Agent Vaughn; I'll just pick up my box and toys and go elsewhere."

TWO

As I go to retrieve my personal effects from my new perch, Garcia stopped right in my path. She held up her hands. "Whoa kid; I may not like the fact you have a mob boss for a sperm donor, but I do appreciate your situation and what happened in Malta. I was up in OPS here when that debacle went down." Well, some conciliation there. "Also, I'm not in a position to judge your pedigree; since my late father was a childhood friend of "Big Joe" Serrano of the Jersey Mob." I nodded with a half-smile. Perhaps Garcia understood me better than I thought. Then she smiled and stuck out her hand. "My friends call me Boop."

"Mine call me Tori; glad to know you, Boop." Good, she and I came to an understanding. That will help me relax much more. "Agent Vaughn, if I may sir, perhaps it might be better if I set my desk up which will further diffuse any tension between me and Bass; provided you decide to keep her on the team. And maybe…I can get to know Boop better?" I saw Jason's eyes shine a little as I made that suggestion.

"An even better, and more mature response; wouldn't you agree with that boss?" Boop looked to Vaughn who insisted I call him Jason when the setting's informal. Jason nodded as he eyed me and went upstairs to his office. Boop smiled. "Come on Tori, I'll help you get your space set up."

I smiled as we walked over to where my desk rested. We didn't have a skylight like the office at the Navy Yard or the new headquarters at Quantico. But the snickerdoodle paint color and outline of dark blue added a calming effect for managing cases. "Thank God no skylight; I hate the sunburst distractions."

Boop smiled as she removed my snow globes. "Same here; I knew I'd like you, Tori!"

"Me too!" A statuesque redhead said as she approached wearing a pink t-shirt and faded jeans. I think I'll fit in better than I thought. "Leah!" She offered her hand.

"Tori pleased to meet you, Leah." As in ATF Special Agent Leah McCoy; wife of team tech guru NCIS Agent Sean "Lightning" McCoy. I looked around and didn't see the handsome half of the McCoy couple. "I'm guessing an op is in progress?"

"Sharp young lady," Leah smiled as she further elaborated. We turned to the flat screen next to Lightning's desk. "NCIS received word one of our carriers had a small Marine MP squad smuggling drugs in from the Med. Two of our female regulars, Lena Ortiz and Casey Collins, are aboard posing as members of the crew while Agent Marcus Valiant works in the dock master's office to check over the manifests. Recognize the carrier, Tori?"

I noticed the carrier's registration. "I sure do. That's CVN-72...the Abe Lincoln; I knew the last Agent-Afloat aboard her." In fact, I'd crossed paths with the late NCIS Special Agent Dumont Talbot. That sweet Georgia bulldog recognized me from my internet matches with my pro wrestling tag team partner Santana Garvin. In fact, NCIS and the DEA used our part-time career as wrestlers as a cover for the Malta op. The thought of our botched op made my rage towards Rhonda Bass resurface. "How much longer do you think Boop?"

"About Jace making a decision on who fills the FBI Liaison vacancy? It's anybody's guess, but I'd say within the next five minutes." I watched as Leah pulled out a ten dollar bill from her left front pocket. "Oh, you have to be kidding me, Leah!"

"I'm willing to bet it'll take less or more time." Leah looked at me. "Tori, you want in on this action?"

I pulled out a ten spot as did Boop. "No sense in being the resident 'fraidy cat' on this team. Put me down for more time. He has two candidates up there to consider. One being a former NCIS agent." Boop smiled as Leah's expression went blank. She forgot about Court; lucky for me I didn't.

"What are we generating a pool of ladies?" The question came from a blonde-haired blue-eyed male with bulging biceps. His rippling pecs under a navy t-shirt with the words *Tech Scares You* printed across his chest. The wording was a dead giveaway for NCIS Special Agent Lightning McCoy. He handed a ten spot to Leah and offered his hand to me. "Sean McCoy."

I shook it with a smile. "Tori Blanton; a pleasure to meet you." I looked at my watch and ten minutes passed as Jason exited his office along with an older man with jet black hair with light streaks of gray in his goatee as well. "I'm guessing that's the aforementioned FBI SSA Cole?" Cole wasn't bad-looking either...for an older man.

"Good eye Tori; yes...that's John Cole. And following him is former NCIS Agent Danny Court." Lightning nodded to Court and I saw a good-looking guy with smart spectacles. His modern light brown short hairstyle with his cowlick swerving upward. And from what some have said, he's a Jersey guy most southern girls would melt into a puddle when he spoke. Yes, Danny Court was definitely easy on the eyes. Then my hottie fantasy went in the pooper when Lightning said, "And hot on John's heels, the Princess of the FBI...Rhonda Bass!"

Now I faced the unsavory image of my damned hatred. She carried herself like a princess with her haughty tan and piercing blue eyes. From the squad room I sensed her supreme arrogance and in her tan suit with a chocolate blouse with fudge-colored boots. When her eyes met mine, she felt the cold steel laser beams piercing her soul as she yelled, "Blanton, who let you in here?"

I was from North Carolina and she was from Philadelphia, PA and full of herself. Her loud-mouthed big city attitude made my blood boil, and how I kept from running upstairs and throwing her off the landing, I'll never know. I simply smiled like *Rosa del Diavolo* and answered with frigid precision. "I'm NCIS Rhonda, I belong here!"

"Ha, one word from my director and I bet I can fix that!" I laughed and didn't stop until everyone from upstairs stood around my desk. Bass marched right up into my face and almost screamed, "What's so damned funny...Probie?"

"The reason why Agent Blanton's laughing Rhonda is she does belong here." The ominous words from SSA Cole forced Bass's shocked look to face him. "Her actions didn't lead to a blown op on a distant island in the

Med, which led to the deaths of two agents of our closest European allies!"
Bass flinched back as Cole turned his angry glare my direction. He stared
straight into my eyes. "By the same token, trusting the daughter of a Dixie
Mafia Capo, I can understand Agent Bass's...concerns. How do you know
she won't turn on you in lieu of loyalty to her father?"

"Because I went to Nashville and spoke informally with Teddy Blanton.
And he told me Tori has no love for him or her older siblings. In fact, his or-
ganization is Tori's other part-time hobby. And that's looking for evidence
the Blantons were behind the deaths of Terrance and Charlene Wayne of
Sneads Ferry, NC." Then Jason stood between me and Bass and faced Bass.
"Court, you're my choice for this team. I'll call the SAC in Houston, the
Asst.

Dir. In Atlanta and Director McBride at the Hoover Building of your
transfer to TFCC; welcome aboard Danny."

"Thank you, Jace," Court said as he eyed me and smiled. "And Agent
Blanton, welcome to Corpus Christi...and back home in the good ole' US
of A!" I smiled and nodded in return. "So, anything besides going back to
John's office for my exit briefing to transfer over here?"

"Not off the top of my head Danny; see you after lunch." Jason smiled
as Cole nodded and left. Bass hung around for a moment. I guess she
wanted to remind me which of us was *Queen Bee* in Corpus Christi; until
Jason glared in her eyes. "And you're still here?" Then she left hot on
Cole's heels. He turned and faced me, "Well done Tori; well done!"

"Yes, that's some moxie you showed by answering Bass the way you
did Tori." Leah's vote of confidence strengthened my resolve to remain
professional in the face of Bass's challenge; even the challenge of SSA
Cole. I haven't been in the office an hour and already I feel like a vital part
of this team. "Boop, if you need to go handle something else, I can help
Tori get settled."

"Probably not a bad idea; it'll give me time to assess the structural
damage done to 'Honest Abe' from that stinger." The aftermath of the attack on *Abraham Lincoln* held as much mystery as to who blew our op and
covers in Malta. Scuttlebutt or rumor had it, the Navy Yard pin-pointed a
hijacked stinger missile was used to blow an eight-foot-wide hole in the

Command-in-Control or CIC bridge section of the carrier. The same missile attack which killed the captain, the Carrier-Air-Group Commander (CAG) and Agent Talbot. I looked at the flat screen photo array and turned my head away. As I sighed, Boop turned back, "Something on your mind Tori?"

"I knew Dewey Talbot; teamed up with him at a couple of Forty-Two tourneys in Naples. He taught me a lot about being an agent as part of that Maltese task force. And I feel…I owe him for that." And I did owe Dewey for his knowledge, experience, an example of an NCIS agent. I watched as Jason and Boop both nodded my direction.

"Okay, I'll have Lightning pull up the satellite footage of the attack and any other data you might need to analyze.

"I'll look over the written reports and the still photos of both cases. Anything else you can think of Tori?"

That imaginary light bulb humans have dancing above their heads just lit up above mine. "Have your team working the drug angle on the Honest Abe, run the fingerprint analysis on that used stinger launcher provided someone recovered it from Malta. We might get prints from a supply troop or sailor or even an ordinance specialist. That gives us a starting point where the Sicily goons got the missile."

"I'll call Casey now Boop and pass on the idea." Lightning smiled as he dialed his land-line phone. "I strongly believe Tori's a keeper Jace."

"I agree as well Lightning…" But Jason's thoughts got lost quickly as a woman my height and about ten pounds lighter, walked in sporting a light gray women's skirt suit with gray pumps and a white dress blouse buttoned up to the second button below the collar. The light brown hair and hazel green eyes mesmerized me as Corpus Christi Police Chief Jennifer Vaughn, walked in with former DEA Agent and my tag team partner Santana Garvin. "Well, well Chief, what brings you over to my office?"

"Since you and I had our usual lunch appointment and you needed a liaison officer from CCPD, I thought I'd have Sgt. Santana Garvin accompany me here." Santana and I nodded to one another.

Santana's fashion sense always included a headband to keep her lovely, and slightly curly bangs tamed. Today she sported a navy pantsuit with a white blouse and black boots? My tag partner expected trouble. I walked up and gave Santana a big hug. "Welcome to the lion's den girlfriend!"

"Feels good to be here Tori girl; how are you doing?" Santana had to ask since we hadn't seen one another in the last two months. We both were on that Malta job, but she managed to escape and return with SEAL Team Two…my hero!

"Good, but you just missed FBI Special Agent Bass." I smiled as if I still wanted to rip Bass apart. Santana's eyes widened as she closed the tight "O" on her lips and nodded. "You would've been proud; I stayed right at my desk and didn't flinch!"

"And she still walked out of this building alive and in one piece? I am damned proud of your girlfriend!" I knew she would be, and I noticed Chief Vaughn's confused eyes. They dart from me to Santana and back again. Finally, Santana stopped Chief Vaughn's tennis match eyes. "I was on the Malta case with Agent Blanton. My apologies Chief; Chief Jennifer Vaughn, this is NCIS Special Agent Tori Blanton. She's filling Agent Darius Coltrane's slot here."

Chief Vaughn nodded in recognition as we shook hands. "My husband said there was an attractive young woman moving into Darius Coltrane's vacant slot. But I think he lied like a rug to keep me from acting like a jealous Georgia Peach." Her sly smile slid Jason's way as he nodded in response. She was already briefed about me being from the Charlotte, NC area.

However, I knew from my study of Jason's personnel file, she made jokes like that to remain civil. And if she had a problem with me, she would address me and not Jason. "I admit Agent Vaughn's cute enough…for an older, former Navy SEAL?"

"But?" Chief Vaughn asked.

"I prefer Force Recon Marines; they're willing to grapple with me anytime!" I got whistles and cat-calls as Jason slowly shook his head and the ladies laughed along with me. Lightning put up a gigantic smiley face that turned red and blinked with a ship's klaxon noise in perfect time. "What's that for Lightning?"

"Just when I was starting to like you Tori; you drop the bombshell of liking jarheads over us poor, abused sailors." Lightning's pitiful gaze did nothing to faze me.

However, my esteemed new boss put Lightning's mocking concerns into a palatable, proper perspective. "Lightning my brother, you have to remember: Tori grew up in close proximity to Camp Lejeune and not close to the Charleston Naval Center. If she had grown up near the Charleston facility, she would have had a better sampling of sailors versus Marines."

"Oh please; she prefers jarheads! Grow up and get over it you two!" Chief Vaughn's declaration received more laughs as Lightning and Jason joined in. Then Chief Vaughn accorded me a special honor; a first-name basis like Jason. "Tori, you'll fit in nicely around here!"

"Now, Tori and I have a little problem to iron out as far as just how useful we can be in task force operations." I knew what Santana meant; our moon lightning job as pro wrestlers could jeopardize current operations like the pending drug bust aboard the *Abraham Lincoln*. And given the fact, our covers were never blown, just our task force op in Malta, the need to maintain said covers, stemmed from our new coworkers knowing those details to make proper adjustments.

Jennifer looked at both of us and asked, "Is that what you meant by… the need to debrief the new team before you two started actually working for TFCC Sgt. Garvin?"

"That's the plan, Jen." Santana smiled and suddenly my nerves went into orbit. "We got this!"

"Let's get Danny back over here and wrap up for the day; then we'll hold a team cook-out at my place. It'll confirm our newest addition's budding fan base!"

The moment Jason said that Boop and Leah turned and faced us more confused than our rollercoaster conversation started. "Fanbase?"

THREE

FBI Special Agent Danny Court met up with us at Jason's house on Greenbriar Drive in a nice, suburban section of Corpus Christi. The two-story red brick home sported a nice red brick short fence with a stone-like courtyard for plenty of parking. The backyard where Jason held court with the fellows and the grill; had a wooden six-foot privacy fence with a thin metallic wire along the top including the gate. Later, Jennifer explained that the house security system also came with a Sensitive Compartmentalized Information Facility or SCIF feature. Even in the backyard under a starry sky, security debriefs could be conducted without the fear of spy satellites listening in on the information. When Boop and her husband, CCPD Homicide Lt. Manny Garcia arrived with Manny Jr and Aryana, the Vaughn's daughter Gracie, came downstairs to entertain the Garcia's children.

The McCoys arrived with their daughters Erin and Katherine as well as the neighbors: in-laws from the Chicago and Dallas areas connected by a Greek family named Papadakis: Joe and Pamela Hampton with adopted children Romy and Leo, as well as Pam's sister Thea Flynn with her husband Mike and their two boys Liam and Sean. As Santana and I worked on a couple of salads for tonight's team meal, Jason came in as Joe Hampton took over grill duties. "Something up Jace?" Santana asked as she finished up her fruit salad and I continued to dice tomatoes.

"Mark, Casey, and Lena are headed home. Apparently, they were able to make an arrest in the drug sting, but the contraband made it off ship prior to the carrier docking at port. The drugs have made their way to Corpus Christi. On a positive note: Tori's suggestion on running prints on that missile tube for the stinger, led to an arrest and one step closer to how your op in Malta got blown."

Good news for a change. But I sensed Jason had undercover designs for Santana and me. Given my age, a college student at Texas A&M-Corpus

Christi would do wonders for my confidence as well as calm my nerves. "So what's the setup?"

Boop walked in with Jennifer and two shoe boxes with undercover documents. "Here's how this party gets going: Santana, you have a college teaching cred for mass communications. With classes starting Monday, Media and TV Presentation will be taught by you as Samantha Wriggle. You transferred in from Florida State to care for a sick aunt and landed the teaching assignment due to Professor Abram's recent assault charge. Tori, you're pursuing a degree in Business Administration and you're filling in elective courses to graduate. You're in need of this class. We decided since you created a great cover personality in Gina Torelli, might as well have you keep it. We went through and solidified the original backstop."

I looked at my transcript and was shocked Prof. Tenshi Myoko awarded me a three-point-two grade point average for her Drama class. "Considering I only spoke sparingly to Prof. Myoko, I'm fortunate to have that GPA. So I'm transferring in from University of North Carolina by way of the University of Tokyo; not bad for a federal agent." Then Jennifer nodded. I'm guessing there's another reason for my new cover. "What?"

"I do…have a selfish reason for coming in here."

"Jen…"

"Damn it, Jason, I'm scared!" When others began to file in, Jennifer turned, "It's okay folks, go back to your grazing the appetizers." She turned back to us. "I'm sorry; ever since Dillon was shot earlier this spring, I've been a little on edge. He's worked his butt off taking summer courses so he can graduate on time in the spring of 2018. So I'm only requesting this, not requiring it. Would you mind checking in on Dillon, when you're able?"

Jason looked over at me; he's making this *my* call. Although, we came over here to debrief the TFCC team, having the kids and Dillon in this mix scared me. On the other hand, having him as a potential classmate, or boyfriend for cover purposes, would protect him and our ongoing casework. "Before I say yes, I have some conditions."

"Name them," Jason said quickly so Jennifer couldn't object. She turned and frowned at him. "You want her to do this; you listen to what she has to say, baby."

Jennifer acquiesced as I rattled off my terms. "First, I decide on how to deal with him while on campus. If he meets me here and doesn't recognize me from my internet matches as a pro wrestler, I give him my cover name and I deal with him in an honest manner."

"Define honest manner for us please?" Boop's question held merit considering this was my...third undercover operation in less than six months.

"I'm erring on the side of caution because I believe Dillon's smart enough to sniff out an undercover cop." The story I heard about him keeping Chief Vaughn's cover a secret from a previous case, became my thesis for this talk. Great, I sounded like a college student again. "If asked, I confirm, but not my real name or identity."

"Good idea," Leah smiled.

"How does not telling him your real name help you both?" Wow, Jennifer's trust level seemed void since last spring. I guess more of the same happened over the summer.

"If asked, he only will know me as Gina Torelli. And I'm sensing he's smart enough to not indicate I'm a cop of any kind. Having grown up around all of you, he'd have the good noodle to not talk out of school on this note." I've only been here a day, and I'm placing my trust in a college kid I haven't even met yet. Wow, am I a risk-taker or what? "Next, if I make enough connection with Dillon outside of class; the campus will have the buzz I'm either a cop or possible girlfriend. If that happens, I'm selling the latter to maintain my cover."

"Do you have to do that?" I groaned as Jennifer settled into the protective maternal mode of her job as police chief. But a corrective glare from Jason and she threw up her hands in surrender. "Sorry, sorry; I guess everyone is still too new to get our bearings straight around here. You don't have to honor any part of my request Tori." One side note: being this was late August. We all wore our favorite beach attire with appropriate shorts and tops for an end-of-summer party. I love how this team gets together.

Then a younger version of Jason entered through the garage awning entrance. He was about ten pounds lighter than Jason and sported one of those dirty beards that caused young women's girly parts to soar into orbit. Dillon Vaughn wore a black *Ocean Pacific* t-shirt with tan cargo shorts and black flip-flops. And under each arm rested a twenty-four pack case of beer. "And the beer arrives; thank Rudy for the assist buddy!"

"No problem Dad." I listened and I heard Jason's voice patterns in Dillon's tones. He spied me and Santana and pointed our direction. "Let me guess: new members of TFCC?"

"Can't get anything past you sweetheart." Jennifer smiled as Dillon put the beer on the center bar and hugged his mother. "Allow me?" Jason smiled as he extended a hand to Santana. "This is Prof. Samantha Wriggle; she'll be teaching the Media and TV Presentation class starting Monday at eleven in the morning."

"I have that class; pleased to meet you…Prof. Wriggle." Dillon shook hands with Santana, and he pulled out what appeared to be a class syllabus. "I noticed the department sent out an email concerning the shortage of textbooks for this class."

Santana smiled. "I spoke with Dr. Argyle the department head and he recommended you order the book online if necessary and catch up on the reading assignments as needed." Boop looked over at her and nodded *nice save Santana!*

"I did some research and discovered textbooks.com offered an e-book version as well and it will save some cost for the class too." Dillon's suggestion helped me since I was one of those students who would have difficulty finding textbooks for my classes. Then he turned to me. *Oh my god, he has pretty green eyes like Jason.* "And you are who? Teaching assistant, registrar gopher, a pretty athlete who needs a Comm. class?"

"The last description sort of fits." I say "sort of" because apparently, he hasn't recognized me or Santana; points for us! "I'm Gina Torelli; I'll be taking Prof. Wriggle's eleven o'clock as well."

I extended my hand to shake Dillon's, but he brought my hand up to his lips and kissed my knuckles. Glad I remembered my moisturizer the last couple of days. I gazed Santana's direction and my jaw dropped wide open. Santana's eyes laughed with silliness as she covered her mouth. I hope no one took a photo of my expression. I probably looked like a twitter-pated dork. "I'm… pleased to meet you, Gina. I hope you enjoy your time with TFCC." I smiled and nodded in response. I might need Santana's class after all. "You okay?"

"Oh, I'm fine, fine; getting better every day!" Okay, so I haven't dated much in the last year. Between my training with Garner and the time in the Med and being aboard the "Ronnie" Reagan, dating members of the male gender hadn't been at the top of my priority list. Dillon…might change that; provided Jason or Jennifer won't give me the "stink" eye for hanging around him. Then again, I mentioned my interest in Marines; Dillon might change that perception as well. "Were you just getting off work for the day?"

"I did; just finished up an end-of-summer party for the Corpus Christi Independent School District's National Honor Society. We catered an event at TAMU-Corpus Christi. The beer was not leftover from that event."

"So you did run downtown and swing by the restaurant to raid the cooler?" Jason's question carried an accusation intended to be funny. Jennifer, however, didn't crack a smile.

"Rudy walked up to me as we cleaned up and said to go by and get the cases he set aside. And here's your change." Dillon handed Jason a wad of cash and some coins. Jason slipped Dillon, what looked like a fifty-dollar bill. I guess even dad's tip their kids who work in the catering business. Mine never did. Teddy always scoffed when I made him honest money as a waitress. Hence why I graduated high school and college early; I wanted out as fast as I could get out. "Are you okay Gina?"

"Me, oh I'm fine; excuse me for a moment please?" I walked outside and stood on the patio facing the back fence. It felt like a week passed by as Santana and Dillon joined me. "Sorry about that; it felt a little claustrophobic in there for a moment."

Dillon nodded. "It's okay. Mom filled me in on what happened to you and…that she asked you to look in on me at school from time to time."

"I take it you're not a fan of that idea?"

"Normally, no; but given the fact you're a new student with no friends, in my humble opinion, is unacceptable; I told her if you chose a *girlfriend* cover option for me, I'm not going to complain." Then Boop ran out as frantic as she was in the office earlier. "Whoa Aunt Boop; where's the fire?"

"Did you happen to look at the driver's license I gave you?"

I answered, "No, not yet!" I whipped out my license from my ID wallet. Yikes; I'm a redhead! "Boop, this sudden hiccup will not feed the bulldog! Tell me you have a quickie solution?"

"I do!" Leah and Jennifer walked out to join us. "I have some coloring and there's a full hair salon setup above the garage here in case we need a quick correction for undercover operations. So, step into my parlor my dear; Mata Hari McCoy will fix you right up!"

An hour later, my hair got washed and rinsed to set my new fiery red color. Dillon walked in as Jennifer finished with the blow dryer. Jennifer turned me around and Dillon's eyes popped out of their sockets. "You like?"

Dillon's evil grin told me all I needed to know. But he said the words. "Me likey!" which told everyone else my new do would be a hit. "You look stunning Tori."

Whoa, wait one second...did he recognize us when he walked in an hour ago? Santana gulped, "W-what did you call her?"

Jason walked in and let everyone off the proverbial hook. "I put the SCIF up the moment you girls came up here to get Tori's hair to match her cover ID. All the kids in this little family neighborhood recognized you from your matches on the internet. So, after a coaching reminder to behave during undercover cases, we will allow autographs and pics with you two."

"Good; one less worry to hang over our heads." And I was sweating bullets until this little hiccup happened. But wow, it was nice to hear my real name uttered from Dillon's lips. Yes, my perception of dating and who was changing rapidly. "Now to make sure the cheese doesn't bind up too much; are we still good with my earlier conditions...Chief?"

"We're good." And the smile from Jennifer told me she wasn't interfering with my case or how Dillon wanted to help with my cover. And the need for Dillon to have a girlfriend came to fruition as Gracie walked in with her Facebook account active. "What's up sister?"

Gracie was one of those lanky, high school basketball players whose metabolism burned calories like a metal fabrication facility. She shared her mother's light brown hair and hazel-green eyes. Although she did have a slight silhouette with a b-cup bra on, her hips weren't as wide as Jennifer's.

But I count that towards her youth and her caloric intake or lack thereof. "I just found out; Tori might want to play up her romantic interest in my goofy brother. Carla's back in town."

"Terrific," was all Dillon said as he shook his head. He faced my confused look. "Carla Baez is my ex-girlfriend from my high school days. She went to Ingleside High and I transferred to Mary Carroll High. Just about the time NCIS moved Dad's current office onto NAS Corpus Christi. Her father Pete became the Assistant Chief of Police for Ingleside PD. So when we travel to Port Aransas to stay at our beach house, we always go around the long way up Mustang Island."

"Don't worry your handsome face, my dear Dillon," I said as I looked deeply into his hypnotic eyes, "Lucky for you, I thrive on competition."

"Let Carla Baez come forth and let her bring some eye candy with her. She will learn why Tori/Gina is a Princess of the Carolinas!"

"Mom," Dillon said, "I think I'm in love!" Woo-hoo…lucky me!

FOUR

Monday, August 29th rolled around, and I met Dillon for our Media and TV Presentation class. I wore a crème-colored t-shirt with faded jeans and black tennis shoes. I put my hair up in a ponytail and wore my dark-rimmed glasses so I could pass for an intelligent college coed. Dillon walked in and sported a TAMU-Corpus Christi Islanders green and a white t-shirt with tan cargo trousers and white deck shoes. He sat down in the front row next to me and set his backpack to his left between us. I smiled. "You shaved!"

"I like to sport a babyface once in a while. Our esteemed professor discovered Carla and her boy-toy from Madrid, Rodrigo Aponte-Sosa, also share our class time here. So, we can either stay up front or move up a few rows." Dillon looked around as the class began to fill.

I checked my phone and received a text from Santana. *Carla and Rod coming your way.* I looked at Dillon. "Let's move up to the very back row; it's too close down here for me."

Dillon grabbed his backpack and my feminine pink backpack. "You lead, I'll follow." We ascend the stairs as Santana walked in. She spotted us and nodded as the class filled and who happened to walk in but Dillon's ex-girlfriend Carla and her new beau Rodrigo. The young Latina wore her bangs in a braid which went down the center of her neck.

Her outfit consisted of a white linen dress tied by a blue sash at the waist and she wore black flip-flops on her feet. Carla's eyes searched for a seat up top but conceded to one of two open desks on the front row. Likewise, Rodrigo took up a desk on the front row next to Carla and he wore a blue t-shirt with stone-washed blue jeans and white Converse tennis shoes.

Dillon and I returned our eyes to Santana as she called the class to order. "Good morning, I am Prof. Samantha Wriggle, and if you have Media and TV Presentation on your schedule, you're in the right place." Santana wore navy slacks with a white dress blouse and navy pumps. She forwent her signature headband and tied her hair back in a ponytail and sported silver-rimmed glasses. She opened her laptop and tapped into the building's wireless network to display her slide presentation. "TV media presentation has been around since the late 1940's. Everything from news, sports, entertainment, and commercials have come to us by a cathode ray tube or a radio the early 1900's. But TV media has come a long way in the last seventy years. With computers, personal data devices, cell phones; our sources of media have grown by leaps and bounds." She stopped and scanned the seats and smiled. "I'm curious; how many of you are not taking this class as part of a degree in communications?" I held up my hand as well as Dillon.

To my surprise, both Carla and Rodrigo held up their hands as well as one muscular guy. He looked like a linebacker to me. Santana smiled. "Good; five out of thirty in my class who didn't lie about this class being an elective. Good, brave souls; come on down to the front so we can all get a good look." We made our way down since we were in the nosebleed section of the class. "That's right, gather around the presentation desk here." Santana smiled at all five of us as she extended her hand to the large guy on the end. "Why don't start with you, sir." Timidly, this giant of a young man walked over and gently took a microphone from Santana.

He smoothed back his shaggy brown hair and held the mic up to his mouth. I could tell he was nervous as he tugged at the green and white polo shirt collar. He looked himself down and all over and then his eyes rose to meet the crowd. "Good morning class, I am Zachary Miller and I'm from Iowa City, Iowa. I play back up Middle Linebacker for our Islander football team." Shouts and applause rang out for our classmate Zachary. "My claim to fame is I intercepted a pass during the Green/White Spring scrimmage and ran it back for a touchdown for the White squad." More applause and whistles as even Santana applauded his efforts.

"I'm impressed; do you prefer Zach or Zachary?"

"Zach, I prefer Zach Professor."

"Okay Zach, I have an observation and a question. The observation is you are an impressive athletic specimen and you have no wedding band on your left hand. Dare I ask, are you seeing anyone or are you currently engaged?" Poor Zach shook his head as my professor/tag team partner did her best to draw attention to his attractive physique.

"No Professor Wriggle; I'm not dating anyone, and I'm not engaged." Zach chuckled a little as Santana's eyes danced with mischief and she shook her head.

"Okay Zach, if you'll see me after class, we'll see if any of these lovely ladies in class would like to apply." Santana, successful in her antics to give Zach a good-natured ribbing, he passed the mic to Carla. The rest of the young ladies seated screamed like Zach was performing a rock concert. Poor guy blushed like a pink rose. "Next?"

"Good morning, I am Carla Baez and I come from across the bay in Ingleside, Texas. I recently won a fashion competition in Madrid, Spain in which the dress I'm wearing has been awarded my own fashion label. I'm working on a Business Administration degree in Marketing."

"Are you planning on featuring future fashion designs Carla?" Santana asked.

"The plan is to introduce not only more dress designs but also some cotton suits for the male gender as well as some children's fashions." Carla looked down the line and noticed Dillon just waiting his turn as I.

She passed the mic to Rodrigo. "¡Hola! or Hello, I am Rodrigo Aponte-Sosa. I am Carla's most recent romantic conquest." I rolled my eyes as Santana shook her head. She started all this nonsense with poor Zach. "My family's claim to fame is we are the oldest family in Spain to serve in the Bull Fighting rings of Spain as well as run with the bulls in Pamplona."

"That can be painful," Santana observed.

Rodrigo smiled and nodded. "For both man and bull alike. The bulls avenge themselves when men get bounced around in Pamplona."

The pained expressions were given in sympathy for those who suffered; both man and beast. "I can imagine; who's next?" Rodrigo smiled like a hungry predator as he passed the mic to Dillon. "And you are sir?"

"I'm Dillon Vaughn; I am a Criminal Justice major with a minor in Business Administration. My claim to fame is I was shot by some Russian mobster back in the spring. I was fortunate my dad bought me a Concealed Handgun Licensing class before, and I was able to prevent this man from hurting anyone else." The crowd roared with applause as I looked at Dillon with mild surprise.

Santana nodded as she signaled the class to settle down. "Are you currently armed, Dillon?"

"Not at this time; the Student Advisory Council, as well as campus administration, is still debating the CHL issue for students and faculty. So until the issue is decided, I've been asked to try and call Campus Police the next time someone tries to kill me." Light chuckles echoed through the crowd and I didn't blame them. Sometimes, campus cops were a joke and not in a nice, funny manner.

"Dillon, aren't you related to Corpus Christi Police Chief Vaughn?"

"Yes I am," he said as he looked over the crowd. "However, like all of you, I must abide by the law and the rules this school dictates regardless of my personal insecurities. So, in conjunction with the Campus Police Department, CCPD, and other law enforcement entities, a local federal task force working closely with the FBI; will conduct constant surveillance of all the colleges and schools in the bay area to prevent something like this from happening in the future."

"I feel safer already," Santana smiled as Dillon handed the mic to me. "And you are Miss?"

I cleared my throat. "I am Gina Torelli and I am originally from Charlotte, North Carolina. I came here via the University of Tokyo where I took Drama courses under the legendary Drama coach Tenshi Myoko. I also have the distinct reputation of being a dead-ringer for one of my favorite female wrestling superstars…Tori Blanton."

Santana looked into my eyes and realized I took a big risk in playing this card. "Do you have…photographic evidence to that effect…Gina?"

"If I may…Professor?" She nodded as I sent her an email with some well-doctored Photo-Shopped photos of me and myself with the red and brown hair. My "twin" and I stood outside the Tokyo Dome in front of a sign for New Japan Pro-Wrestling. Also, another photo of "us" in front of the State guest House Akasaka Palace. Several other popular locations including a Japanese Tea House in downtown Tokyo. "She even signed an eight by ten publicity photo to commemorate the meeting."

"Nice Gina; very nice," Santana smiled as I looked around and saw Carla's eyes locked on me. Great, another cop's kid giving me the business. "Something wrong Carla?"

"Oh, nothing Professor Wriggle; nothing important." Carla smiled like a she-devil.

Santana began to get unnerved by Dillon's ex-girlfriend. "Well, until you have solid evidence to the contrary that Gina's…photo array is a facsimile, I'm willing to believe her at face value. Doppelgangers are quite unusual; even in this day and age." She looked at the clock. "We're out of time for today; please refer to your class syllabus and read chapters one through five by Wednesday and be prepared to discuss concepts of presentation on radio versus television."

As class broke up, I retrieved our backpacks and when I returned to Santana's desk, Carla was smiling at Dillon. She spoke, "So, is Gina your girlfriend or is she some kind of professional actress just playing college coed?" I walked up and handed Dillon his backpack and took his arm lovingly. When Carla noticed my actions, her smile disappeared. Ha! Serves her right for being invasive and rude! "Hello, I'm Carla."

I smiled and extended my hand. "Gina; it's such an honor to meet you, Carla. And I am thoroughly glad to meet an authentic Spaniard. Are you a Don after a fashion…Senor Sosa?"

"No, no Dons in mi familia Senorita Torelli; just bullfighters." Dillon listened intently as Rodrigo noticed Dillon's attention divert over to Zach. "Am I boring you…Senor Vaughn?"

"Not at all…Senor Sosa." Dillon smiled as he shook Rodrigo's hand. As the two gripped tighter, Rodrigo began to falter. Dillon let his grip loosen a bit. "My apologies Senor; I work at my family ranch in West Texas during some summers and holidays when possible. I forget not everyone's bodies are strengthened by the same activities in which I participate. I hope I didn't cause you any…unnecessary pain?"

Carla's laser beam eyes glared at Dillon's smile. Rodrigo smiled and chuckled. "No, the pain has subsided already. It's nice to test a man's strength from time to time." Then he asked as if to fish for Dillon's weaknesses. "Any old embers for Carlotta?"

"None." I saw Carla's eyes; his one-word statement cut her to the quick.

As we turned to leave, Carla called out. "I don't believe you, Dillon Vaughn. I don't believe you just…moved on like that!"

"Your father helped that along Carla, and you followed his advice and left here. You, not him, made that decision. Move on and stop throwing your conquests in my face. I don't have time for childish antics anymore." Dillon turned and a burning anger she never saw in him before; pierced her soul. "I almost died last spring. You know what your father told me when he came to visit?" She shook her head. "He said with Rodrigo's smug arrogance, '*Too bad the Ruskie missed; one less Vaughn in the world would do it some good!*' Take your bullshit elsewhere Carla; I have no time for it!"

He walked away and I followed hot on his heels. He took short, quick breaths as he rounded a corner and hid from everyone but me. "You okay?"

"I'll be okay. I think Carla's playing a game, but I don't know on whom." Then he looked deeply into my eyes; then embraced me. "Thanks for sticking around."

"Anytime my dear." I took his hand as we walked out of the building. "You were pretty rough on her."

Dillon shook his head. "Maybe seeing her did push my buttons a little, but to join this class, this semester? I don't know…Gina." He said my cover name as Carla and Rodrigo exited not too far behind us. "Want to go visit Dad for lunch? I think I might have something for your case from my Organic Chem class."

"Sounds like fun, but let's take your car. I parked mine at my cover apartment across from the campus."

I looked out the passenger-side mirror and noticed a black Lexus SUV tailing us in Dillon's classic-looking '65 Chevy truck. "Who do you think that is?"

"One way to find out," Dillon smiled as we rolled up to the south gate. "Good afternoon Cpl. Motts."

"Good afternoon Mr. Vaughn and this is…?"

"Gina Torelli; I believe Agent Vaughn has me on the access list with Mr. Vaughn as well?"

Motts looked over the list and found our names. "You're good to go; enjoy your lunch with your dad Dillon."

"Thanks, Dan; keep up the good work." Dillon smiled as we were waved through and the black Lexus was stopped at the gate. Dillon punched up to the station speed limit of forty-five miles per hour and drove straight to NCIS. Dillon and I looked back as the black Lexus was turned away from the gate. "Yep; just as I suspected; Carla and Rodrigo!"

FIVE

Jennifer joined us as well as a tardy Santana. She laid her laptop over on the leather sofa and removed her glasses to relax. Pizza of different flavors filled the center of the conference table in Jason's office as Santana retrieved her laptop and uploaded the footage. "By the way, those old Photo Shop pics worked like a charm. Glad you still have that Gina Torelli Facebook account active."

I smiled as I bit into a Veggie Delight from *Mario's Pizzeria* from the Base Exchange. "Boop and Lightning did a bang-up job of reinforcing that backstop on my cover ID. My Twitter presence as Gina's picked up a few new followers: Zachary Miller the linebacker as well as the new Spanish couple of the moment; Rodrigo and Carla."

"What?" Dillon yelled as he peeked at my phone. "Okay, now I am ticked off!" Dillon got up and paced over by his father's desk like a caged animal. I'm guessing here, but Carla was playing some game with Dillon's emotions, and she was winning the war. Dillon's discomfort aside, if she recognized me or Santana, our op to discover where the Speed went from the carrier, would be down the toilet. We needed some breathing room.

Fortunately, Jennifer gave us an idea. "We might be able to legitimize your cover."

"How do we do that babe?" Jennifer successfully piqued Jason's interest; for that matter…mine too. Her smile gave away the punch line: my dad, Teddy Blanton, was in Corpus Christi. "How long has he been in town?"

Jennifer punched up some keys on a keyboard and put the surveillance footage on Jason's big screen. "Even though you and John Cole have a shaky relationship right now, he and I are copasetic. According to sources with the FBI, Teddy's looking for investment property. He's calling it, his retirement nest egg."

Could it be; is it possible my dad is going legit? Is he leaving his prized businesses in the Carolinas to call it a career? But why would he give that all up? Then I noticed everyone stared at me. Even Jason smiled a weak smile to wake me up to a possible hope or dream for my dad; he still loves me…and he's scared. "He's doing this…for me. My dad's getting out… for me?"

"It's possible Tori." Jason's words gave both hope and doubt. Teddy's broken my heart one too many times to believe it's possible. But if he heard what happened on Malta…huh, Jason's conversation with my dad in Nashville. I looked deep into Jason's eyes and he nodded. "Yes, to your un-asked question; yes, I told Teddy about Malta. I also told him you received citations from England and France for bringing home their lost operatives." Jason gave my dad all the de-classified details about Malta. "He shed tears, prideful tears in a daughter's accomplishments. I think he's changed…for the better."

"But why come here now? Why put himself in a position to be arrested by other federal law enforcement? That's the part I don't get! Has his relationship with my older siblings changed to where they want him…dead?"

"Only one way to find out girlfriend; talk to the man." Santana's right; I wish she wasn't. Maybe…it is time to bury the hatchet with Dad…and not in the back of his neck.

After looping in the FBI and other related federal agencies interested in the Dixie Mafia's business interests, my dark-rimmed glasses were traded out for a pair wired up for visual and audio magic. I wore a green TAMU-Corpus Christi Islander long-sleeve tee and a pair of green sweatpants to match my shirt. Just an hour prior, we briefed all agencies on the purpose of the meeting with my dad, 'Tough' Teddy Blanton. I took the lead. "Teddy Blanton, allegedly, has been a main-stayer with the Dixie Mafia for the last ten years. In the last six or seven, his profits have slipped; thanks to the outstanding work of our federal law enforcement system. But we believe an unforeseen consequence of this activity has arisen due to these losses. My older siblings; are forcing my father into retirement."

"And how does this help us?" Agent Cole's question had merit. I held up a blank flash drive. "What's that?"

"It's a drive similar to the one Mr. Blanton has in his possession. After his conversation with Agent Vaughn in Nashville, Mr. Blanton called the NCIS office in Memphis and made a deal with the agency as well as the US Attorney General's office in Washington. On that drive, is all the financial information, business interests and employee roster of every interest with the Dixie Mafia. The information extends from Kentucky, all the way down the southern gulf coast states where the Dixie Mafia resides."

"What kind of deal? Please tell me the DOJ didn't give him a country club-like sentence for life?" Bass asked and she did this to simply annoy everyone. Something happened between her and my family to warrant all this bitter hatred.

The time came to air this out. "Please Agent Bass; please share with the rest of the class why you feel a win-win for federal law enforcement is a bad thing in this instance?"

"Allan Bass–DEA; look up the case file. He was my husband!"

After that…entertaining briefing and the discovery the Dixie Mafia might have killed Bass's late husband, I understood why Rhonda hated my family so much. I can't blame her; I hated them too. But if my dad didn't have any dealings with my mother's death or that of Allan Bass; we had to find a way to confirm that theory. It also explained two points: one, why Rhonda blew our op in Malta on purpose and; two, why she wanted to punish my dad for my…potential loss to him. Agent Cole assigned her to monitor the show from the joint-surveillance van.

I checked myself over in the mirror and looked into Jason's confident eyes. "You ready to knock this one out of the park slugger?"

"Throw the fastball down the middle Big Papa; I'm ready!"

We chose the Oso Bar and Grill near Oso Pier to meet with my dad, Teddy. I sat in a booth close to the front door so he and I could be seen with the backup he and I could muster. Then a familiar shadow loomed at the door to the grill.

I stood from my perch to take-in the stature of my father. Dad sported a bald head with old, tired brown eyes and a sad smile. He stooped slightly due to his age and he walked with a slight limp these days. Jason told me he suffered from Rheumatoid Arthritis. He was definitely not the tough, old codger I remembered three years ago. Age had caught up with my dad and now I understood his reasons for retiring; he wanted to make amends. "Mr. Blanton?"

"Gina…right?" I nodded as did he with the biggest smile I'd never seen before. I invited him to sit in the booth with me, but he preferred a table in the back so no one could sneak up and do us harm. Can't say I blame him, and the surveillance crew made sure we were covered for such contingencies. "How's Tori? She told me her last assignment left her drained."

"She took a sixty-day break to debrief and then she came here. Went right to work."

Dad removed his gray-tweed sports coat and straightened the collar of his light green dress shirt. "Rotten kid of mine; she faces her fears head-on…just like I did when I was a young man. I never told her…how proud I was when she went against the grain and chose to be a federal agent." A tear escaped my eye as my dad…wept. I spun around the table and…embraced him for the first time since I was a little girl. "Do you think, Gina, Tori knows…how proud I am of her and how much I do love her?"

As I held him, I heard Jason whisper in my earpiece. *"You still love him Tori; just tell him so."*

I nodded as I held my sobbing father in my arms. "She knows Mr. Blanton; she knows." I couldn't help but shed a few tears of my own. He, Teddy Blanton, was not responsible for my mother's death. And he was blameless for Allan Bass's death as well. Then I released the embrace and asked, "We need to get down to business. Do you have the silver thumb drive like this one in my hand?" I held it up as he smiled and held up his version. We exchanged drives and I plugged his drive into my laptop. "I was asked to confirm the information." When the data loaded, a password screen popped up. "Mr. Blanton, did you password protect the thumb drive?"

"No, but Rex; the kid I asked to load the drive with the information I needed to hand over, might have been paid by my daughter to trap it…as he called it once." Damn, my poor dad was done in by my older sister Tessa. Her paranoia rivaled any don or debutante in the Dixie Mafia! "Can you figure out the first password?"

"The first…password?" Oh no, Tess had Rex build-in a two-level password encryption. "Wait, wait, wait…the first password would be something special to you. What did you call Tori when she was a little girl; a special nickname?"

Dad smiled. "It's 'honeybee'; all lower case letters." I put in my childhood nickname and a video file of my older sister Tessa appeared. Her dark eyes and straight black hair made her look like an old Smoky Mountain Witch my mother once described to me.

"Congratulations; you made it past the first level of the two-level password encryption. That means baby sister is handling the data transfer. Nice to know you survived Malta kid. I wanted the pleasure of doing you in myself since you gave me one of those damned tattoos. Here's your next clue smarty pants. it's something Dad would never order, but the bros and I… relieved him of the betrayal issue. You have two minutes to put in a guess after the video stops. If you fail, the data and your hard drive will be wiped by a security virus we installed on the drive. Yes, we drove Dad out of the business and that was being merciful. His pain will be to watch you die before his ancient old eyes. Ta-ta lil' sis!"

Then a timer appeared as the data was trapped behind the timer and a nasty virus. Timing was critical as I remembered she made the smug reference to betrayal. Dad's divorce from Mom and Mom's marriage to Terry. I put in 'KiLlM0m' in that sequence and the timer stopped. Files upon files of data opened and an upload program began. I took in a sharp breath as Dad smiled. "How did you know to put in that password and that sequence?"

"Your daughter Tessa does have some brains; not too many, but some. She always puts a one and a zero in her passwords." As I watch the upload, I disconnect my laptop from the Wi-Fi network.

Lightning yelled in my ear, *"Tori, what are you doing? We didn't get the complete upload."*

I showed my laptop screen to Dad. "Notice anything…hinky about the screen?"

"The documents look like a mirror image."

Then Lightning understood what I did. "*I didn't even notice they tried to mirror your hard drive. Nice job kid!*"

I smiled as the upload to my laptop continued. "Tessa wanted to clone my hard drive by the upload, but when I severed the Wi-Fi link, I prevented the cloning process. Their version will be incomplete and corrupt whatever device they used to collect my data." Then I watched as people in dark clothing began to move towards us. "We have company." Then I looked at Dad. "Are you armed?"

He shook his head. I heard Jason yell, "*All units move, move in now!*" I closed my laptop and handed my case with it to Dad and motioned *Stay close to me, I got this!*

Dad watched in horror as two men I knew marched toward us with Remington scatterguns pointed at our heads. My brothers Tad and Junior raised their weapons as I drew my service Sig-Sauer pistol and fired. My brother Tad, the curly-haired older brother snapped back and fell to the floor as Junior yelled, "Tad!"

I yelled, "Drop it and kiss the floor now Junior!" He raised his shotgun again as I fired. I hit him on the right shoulder and Tad in the left arm. Then I turned to face Dad as I saw my sister take aim at him. "No!" I yelled as I held Dad's head down and fired. To my own horror, my last round went through Tessa's forehead. Her eyes rolled back inside her head as she fell backward with a sickening thud. I cried, "Oh God no!" Agents from our detail rushed in from all sides as Dad rose and saw I shot…and killed my sister. "I'm sorry Daddy; I'm so, so sorry!" I sobbed as he held me close and put my pistol on the ground next to us. Lightning and Danny came over and secured my weapon.

Danny whispered, "You did your job Tori; no one will fault you. At least, I hope not."

"I won't son; not one iota will I fault my baby girl."

33

SIX

I felt numb while the EMTs checked me over for illegal substances via blood sample and I was given a breathalyzer. When any non-FBI federal agent is involved in a shooting incident, fatal or not, the Inspector General's Office was called in to take statements and draw conclusions as to whether or not, that agent was justified in their actions. The checks for foreign substances in my bloodstream as well as the breathalyzer to record if I had any alcohol in my system; were also standard operating procedure.

A thin man with a close-cropped dark hair-style walked up with a file folder in his hand His dark business suit with black tie, gave me the impression he was trying to resurrect the character Agent "K" from *Men in Black*. He noticed Jason and asked, "So SAC Vaughn, who is the agent who did all this damage?"

Jason pointed to me as I sat with the EMTs on the ambulance bumper. "Nick?" Jason called to IG Officer Nicholas Thorn and said, "Go gentle on this one, please? I just got her in last week." Jason had some idea on how I felt. I wonder, how many times with NCIS, did he kill someone? Jason gave me a confident wink and I remembered he did extensive research on me. He knew I went through one of these before.

The man shook his head with a half-smile as he walked up to me. "Agent Tori Blanton, Officer Nick Thorn–US Inspector General's Office. I will be conducting your shooting case. Care to replay the incident from the moment you drew your weapon please?"

I replayed the whole story from the moment I drew on my brothers to when I killed Tessa to protect my dad. I discovered my brothers told Thorn I drew first which prompted them to draw on me. However, witnesses in the grill confirmed I drew after their shotguns were drawn. "Then I turned to find Tessa Blanton pointing a gun at me and Mr. Blanton.

I turned my weapon, pointed upward, and fired. It happened in a split-second." Thorn gave me a sideways glance.

"And you think based on the last four months, in your experience, you were healthy enough to make a split-second decision like that Agent Blanton?" I'd gone through this before with an IG investigator in Germany after Malta. Same vocal inflection, same smug attitude believing they are superior due to holding someone's career in their hands. I'm betting this klutz never fired a weapon in the line-of-duty in his life. "Well, Agent Blanton?"

"Yes, based on the last four months, in my experience, I was healthy enough to make that split-second decision. The witnesses all confirmed my version of events; even to refute what Thaddeus and Theodore Blanton, Junior claimed were my actions. Even Theodore Blanton, Senior informed you those events were as I said. So I have to ask, are you taking this more personally than I am? What do you fear Officer Thorn?"

"Tori!" Jason yelled in a corrective tone.

"I'm trying to make sure this team has no more loose cannons assigned to it, Agent Blanton! And given your recent experiences in Malta, you especially need a thorough review of your actions to make sure you're healthy enough to be part of this task force!" I glared into Thorn's eyes and I saw it...he feared anyone who could fire a weapon to protect life, limb, and property if necessary. "What Agent Blanton?"

"Just out of curiosity, for my own curiosity, have you ever shot a weapon or killed someone in the line-of-duty; Officer Thorn?"

I saw the stress on his face and the horror in his eyes. I looked over my shoulder and saw Jason glaring at the both of us; but more on Thorn than me. Finally, he answered my query. "No, I never have fired a weapon in either case."

I looked back to Jason, who nodded for me to continue. "Then I have to ask; do you feel, other than you're paid to do this job, that you are qualified, based on your lack of experience in this situation, to determine who might and might not be, a loose cannon or a competent agent; Officer Thorn?"

"I go by the reports of others in that situation!"

"Oh my god; are you an investigator or a bureaucrat Thorn?" Thorn's jaw dropped wide open as he turned away. I looked back at Jason who smiled, shook his head and chuckled. Then Thorn faced me as Jason's stoic, serious expression returned. "Allow me to ask again: given your apparent lack of field experience of firing a weapon or killing someone in the line-of-duty, do you feel you, not someone else before you, you are qualified to render a conclusion of someone's competency to be a field agent with a sidearm?"

Then I felt Jason edge up behind me with his arms crossed over his chest. "I'm curious as to your qualifications as well…Nick!"

Nick Thorn realized his less-than-professional behavior towards me a moment ago, just made me and Jason, angry. But how I held my anger and questioned his competency was professional right down the line. He quietly answered, "No, I'm not; but no more so are you."

"We'll agree to disagree Officer Thorn." I calmly said as I looked deeply into his big, brown eyes. "However, food for thought: before you ever, and I mean ever, speak to me in that arrogant, condescending voice concerning my professional standards again, walk a mile in the shoes of those agents you cleared or condemned, not based on the findings of others. You'll have a clearer perspective on what agents in the field; deal with on a daily basis. And…one more note: before you conduct anyone else's shooting review for this team, avoid speaking with the FBI prior to your investigation; it'll make your findings more…professional."

"And if Officer Thorn does that again, speaking with the FBI prior to a shooting investigation involving TFCC agents, I'll use every favor I have from Washington to Houston to remove you from the IG's Office! Are we clear…Nicholas?"

"Crystal clear Agent Vaughn," Thorn said sheepishly as he glanced Rhonda Bass's direction. "My initial findings are; she's cleared, but she needs to schedule and attend a post-shooting incident debriefing as soon as possible."

"I'll call the office psychologist and schedule it ASAP."

"Good," then Thorn looked back as he left. "By the way, that's the most courteous, and professional ass-chewing I ever received from someone I've investigated Agent Blanton. Well done!" He smiled and left.

I smiled and turned to face Jason, but my smile soon disappeared. Jason glared at me like a disappointed father; whose daughter stayed out late on a date. "You won a battle, but you lost the war. If you ever disrespect some-one in the chain of command like you did again, it's a fifteen-day suspension without pay. You do it a third time, I fire you...clear?"

"Yes sir," I said quietly. Just as fast as I'd won him over, I experienced Jason's wrath. Maybe...going undercover this close to Malta's close, was a bad idea. I killed my sister. Then I looked around and discovered my backpack was missing. "Where did my backpack go?"

"Lightning and Leah secured it prior to their departure. Teddy went with them to give a statement as to the drive's authenticity." He took a moment and I heard him sigh. I guess the years of government service wore him down.

"I chewed you out a moment ago to signal the FBI, I wouldn't tolerate insubordination. But in light of that little scene, I acted just now, I also chewed out Thorn for prejudicing himself prior to conducting your shooting investigation. He won't make that mistake again; I won't let him!"

"So Bass did try to get me fired just now." No surprise there, but I've tried beyond my capacity to remain professional, have avoided being a jerk to Rhonda after discovering her DEA-husband Allan, died at the hands of the Dixie Mafia. I guess some people need to learn the hard way. "Uh-oh, heads up." Jason turned to find Cole, Bass, Carla with Rodrigo, and an older Hispanic male I'd never seen before.

"Danny, take Tori and get her back to the barn." I started to protest but Jason held up his hand. "Trust me now, please?" I nodded and followed Danny as Jason called Boop. "Boop, we may have a little problem!"

Two hours later, Jason arrived with Cole, Bass, Rodrigo, and members of the Baez family. The older, bald Hispanic male, I discovered, was Carla's father. His long face and nose denoted possible Italian descent, but the skin tones and speech patterns defined the Latino heritage of Ingleside Asst. Police Chief Pete Baez. The nameplates for me and Santana had changed to match our covers at TAMU-Corpus Christi. "Ladies and gentlemen," Jason started off, "I believe everyone here is familiar with Agents Bass, Cole as well as Carla and Asst. Chief Baez?" Everyone nodded. "This other young man is Carla's boyfriend Rodrigo Aponte-Sosa."

Danny rose from his desk and never broke eye-contact with his fellow FBI agents or the Baez family and Rodrigo. "So Jason, allow me to get this whole situation straight in my head for a moment…" Uh-oh, when an FBI agent connected to TFCC started an observation in this manner, someone's about to lose their jobs. And for once, no one glared at me in that tone of voice. "Members of my own parent agency, along with a local, small-town assistant police chief; his daughter and her Madrid boyfriend; may have just jeopardized two new investigations initiated by this newly formed version of TFCC? And one we inherited from NCIS-Naples? What were you people thinking?"

"We didn't know about the drug investigation and its companion case at TAMU-Corpus Christi, or at least I didn't," Cole said as he gave Bass the evil eye. When she started to squirm, I almost jumped out of my seat. However, I stayed where I was as Cole asked Bass, "Tell me you didn't blow any current undercover operations conducted by this task force?"

"No, I haven't; tempted to, but not yet!"

Slowly I stood as Boop moved to keep me from ripping Bass limb from limb. Unfortunately, someone forgot to cut Santana off. She reached Bass and put her right arm in an upright Fujiwara armbar. It's a wrestling arm lock that can break the arm at the elbow if the proper leverage was applied. "I will ask you once; after that, I start breaking limbs Agent Bass!"

"Sam?" Jason asked cautiously.

"No Jason," Cole said which surprised all of us. "I want Prof. Wriggle to ask." Santana looked into Cole's eyes. "If she's dirty, I want to know Sgt. Wriggle. If she doesn't answer, break her left leg next!"

"Who did you call in the Med to blow our op on Malta?" Bass struggled as Santana bent the elbow further. "Who did you call?"

When Santana applied enough pressure on Bass's elbow, she screamed, "NCIS Agent-Afloat Dumont Talbot!"

I walked passed Boop and bent down in that traitorous witch's face. "Why, why would Dewey Talbot take that call and blow us and then die in a stinger attack on his own floating airport?"

"He owed me for some gambling debts his father accrued from a gambling house in Savannah, GA. I busted the racketeers and discovered they were front for the Blanton family of Charlotte, NC." I glared into her eyes. If she ratted me out again, Santana would have to hold me back from breaking her neck and carving a bloody rose over her heart. "You know the family…Agent…Torelli?"

I smiled because I had her and now she owed me! "I know Tori…quite well. She wrestled for a women's tag-team title in Japan when I served as Agent-Afloat board one of our carriers. She left her family because of their criminal activity. Tori…always suspected one of her siblings of killing her mother, step-father, and her younger twin siblings. Do you know which one called that shot?"

"Tessa did, and she was damned proud of her evil. But…she took her cues from a shot-caller from the Detroit Mob; who I don't know. The FBI might know, but I don't." As I rose and Santana let her up, Bass dared to cry out. "I'm sorry; about Dewey…about all of it!"

I handed Boop my weapon and my shield. I turned back around and slapped the hell out of Rhonda Bass. "I don't care who does it. Take her shield, her weapon and get this traitorous bitch out of my squad room, building and off my station. If I see her again Agent Cole, I'll take her kicking and screaming to Tori Blanton, and watch her carve a rose above her heart…alive!" I turned and ran from the squad room to cool off and mourn those who Rhonda Bass betrayed.

As I fled the squad room, I heard Jason yell at Carla, her father, and young Sosa. "Now for you three!"

SEVEN

A crib in a police or federal agency office served as a place of rest when law enforcement was required to remain at work to complete investigations. Usually, these places were enclosed with several feet of concrete blocks and housed several beds and bunk beds like at a police academy or basic military training dormitory. In this crib at TFCC HQ, I fell into a lower bunk bed across from the door, rolled up in a fetal position and cried my eyes out. My first official day with TFCC and I almost resigned a couple of hours ago.

I had to come here, get away from everyone, and try to process every-thing...and failed miserably. And the fear, doubt; everything someone in my job dealt with, hit me with a vengeance. Maybe that jerk Thorn was right; maybe I am a loose cannon. I just didn't know anymore.

"Tori, Tori are you in here?" I looked up into the darkness and saw Santana as she stood in the doorway. She turned on the light as I hid my face. I didn't want to see her or her see me. But she came over and sat on the lower bunk where I was curled up. "Hey, come on girlfriend; we've all had rough days on the job. You know that."

"Not like this one; not when I killed my older sister...the bitch!" And Tessa was a bitch.

"Now's not the time to hide out in here; moaning, groaning and carry-ing on baby-doll." I looked up again and saw Jennifer with Boop and Leah in tow. But the fourth woman, I didn't recognize. She was a black woman tall and proud, like a weapon prepared for war. Her soft, brown eyes com-plimented her bright smile and her powdered blue dress with black pumps. Former FBI Special Agent Cassandra Coltrane marched over and sat down on the bunk opposite of mine. "Well, well, well; I am certainly blessed to make your acquaintance Miss Tori. I am former FBI Special Agent Cass Coltrane." She took my trembling hands into hers. "Ah, adrenaline; it's a cop's best weapon in the face of danger.

You never feel the tremors until after a shooting review or a word with the agency-appointed psychologist. Or in your case when someone like me comes along to hold your hands."

"I feel…completely useless right now…Cass. I don't know which end is up or right…where do I go from here?" I'm sure I looked like a lost puppy to Cass Coltrane. But her smile shined brighter than the lights inside the crib. "What happens now?"

"Now, Rhonda gets an opportunity to spend the rest of her life in a "Club-Fed" facility, or testify to what she did, against the Dixie Mafia and possibly WITSEC," Jennifer mentioned WITSEC, an acronym for Witness Security…or commonly called the Witness Protection Program. Once Bass testifies in open court as to her participation in the debacle of Malta, the attack in the *Abraham Lincoln,* and her constant harassment of me in the performance of my duties, she will be given a new identity with documentation, a job, and relocation to a place where no one knows her. The US Marshal's Service will watch over her…until the day she dies.

"If that hussy's smart, she'll choose option two and testify. We might find who in Detroit setup, everyone, to die in Malta." Boop's words brought comfort and pain. Dewey helped her betray us all, and his reward was a quick, painless death. He's the lucky one in my opinion.

"Tori?" Santana asked as I snapped out of it. "Where were you girlfriend?"

"Every time someone mentions Malta, I drift back to that damned dungeon. The beatings, the torture, the watching of that stinger fired into the harbor; hitting the Abe Lincoln. The SEAL team's arrival and…my own savage escape from captivity. And the…sadistic smile of satisfaction as I watched three big bruisers from the Beluga Crime Family of Sicily, slowly die…clutching the bloody roses I carved into their chests." I took a breath before I continued, "I looked at myself in the mirror after the… deaths I committed, and asked myself, 'Are you that cold? Could you be like your family if pushed beyond your tolerable limits?'" I turned with tears in my eyes and looked into the eyes of these…sisters of the shield and nodded. "I discovered I could be that cold, and heartless. And…it scared me!"

"If it never scared you Tori; we'd be worried about you...Jason too." Jennifer's words reminded me of just how Jason's harrowing experience mirrored my own. I guess that's why my boss liked me so much. He found a tenacious, honorable, female version of himself. But I was still too new to the job to pull some of the nonsense he pulls to keep us working cases. Hence, why he chewed me out about my shooting evaluation with Nick Thorn.

Then Jennifer embraced me and held me firm. "Come on girl, you have a job to do and a case to finish."

"Okay, I'll do it. But after these cases are in the books, I need to go out and cut loose. I've been taken my job way too serious this past year." I laughed as did everyone else while we made our way to the squad room.

We returned as Jason set out to rip into Asst. Chief Baez, his daughter Carla and the young toreador, Rodrigo. "Do you three have any idea what you almost did? You came close to jeopardizing a federal investigation; by simply tailing Dillon here to TFCC!"

"Dillon was rude to me and Rodrigo after class!" Carla yelled, "I wanted to give your bratty son a piece of my mind!"

Jason laughed as he put up the surveillance footage from this morning's class. He cued it up to the point where Rodrigo introduced himself to the class. *"¡Hola! or Hello, I am Rodrigo Aponte-Sosa. I am Carla's most recent romantic conquest. My family's claim to fame is we are the oldest family in Spain to serve in the Bull Fighting rings of Spain as well as run with the bulls in Pamplona."*

"I was able to confirm that much from Interpol's office in Madrid concerning you, young Senor Sosa. But this outburst as a result of Dillon's answer to Rodrigo's question concerning his alleged unrequited love for Carla is what set this whole situation off."

He fast-forwarded to Carla's outburst and Dillon's...alleged rude response. *"I don't believe you, Dillon Vaughn. I don't believe you just... moved on like that!"*

"Your father helped that along Carla, and you followed his advice and left here. You, not him, made that decision. Move on and stop throwing your conquests in my face. I don't have time for childish antics anymore."

42

Jason gave Asst. Chief Baez the evil eye as Dillon further elaborated. *"I almost died last spring. You know what your father told me when he came to visit?"* I watched her head shake again. *"He said with Rodrigo's smug arrogance, 'Too bad the Ruskie missed; one less Vaughn in the world would do it some good'! Take your bullshit elsewhere Carla; I have no time for it!"*

Jason paused the tape and then stood nose-to-nose to Asst. Chief Baez. "'One less Vaughn in the world would do it some good?' Wow, I had no idea my family offended you so grievously Asst. Chief Baez! And what business did you have visiting my son during his convalescence in the hospital? Who were you really visiting that day?"

"Maria was diagnosed with Lupus a year ago. She was in the cancer wing for Chemotherapy. I heard about the incident at TAMU-Corpus Christi and that Dillon was shot. Maybe…I should have just left him alone." Jason gave Baez an angry, doubtful look.

"Why didn't you just leave him alone…then?"

Jason's angry green eyes never broke eye-contact and Baez stood there…stone-faced. Jason shook his head and chuckled bitterly. "Still holding on to that old, fear of my family being too controlled and too disciplined to let someone like you get under our skins. Carla finally succeeded in getting under Dillon's today, but in doing so, has landed her, her new beau Rodrigo, and you; in boiling hot water. Let go of this nonsense Pete; it'll ruin your career and your family."

Jason turned to Carla. "And you…*chica*; your continued harassment of Dillon and my undercover agent he's with, will get your cute little ass thrown in the station lockup for obstructing a federal investigation. Are we crystal clear on your scholastic objectives for this semester young lady?"

"Yes, sir." Carla's response was so quiet; she feared Jason would throw her in the station lockup that moment. She gave me a passing glance and turned her eyes away. "Rodrigo, you need to sign the form on the desk. It's a US Justice Department Title Eighteen form. Dad and I signed ours already."

"And I should sign this form…why Senor Vaughn?"

Jason smiled as if he swallowed the proverbial canary. "Failure to sign this form guarantees you will be red-flagged by the US Government as a national security risk. I will then, have your student visa revoked and deport you back to Spain. *¿Esta comprende chico?*" Jason's command of the Castile dialect of Spanish surprised even Rodrigo. The young man nodded. "Excellent; sign and leave with the others!"

After Rodrigo signed his Title Eighteen, all three turned to leave. But Carla turned back and asked, "What about Dillon?"

From behind the crowd, my undercover lover, *jeez I need a life*; Dillon approached and stood next to Jason with Jennifer flanking Dillon. "What about me Carla?"

"Honey…" Baez began.

"Papi; you and Rodrigo wait for me downstairs please?" Baez and Rodrigo went downstairs as Carla turned to face Dillon and his parents. "What my father said last spring; he was out of line. And you never answered my question, which I felt was rude. But I see now, she can't be your girlfriend; not while she works for your father."

As I was about to put my size-eight boot up her ass, Dillon calmly smiled. "How do you know what my social life is like where my father's business is concerned…Senorita Baez?" Carla's eyes widened with obvious shock as Dillon continued, "Furthermore, how do you know in the last two years, I haven't taken dual credit coursework and completed law enforcement training at FLETC to work for my father…Senorita Baez?"

"I don't, but I'm willing to bet you haven't…Senor Vaughn." Carla's neutral expression told the story. Dillon's mental discipline and calm, controlled demeanor returned and it unnerved Carla. "However, regardless of any…career aspirations at this point, if Gina is your choice…for love; who am I to chime in on your life? I hope she makes you happy." With that final word, Carla Baez followed her father and lover…downstairs.

Jason dialed his cell phone and spoke briefly. Then he looked to his family and to me. "Blanton, upstairs in OPS with us now. Vale needs a word!"

Dillon stopped him and asked, "Did I just cause a problem, Pop?"

"I don't know. What I do know, is Cole called the Navy Yard and expressed…concerns as to the new make-up of TFCC. Your bluff a moment ago; probably the most ill-timed smart-assed play in history." Dillon and I both groaned collectively as we journeyed upstairs to OPS.

EIGHT

The OPS center of an NCIS office for our size is a mini version of the Multiple Threat Analysis Center or MTAC at NCIS-Washington, D.C. On the big seventy-two inch screen, the image of NCIS Asst. Dir. Leo Vale appeared. He was a distinguished black man in his early fifties with a bald head, silver round-rimmed glasses slightly shaded, and a thin goatee which framed his pearly-white teeth admirably. His tan two-piece suit with white dress shirt and dark blue tie made for a palatable image for a vid-conference. *"Welcome to the region Agent Blanton. You've had a, shall we say, colorful past six months as an NCIS agent with only a year under your belt?"*

I sensed this conference headed south from the get-go. "A very...mild description of the past six months...sir." It was the only response I had under the circumstances. Then another man, distinguished in his appearance, appeared next to Vale. He was slightly taller with gray sideburns and sported a dark gray two-piece suit.

I watched Jason shake his head as he viewed the monitor. "Vincent Darrow; let me guess...SEC-NAV hates me now!"

"No, she loves you...which is why I'm here; Malta and Abe Lincoln issues aside."

"Come on Vince; don't start with the riddles now. Those two cases are connected to the Dixie and Sicilian mafias with a foreign crystal meth supplier. But the Dixie Mafia's falling apart. And their Detroit Mob sponsors are about to scatter."

Recently appointed NCIS Director Vincent Darrow nodded. *"You always knew how to fine-tune a conversation Jason; I missed that not dealing with you for the last ten years. As you can see, SEC-NAV Elise Marcum asked me to come back to lead the agency; primarily because of our prior experiences. She also expressed concerns of you accepting Agent Blanton's transfer to fill retiring Darius Coltrane's slot.*

45

May I ask why you didn't consider anyone else or...keep FBI Agent Bass?"

Jason looked to me; and back to Darrow. "Former FBI Special Agent Bass's...treasonous actions led to the Malta op being the disaster it became; which led to the tragic deaths aboard *Abraham Lincoln*. Need I explain that particular can of worms sir?" Jason knew Darrow well, but in my experience; when old friends become formal, the tension from some higher up affected this reunion.

"The issue of her crimes isn't the problem; it's how it was allowed to come to fruition. But as I explained to Marcum, every agency has its mavericks that get the job done. You're an NCIS maverick, but you work within the rules more often than not. And that annoys some politicians and some of my fellow bureaucrats on the beltway. I also told them when they support compromises that their legality can be challenged; you excel at being a pain in the ass."

"Well, now they know if they didn't before." Jason smiled as did Darrow. "But I'm assuming we're about to discuss what happened moments ago in my office?"

"The fact you called Leo and I was here to consult; probably will save us loads of headache in the long run. Dillon, what were you thinking?"

Dillon eyed Director Darrow and switched off between him and his dad. Finally, he answered, "My words were inappropriate at the time sir. My intentions were to impress upon Miss Baez her continued interest in my personal life, would not be tolerated. I apologize for misrepresenting federal law enforcement and myself, sir."

Darrow nodded as a short, black woman entered the monitor. Her dark, shoulder-length hair complimented her dark blazer with red dress blouse. Secretary of the Navy Elise Marcum smiled. *"Apology accepted Mr. Vaughn; you do have your father's personality as far as your careful words, thoughtful diction in your phrasing and an obvious repentance when you've done something wrong. And before you ask Jason, yes, we're all here at the Navy Yard. We flew to Norfolk so we could view the damage done to Honest Abe by the illegally procured stinger. Before your regular team of investigators began their journey back home, I complimented them on their speedy actions and initial arrests in both Malta and the crystal meth case. So I asked Vince and Leo to allow me to sit in on this part of the briefing.*"

Jason nodded to me as Lightning loaded the footage from Dillon's phone. I took it from there. "What you're about to see, ladies and gentlemen, is a senior for the TAMU-Corpus Christi football team, acting as if someone gave him happy pills during class." We watched as the young man began dancing around the class and speaking out loud exerting little or no control over his actions. Then he collapsed. "Young Mr. Vaughn stopped filming the footage and dialed 911. When Donovan Corey collapsed, we received updated intelligence from the Med indicates this batch of crystal meth will incapacitate or kill with only a five or ten cubic centimeter dosage. It's extremely potent and potentially lethal."

"My God; lethal speed to create a worse epidemic than Ebola, sarin or anthrax! And if it was sold to sailors, Marines and civilians alike...?" Marcum asked.

I confirmed Secretary Marcum's fear. "We might be looking at a potential national security threat on the same level as a chemical, biological, or nuclear attack. The exception: someone looking for recreational pharmaceuticals might get themselves killed in the process."

"And killer speed is scary enough! Young Mr. Vaughn; well done and good thinking; you might have assisted in busting this case wide open. Anyone new appear at TAMU-Corpus Christi that coincides with this incident?"

Dillon dropped and shook his head. I knew what he was thinking, and I prayed I was wrong. The moment he spoke the words, my fears were founded. "The only people who appeared here that coincided with this incident is the appearance of Carla Baez and her new boyfriend from Spain– Rodrigo Aponte-Sosa."

"The moment he was mentioned, we did a Class One background check with Interpol-Madrid on the Sosa family." Lightning smiled as he inputs more information. "A deeper check resulted in the Sosa family of Madrid's connection to several in-country pharmaceutical companies. Some of the chemicals analyzed from the speed found on Mr. Corey come from the mountain regions near Madrid."

Darrow shook his head. *"That's too close of a coincidence to ignore. Jason, between SEC-NAV and I, we will contact the Spanish government as well as have the State Department speak with Spanish diplomats to inform them of our need to expedite a conversation with Mr. Sosa since he's been served with a Title Eighteen form. Also, as it pains you to do so, speak with both Asst. Chief Baez as well as Carla. They might not know who she's dating or if so, why they failed to report his sins."* Then Darrow said, *"Dillon, you know Carla better than anyone there, is it possible she's in bed with this guy?"*

"It would be a guess, but I doubt she'd come back here a criminal in this instance."

"Spoken like a man with a future in law enforcement; honest with an innocent until proven guilty *mentality."* Marcum smiled, but she saw as I did, the blank neutral expression on Dillon's face. *"But you don't believe it or the situation."*

Dillon nodded noncommittally his head from side to side. "Carla might be innocent, but I agree where Rodrigo's concerned. Asst. Chief Baez believes I'm not normal because I try to make life easier for my folks by living a controlled, disciplined life. So it makes me think maybe Rodrigo's too perfect and because he's from Old España; perhaps it's blinded Chief Baez to the point…he's too perfect and can't see the blemishes."

I observed Dillon's manner, eyes, vocal inflection; he was clear, concise and totally analytical. Jennifer noticed it too, so she asked point blank. "So, you're not jealous of this new boyfriend of Carla's? And all this circumstantial analysis you're offering has nothing to do with the Baez's prejudices towards our family?"

"My analysis has nothing to do with that knucklehead chief or his bratty daughter. Her mother's illness would bring her back home from Europe. And yes, she might bring a boyfriend to experience the American University Educational System; but if she only met him in the last six months to a year? That's a red flag to anyone who knows Carla. And anyone who knows Carla knows her father's extremely prejudiced towards anyone here who isn't Latino. Mom, when she left on his advice, I supported it. Why, because she needed the life experiences. My reaction to this shocked him more than it did anyone else. He wanted her away from me and got his wish." He took a breath. "He thought I'd act all heartbroken. I was, but it wasn't my decision for her to study in Madrid; he encouraged her, and she chose it. So I'm not going to mope around and miss her while she's romanced by some young Toreador. I have a life too."

"Who are you and where did my son go?" Jennifer asked tongue in cheek.

Dillon smiled and kissed Jennifer on the cheek. "You're son's still here Chief; he grew up and assumed a man's responsibilities...as well as a man's consequences. Getting shot last spring for doing the right thing; an example of accepting a man's consequences." Jennifer's sudden sharp breath caused Dillon to gently grab her shoulders. "Mom, I said that because you think someone's going to target me again. Even the folks on the screen know of our family's struggles to live a normal life here. Carla's a phase in my life I'm over. If something develops with Tori Blanton; it will, and I will make sure it never interferes with my schoolwork or her job. If and when that does, I will tell her enough. And she and Dad will be there when that decision is made."

Secretary Marcum chimed in, *"Chief Vaughn, I believe this case will work out one way or another. Dillon's made smart decisions for the most part; so has Agent Blanton. There were some minor bumps so far, but nothing that wasn't handled in the proper light and format. Agent Blanton, listen and learn from your SAC. I believe his career highlights will help you avoid career pitfalls he's already endured; including dealing with no-account bureaucrats like us!"*

I shook my head as Secretary Marcum smiled. "Madame Secretary, I would never, ever call you a no-account bureaucrat ma'am. You've done too much for the Navy and this agency to insult you in that manner. Please keep up the good work and we'll do our jobs the best we can."

Marcum smiled. *"You're a keeper Agent Blanton; regardless of the feelings of Dir. Darrow or Asst. Dir. Vale. If you're willing to give me props, you're a keeper."*

"I'd give props to any former JAG attorney who allows for trafficked women of our armed forces to be rescued and returned home safe and sound ma'am." Yes, I had heard the story of Captain Laquita Boggs and her harrowing experiences. And how this team brought down the Private Military Contractor and those who committed those atrocities. Wish I'd been there.

NINE

After our meeting with the upper echelons ended, we looked at the clock and it was time to go home for the day. Before I was able to gather up my gear to leave for the day, an older woman with sandy brown hair and blue eyes approached me. Her canary yellow blazer with a maroon blouse and black slacks gave my eyes a focusing issue as TFCC Unit Psychologist Dr. Amanda Wise smiled. Her dark-rimmed glasses dropped to the end of her nose. "Agent Blanton; I'm Dr. Amanda Wise. What time would you like to speak concerning the shooting incident?"

"I'm available tomorrow afternoon at 1500 hours if that will work for you Dr. Wise?" I'm hoping the time would because I promised the Vaughns I'd have lunch with them after my morning Kinesiology class (which I needed to make up from my original college years due to going to FLETC). So, I get an actual college credit here and there. Helped legitimize my cover as Gina Torelli.

Dr. Wise looked at her schedule. "1500 works great for me. Would you like your father present Agent Blanton?"

"No Doc; the post-shooting exit debriefing is my burden alone to bear ma'am."

"Are you sure?"

"Dr. Wise, is there some kind of concern as to my state of mind due to my family issues?" Yes, I'm asking because my career was my own and no one else's. I sighed, "Look Doc, my dad and I are good. We've basically reconciled after three years of no communication. IG Officer Thorn's concerns aside, my sister tried to shoot one or both of us, I ducked my father behind me, I pointed, fired and my sister's dead. If any discussion is further needed, I'll see you tomorrow afternoon. Excuse me please?" She nodded as I grabbed my backpack and headed to the elevator.

"Tori wait up," Santana yelled as I held the elevator door. She slid inside and I pushed the one button. As we headed down to the lobby, she asked, "Are you okay?"

"Unit psychologist; wants me to meet with her about the shooting incident. She wanted to know if Teddy needed to be there. I told her no." Santana nodded. "You disagree?"

"No," she said without facing me. Then she turned to face me. "Your sister chose her path; so did you. Yes, your dad pushed you away and it shaped your decision-making to become who you are now. If he hadn't done that, we never would have met on the Independent Wrestling Circuit, you wouldn't have gone to FLETC, and we wouldn't be here now. And your dad said he hates that you had to shoot Tess, but he doesn't blame you for your siblings being stupid. They chose to force him out and to come after you both. They must live with the consequences of their actions. You did your job and have done nothing to be ashamed."

When the elevator door opened, Dillon and the Vaughns waited for me. Dillon took me into his arms. Jennifer smiled. "He didn't get to speak to you after you shot Tess. He wanted to wait for you." And I didn't complain once about a handsome man's embrace.

Then Dillon kissed my forehead. "I'm glad you're okay."

"It's nice to have someone thinking about you besides a rotten old parent." I laughed.

Jason and Jennifer walked up, and Santana followed. "The moment I met you, Tori Blanton, I knew I could count on you to be a valuable asset to TFCC. Even in your down moments today, you have bounced back with the poise and maturity of a seasoned investigator. I will say this; you are still a young woman. And as a young woman, you have needs and desires that go beyond the scope of your job here. So I'll ask, where's your head and your heart?"

I smiled as I let go of Dillon and faced Jason. "My head's still in the game Coach. We have a plan; it's being implemented in steps and we know who might be supplying the crystal meth. I've scheduled my post-shooting exit debrief for after lunch tomorrow, and I haven't been fired. As my heart goes, it's slowly being stitched back together with a loving, supportive team…and adoptive family. Where Dillon fits in, that's still a work in progress due to the cases at hand. I want to say, I'm falling for him, but I'm afraid to say it." I looked into Jason's eyes. "Do you understand?"

Jason nodded as Jennifer embraced me. "I do too. And the reason why Dillon wanted to wait for you here is he feels the same as you. He wanted to make sure you were okay after hearing you were in a shootout."

I nodded as Dillon took me in his arms again. I whispered, "I guess I sold my cover too well?"

"Maybe; maybe meeting you last Friday night, I sort of knew this might happen." Wow, I knew I could get guys to fall for me, but I wasn't expecting this…much attention. But when Dillon's lips met mine, I saw skyrockets. I witnessed a new kaleidoscope of colors and I finally relaxed. All the tension left my body like the air that leaked from a balloon. I felt… at home now. "How are you doing now?"

You couldn't knock the smile off my face with a forearm shot to my jaw. "I'm doing much better than I was an hour ago. And I'm getting hungry. Do you people ever eat supper around here?" Everyone laughed as we headed out and met Gracie at the Pizza State.

The next morning I met Dillon for breakfast at Einstein Brother's Bagels on the TAMU-Corpus Christi campus. We both had electives at the gymnasium with my Kinesiology class while Dillon was taking a fencing class. When we arrived, Dillon kissed me goodbye as I headed upstairs to my classroom. When I arrived, I recognized a woman about twelve years older than I was sitting in the row where I wanted to sit. Her dark hair and full blue eyes smiled as warmly as her lips did and she nodded to me. She wore sweats and a white university long-sleeve tee as NCIS Special Agent Lena Ortiz nodded for me to join her. "Hi, I'm Lena Ortiz and you are?"

I used my cover ID. "Gina Torelli." We shook hands and I leaned in and whispered. "Jason sent you?"

She nodded. "Which is why I'm using my real name, and the fact I need the course credit for this class."

"No kidding…me too! My original minor at UNC was Phys. Ed. I needed the course to complete the minor. So, shall we meet up to study after our initial reports are written?" I smiled as Lena smiled and nodded. "Cool, I'll tell you about my...extra-curricular activities and you can tell me about your mom. Hear she's an NCIS legend."

"Sounds great; you know why I'm here besides you and the class right?"

"Look after Dillon?"

"Part of it; another part is Title Eighteen Enforcement."

I groaned, "Which of our two problem children is taking this class with us?"

Lena smiled devilishly. "Our brave, Old World Toreador Senor Rodrigo; feel like flirting with him to test his fidelity?"

"Nah; his hands and general constitution don't impress me." Lena's eyebrows furled downward. "Dillon almost broke his hand shaking it in our TV Media class yesterday."

"Well, that blows my Spanish Machismo fantasy all to hell!" We laughed as the class filled up and Rodrigo noticed me as Lena, and I sat at the back of the class. He headed our direction and took a seat next to Lena. Rodrigo sat down as Lena greeted, "¡Hola Senor!"

Rodrigo eyed me carefully and nodded politely to Lena. "Hola Senorita; forgive me, but I might need to move to another seat."

"Did I offend you Senor...?"

"Sosa, Rodrigo-Aponte Sosa; no Senorita you did not offend me. But somehow, I have offended your friend here and desire to not be a source of...irritation?" I smiled like a hungry crocodile as Rodrigo got up and left.

"What happened at the office yesterday afternoon to scare him like that?" Lena asked as I shook my head. Rodrigo looked back at me and I smiled devilishly. Suddenly, he got up and left the classroom just as the professor entered. "Are you about to tell me one hell of a story...Agent Blanton?"

"Something like that Agent Ortiz."

We met Dillon after our nine o'clock class. "Ah, I see you two met."

Lena smiled. "We did and scared Rodrigo right out of Kinesiology."

"We weren't trying to scare him off...honest!" I smiled.

"I don't know if Rodrigo needs the class or not, but Tori and I need it for our minor degrees. I guess he thought he could try something funny and she scared the bejesus out of him." Lena looked at Dillon who nodded. "What did she do?"

Dillon smiled and expounded on my joint exploits with Santana Garvin. "Well, her partner from a Mediterranean operation put former FBI Agent Rhonda Bass in a standing Fujiwara armbar. And after she yelled her confession to a shocked squad room, Tori handed her gun and badge to Boop, walked over, and slapped the piss out of Bass. Then Bass was relieved of her gun, FBI shield, her agency ID, and was arrested for treason. I think seeing that, scared him and my ex Carla to silliness."

Lena smiled and nodded her head thoughtfully.

"So, that's what this is all about huh? You exert a little…stress relief from the Malta incident and two college kids get a reality check."

"Not exactly; they know I'm an agent; just not my real name. That's the real reason for the Title Eighteen; as well as Carla's father Asst. Chief Baez across the bay." I gave Lena the full story along with Dillon as we noticed Rodrigo and Carla. Carla wore a green Islander t-shirt, blue jeans, and tennis shoes and glared menacingly at the group. She handed her fencing foil to Rodrigo and marched over with purpose in her eyes. She stopped and stood there daring someone to speak to her. So, I do. "Is there a problem?"

"You have Kinesiology at this time of day as well? What is it with you two? Are you and Dillon spying on us?"

Dillon slowly shook his head and asked calmly and collectively, "How did you register for your classes Carla?"

She fidgeted for a moment; then answered, "I registered online prior to returning home."

Dillon asked, "Rodrigo register in the same manner?"

"Si, why is that important to this discussion?"

"I registered in person prior to the fall semester beginning. From what I was told, so did Gina. According to the university bylaws on class and attendance; students who register in person, get first priority on class schedule and lab time. Since you registered online and not in person, the computer placed you based on class size and not according to your personal preferences."

Carla nodded her head from side to side as she carefully thought the matter through. "You're right; due to time zones and the way the Spanish network is set up, I got general class information, but failed to adjust my preferences when I returned home. Okay, you're not spying on me or Rodrigo. My apologies if I've been a jerk to you and to Gina. By the way, any of you have a remedial composition class before lunch?"

"I don't." Dillon smiled.

"Not me." Lena looked at me.

"I have a Quick Books class at eleven o'clock," I responded.

Lena's eyes lit up. "So do I…with Dr. John Mallard."

"Oh my lord; I found my Tuesday/Thursday study partner!" I said as Lena and I squealed with delight. Rodrigo and Carla closed their eyes and their faces soured with disgust. "What?"

"You two act like drippy college students," Carla said with disdain in her voice. "Dillon, you can have those nerds, I'll keep Rodrigo." Then Carla let her exposed fencing foil rest over Dillon's heart.

To her surprise and ours, Dillon disarmed her and pointed at her heart. Then he handed the foil back to her with the blade facing him. "Point that weapon at me again, I'll break it in half and spank you with it; clear… chica?" She nodded as he looked at Rodrigo. "Take her and go!"

TEN

"Was disarming her necessary Senor Vaughn?" Rodrigo stepped up and stood nose to nose with Dillon.

"What I did, was demonstrate to Carla when you point a weapon, any type of weapon at another person, be prepared to use it as a weapon. She violated a safety rule for the class. I simply reminded her I was prepared to use it against her if necessary." Dillon stood his ground and didn't move.

Finally, I had enough of this machismo demonstration. "Okay boys, that's enough. Senor Sosa, I strongly suggest you escort your girlfriend from the building and go on to your next class before I take you in for disturbing the peace." Then I glared into Carla's eyes. "You broke a safety rule; go report yourself to the professor who instructs you in the class. If not, I'll get Dillon to tell me and I will report you...go!" Both left as Dillon took in a deep breath. He walked over and sat on a bench outside the main gym of the athletic complex. "Are you okay?"

"They still want to push issues and limits. I'm not sure who is pulling whose puppet strings. I'm confessing here; both are now getting on my nerves." Lena knelt down and put her hands on his shoulders. "Some tough guy I am...huh, Aunt Lena?"

"You'll be okay buddy. However, I suggest we get you over to NAS Corpus Christi and have another talk with your dad about those two." We all nodded as we went the opposite direction and loaded up in Lena's G-ride. Then we headed to the office.

We arrived as Jason met us in the squad room. "Lightning caught the latest incident with Carla and Rodrigo. How are you holding up buddy?"

Dillon shook his head. "I almost played *El Zorro* with Carla Dad. My nerves are fraying!"

"Okay," Jason said as he wore a light blue dress shirt, tan khaki slacks, and brown loafers. Gently, he put his hands on Dillon's shoulders. "I want you to withdraw from those two classes. We have coverage on Carla and Rodrigo. Keep your other morning classes you have and…you can earn some extra credit towards your bachelor's in criminal justice."

"How?" That's what I was wondering…how?

"Well, you actually gave Darrow and Uncle Leo the idea yesterday with that nonsense you spouted off to Carla about your perceived law enforcement creds. Darrow and Vale had a little conference call with Dr. Desoto early this morning. He agrees with us these two are here to primarily upset your applecart for some reason. But he also came to the same conclusions about the crystal meth case we did and Rodrigo's timing to attend classes here in the US. The water lines are being replaced this semester from all the main water lines to the city. With all the construction around the campus, no one would suspect a second water utility truck of being a surveillance van for our case. We want you, Dillon, to assist with the on-campus surveillance."

"How do we deal with Rudy and my work schedule with the catering business?"

Jason smiled as I watched him work his magic. "Your mom will go speak with Rudy about this new wrinkle in working towards your degree. He won't penalize you for the time you spend working for us on this little assignment."

"Okay, Rudy will be on board; now, how's Mom with this little assignment?" Dillon asked a valid question considering Jennifer's anxiety.

"I'll handle your mother." Dillon shook his head and chuckled. "What, you doubt me?"

"No, I don't doubt you Dad; I doubt how calmly and coolly she'll take your reasoning. Remember, before I turned eighteen, I wanted to go to Annapolis; then become a SEAL?"

"Oh yeah, she's still kicking my ass on occasion about that." Then I saw in his eyes he found a solution to the problem. "Maybe what I need to do with you along, is to give Chief Vaughn a Demonstration/Performance briefing on the surveillance operation."

"Involving travel through the sewer and maintenance tunnels under the university street system?" Dillon smiled his question.

"Exactly!"

An hour later, right before lunch; a city water/sewer van was parked just outside the University Bookstore catty-cornered from the Dugan Wellness Center and across from the Computer Lab.

I took the first shift with Lightning and Leah as we tapped into the TAMU-CC's Security Camera System. Leah wore a light-weight city water denim uniform shirt with blue jeans and tan work boots. Lightning wore the light-weight coveralls with tan work boots as I wore a university facilities polo shirt with tan khakis with black work boots. "Jason, Jen and Dillon should be here soon."

Leah looked at Lightning as she zoomed in on an image of Rodrigo as he exited the computer lab. "Wasn't Sharon coming along to give Jen some…moral support?" I gave her a confused look. "Sorry Tori, Sharon is CCPD Tech Response/Cyber Crimes Chief Sharon Lester. She's a top computer forensic specialist. Sharon cut her computer chops as a teenage hacker from the Okefenokee Swamp near the Florida/Georgia state boundary. She made a deal to help the FBI Cyber Crimes Unit in Atlanta to track down hackers like her and then as a condition to her rehabilitation, she went through the Atlanta Police Academy when Chief Vaughn did. They've been friends and co-workers ever since."

"Wow, I'm getting to know the full gambit of law enforcement here in Corpus Christi." I thought of it an honor to work alongside Jason and TFCC. What no one expected, was Dillon's ex-girlfriend, Carla, to complicate our undercover operation to sniff out the crystal meth suppliers or dealers. Now Dillon's had to withdraw from classes he needs to satisfy our operation needs and keep the diplomats from going to war. But on the plus side; SEC-NAV Marcum, Director Darrow, and Asst. Dir. Vale agreed Dillon's participation in our surveillance on campus was beneficial. So, he got temporary creds and a shift in the van; sort of a paid intern. However the sticky point: alleviating Chief Vaughn's insecurities about said participation.

Then we heard a knock from the van's undercarriage. Lightning opened the door and up popped Dillon with Jason behind him. "Good afternoon all. We have Chief Vaughn and Asst. Chief Lester joining us today." I offered a hand to a raven-haired woman with hazel brown eyes and her hair tied back in a ponytail. She wore a city water/sewer polo with tan khaki trousers and tan work boots. Yes, this was how I pictured Asst. Chief Lester while undercover. "Chief Sharon Lester, this is NCIS Special Agent Tori Blanton.

"Tori, Chief Sharon Lester of CCPD."

"Pleased to meet you, Chief Lester." We shook hands after she climbed up into the van. Next, I helped Jennifer up. "Howdy Chief."

"Howdy; how is Jason's newest agent in the office as well as my son's new girlfriend?" The Vaughns, Dillon and I just smiled as everyone else's heads turned in curiosity. "Yes, you heard me correctly."

"Oh boy; does everyone else in the office know?" Leah asked as she gave me a low stare.

"They do; we're all good on that note," Jason said as Sharon shook her head. "What Sharon?"

Sharon looked at me and back at Jennifer. "Have you bothered to ask Grady, me or Stacy about this relationship since we're also adoptive aunts and uncles of this young man?" I could hear the doubt and the leery tones in her voice. She might have read about my exploits or seedy rep of my affiliation with Teddy Blanton. Jennifer's corrective glare made her nod her head. "Sorry, I had a blood relation who suffered from a few…visits from the Dixie Mafia for protection payments in Macon, GA. Any southern cop you run into where that organization has tentacles will have someone suffering at their hands."

"Which is why I left when I was a teenager Chief Lester; I grew tired of my older siblings taking pleasure in the suffering of others. But before I left, I showed them what bullying the baby sister led them to receive; each got a bloody rose tattoo from me. And I did it while having them wide awake, tied down to an old medical exam table with birthing stirrups to hold them in place." There, I finally peeled back the mystery of my dead sister's haunting words of her tattoo origin. "You see, my sister confessed on a video file, she killed my mother, stepfather and twin step-siblings. That's why she got her memento from me."

Leah chimed in, "Hell of a way to send a message Tori."

"It was, and that's what caused the initial rift between me and Teddy. He told them to leave me and Mom alone with our new family. And they felt too betrayed to honor his word. So, Mom and our new family died; and I avenged them by carving up my living, yet estranged siblings. I doubt Tad and Junior will forgive me for killing Tess. I'm still working on forgiving me for doing that."

Then to my surprise, Lester chimed in again. "Forgiving yourself when you take a life in the line-of-duty; is the toughest road to travel." Then she extended her hand to me again. "My friends and coworkers…call me Sharon. If you let it slip and place 'Aunt' in front of that…well, I won't bone you for it."

"Mine call me Tori; glad to know you, Sharon." Then Dillon sat where I was, and I guided him through the procedure. "Remember: anyone who meets up with, or makes exchanges with Rodrigo or Carla, are persons of interest and get their faces. Once you have those, run them to facial recognition to see if we get any hits. Any questions my dear?"

"Just one, and not about this…how are you holding up?"

"I'll be better once I speak with Dr. Wise and get it out of the way. You behave yourself, mister!"

"He's not the worry Tori; I'm too old to be fooling around with my boss's son. Besides, he's got you!" Sharon laughed as we all did. "See you later."

Before we were completely into the maintenance tunnel, Jason asked Jennifer. "Are you good with the surveillance security babe?"

"Yes," Jennifer said so Dillon could hear her confirmation. After we're a few feet away, she said with an honest tone. "I am good, but…if young Sosa is running this operation…?"

"Trust me babe; if this young Toreador is running an international crystal meth business; he doesn't want to tangle with your son. Why? Russians tried to kill Dillon in the spring. He returned fire and took out a top Russian Mob hit man. Everyone in the underworld fears the name…Shadow Wolf now. Even Carla's a bit unnerved by that little incident last spring. That's why she's constantly trying to get under his skin and testing him. Her father's pushing this as well."

"Title Eighteen's got him running like a scared rabbit at the moment," I chimed in as Jennifer took in a deep breath. "Asst. Chief Baez won't directly challenge anyone. He's a bureaucrat with a badge and he's in deep trouble with Chief Forsyth. I listened to you whispering in the background while Sharon and I talked. Jen, Dillon's not worried about Baez; neither am I. Is this some concern over Carla's mother and her lupus?"

"It is," Jennifer said quietly, "Maria's lupus is in stage one; very treatable and she's getting stronger. But if she finds out Carla or Pete's in serious trouble, she could relapse and go into stage two. Then her treatment options become limited."

Jason chimed in. "Then I suggest you talk to her with Carla present while her husband is at work; go visit her at the hospital and make sure Rodrigo's not present during the conversation. She might know of Dillon's incident last spring and understand your...concerns for his safety."

"Good point," Jennifer smiled. "Tori go on to your appointment. I'll let you know about that conversation later." She's right; it's time I faced Dr. Wise about my own troubles.

ELEVEN

I made it back to NAS Corpus Christi by 1500 (3 p.m.). I walked in and met with Dr. Wise. Her sandy brown hair she wove into a tight bun and wore a navy pantsuit with what looked like canvas deck shoes. Given her petite frame, the look denoted cuteness like a pixie with glasses. She sat with her legs crossed and a legal pad in her lap. "Okay Tori let's begin. You were estranged from your family for most of your teenage years when you moved in with your mother and stepfather…Terry…was it?"

"Yes."

"Not long after you moved in…what, a year later…they were murdered. Is that correct?"

"Yes." This was old news; why was she bringing this up again?

Then she took off her glasses. I guess she felt I needed to elaborate further. "Look, Tori, I know you think re-hashing your history at this point, is a pointless exercise. I need to know how you're feeling before all that business went down yesterday in order to help you deal with it if I can. According to your file, the FBI wanted to recruit you as well. Why not Quantico?"

I took in a sharp breath. "The FBI…was the agency that investigated my mother's death. I answered their questions about who I thought did this. Dad wasn't near the crime scene." Oh god, I thought this would be easy, but it's not. "When I told them of my sister's angry rants and how I thought my older siblings did this; you know what the lead agent said to me?" Dr. Wise shook her head. "He told me, 'Brilliant deduction kid; now do you have corroborating evidence to support your accusation?' He used a bunch of five-dollar college words to insult me rather than ask if I had proof my older sibs did this. So, I decided rather than join a top-notch, elitist crime-fighting club like the FBI, I thought one of the B-teams would be a better fit, and it has. So, if you ever worked for the FBI and I just insulted you now Doc, I apologize.

63

The stench of Rhonda Bass's betrayal of Malta and her attempts to insulate herself by getting me fired, are also points of distrust in the FBI...except for Agent Court."

"A former NCIS agent who made good replacing Cass Coltrane; and focusing on cleaning up one mess made by a dirty federal agent; impressive." Dr. Wise made notes as she took off her glasses again. This time, she put her legal pad on the coffee table that separated us. "One of the reasons why I was asked to speak with you in this meeting is your sharp, but professional critique of IG Officer Thorn's investigative method. I agree with you Tori; anyone who has never fired a weapon or killed anyone in the line-of-duty; has no clue how an agent or cop deals with the aftermath of the incident.

"And you're correct; I once worked for the FBI...as a Behavioral Analysis Unit member. And in my pursuit of serial killers and dangerous unsubs, I have fired my weapon and have killed in the line-of-duty. And I discovered the toughest road to travel, is the one where forgiving yourself for those situations, becomes a survival tool. Your particular situation is a double-edged sword because the perp you killed, was family to you; estranged or not." Wow, a psychologist who has traveled down the road I'm on...well, not exactly, but close. "And I can only offer my door to remain open to you if you need someone to listen when it gets difficult to navigate."

"I'm sorry I had to draw my weapon period. Am I sorry my dad was there, and he witnessed the aftermath, yes. Am I sorry she forced me to kill to protect others, yes. Am I sorry the person I shot is dead, no. Tessa chose a path of darkness, and I chose a path of light. And light can't exist without darkness in this world." And I never thought I'd say this, but what came next, didn't seem to faze Dr. Wise one bit. "And...I hate her for making me shoot to kill in that situation."

"And that attitude is shared by most LEOs who are forced to fire and kill in your situation. Doesn't matter if you're a federal agent, State Trooper, County Mountie, or city officer. Anyone with a badge or shield who must fire a sidearm to kill, to preserve others, always hates the one they've shot in that instance." She nodded and invited me to stand. I joined her. "Nothing wrong with you time won't fix…or heal. You're cleared for full duty Tori, but I am serious about that open door invitation. Come by if you ever need to talk, okay?"

"I'll keep it in mind Doc; you have a nice afternoon." Once I left Dr. Wise's office, I checked my watch. *Only fifteen minutes; wow…that has to be a record for Doc Wise!*

As I walked into the squad room, Jason and Jennifer noticed my smile. Boop, Mark Valiant, and Casey Collins did as well. Lena Ortiz walked in and noticed my smile too. "There she is guys, *Rosa del Diavolo* in the flesh. Tori, I'd like to introduce to you my cohorts who made those arrests on your tip here; NCIS Special Agents Marcus Valiant and Charlotte Collins. Mark's from L.A. and Casey's from Gatlinburg, Tennessee." I first shook hands with Casey Collins. She was my height, darker sandy brown hair, and brown eyes and wore tans and chocolates in her suit attire.

"Welcome aboard Tori, and nice job on those tips with the stinger." Casey smiled.

"I agree Tori, and I found something…Dewey might want you to have." Mark Valiant was as valiant as his name portrayed. Tall, dark as a caramel mountain with a nearly bald head and wore a light gray suit. His hands were bigger than anyone else's in the office, but he was as friendly as the day was long too. He handed me a brick-like container and inside was the championship set of dominoes Dewey won from our last tournament. "He left a note: that if anything happened to him, he'd want you to have this."

I took the seemingly small box and held it to my chest tightly. And I said barely audible to anyone else. "Rest in peace my friend, Dewey Talbot; we caught the traitor. Rest in peace." When I turned to face Jason and Jennifer, another couple walked in and stood next to them.

The woman looked almost like Jennifer, except her hair was darker and her left eye seemed more blue than hazel. Her husband had light brown hair, blue eyes and wore dark slacks with a powdered blue dress shirt. Then, I recognized the couple as Dewey's cousin and his wife: Grady and

Kate Talbot. Kate stepped forward and nodded. "Jen, I can see why Dewey liked her; she's a real pistol."

"She has her good points; for a youngster. Were we ever that young Katie?"

I heard the tongue-in-cheek humor between the identical cousins. I felt like I was watching a modern-day episode of the *Patty Duke Show*. "I was never her age; I was born middle-aged!"

"Jace, you have repelling ropes in the ceiling? I have a funny feeling it's getting deep in here!" Grady smiled as Kate looked at him and slowly shook her head. "You were the one who said you were born...middle-aged."

Kate looked at Jennifer. "And you think you and Jason have marital problems. See what I deal with on a daily basis?"

I didn't find it difficult to follow the humorous exchange between the cousins and their spouses. One aspect I found refreshing, was Kate's Midwest accent. She was definitely not from the south. And I heard similar tones in Grady's voice as I did from Dewey's voice. Both Georgia Bulldogs and I found them both intriguing. I walked up as they stopped trading barbs to pay attention to me. "Asst. Chief Talbot, I'd like to express my condolences on Dewey's loss."

To my surprise, Asst. Chief Talbot responded as he took my hands in his. "And in return to you and your father; I'd like to express my condolences on the loss of your sister Tessa." Before I could say anything, he held up his hand. "I know...you shot your sister. But you did that to protect your father, and several other folks in that restaurant at the time. And I know Dewey's smiling proudly at your accomplishments thus far Tori."

"Thank you, Chief Talbot."

"No, no formality Tori. As Jennifer has indicated, you're family. And in this...large law enforcement family, it's always first-name basis."

"Thank you...Grady; so you also have killed in the line-of-duty?"

"I did; first as an Army sniper; next as a cop much later in Savannah, GA. Also, I had a specialty as a CSI. So I know first-hand how to collect, analyze and disseminate evidence. And something I might have for your drug case. Dewey sent me his laptop; after he received a call from FBI Agent Rhonda Bass." Grady handed the laptop to Lightning as I looked at him. "There are times Dewey and I didn't always get along with you and your family; but when he became a federal agent, we'd bounce casework and scenarios off of one another. He told me if he ever got into a situation where he'd compromise his principles; he'd send me the evidence to bury his betrayers. Hence, he sent his laptop and I'm turning it in."

"Thank you, Chief Talbot, for your assistance!" Jason smiled.

TWELVE

While Lightning worked on Dewey's laptop up in OPS, I returned to TAMU-CC to relieve our surveillance team of Dillon and Sharon Lester. Leah came with me since the basic workings of the computerized equipment were familiar to her. Also, Lightning was very astute to teach her all the contingencies. It's like training your spouse in hacking, but no actual experience in hacking...scary huh? "Relief crew gang; time for you to go home for six hours and rest."

Sharon logged off and Leah logged on. I looked over what Dillon watched on the monitors and fed new information into the matrix. "So, are you bored with stakeout duty yet?"

"On the contrary, I found it quite engaging. And yes, I sound like I'm speaking Old World English terminology, but it's how I feel. Sharon and I used the time to play *I spy* on our targets and possibly other suspects." Dillon replayed his portion of the surveillance footage. He noted Carla's and Rodrigo's movements throughout the day. Carla met mostly with girls in her classes. But Rodrigo, men in two or three-piece suits met with him at different times before or after his classes today. "So, either all those guys are his academic advisors...?"

"...or those are dealers, other suppliers, or possibly Spanish government minders for Rodrigo. We need to find out who these guys are and their place of employment." Leah nodded.

Mark came and relieved both Sharon and myself as I accompanied Dillon back to NAS Corpus Christi. We walked in as Jason met us. "Good work on that surveillance kiddo. Lightning already uploaded the surveillance footage of Rodrigo's meetings he thought no one noticed." Then Lightning called down to Jason. "Vaughn, go Lightning. Yeah, okay." Jason ended his call and looked at us. "Come on, let's go up to OPS."

When we get up there, Santana joined us along with Danny Court, and Lena Ortiz. Lightning put up the surveillance footage Dillon siphoned off. "Okay boys and girls, the life and times of *Rodrigo Aponte-Sosa*. These four men who met with him before or after his classes, Spanish Government Security–Diplomatic Security Forces."

"All four of them?" Dillon asked shocked by the revelation. "Dad, is this their government's response to the Title Eighteen you had him sign?"

"No clue, but suddenly, we have a Spanish National with Diplomatic security out of the blue? Someone in Madrid's nervous. Maybe the Sosa family?" Jason looked at Lightning.

"Okay boss; Level Two security background check. But I might have to go dark this time." They gave one another a low, but conspicuous stare.

"Call into Darrow, not Leo, Darrow; and if he approves, whatever it takes!" Lightning nodded as he made the call. Jason turned to Dillon. "Your mom still here?"

"Yes, so is Grady and Cousin Kate; they're up in your office. Gracie arrived a few minutes ago."

"Good; go in and turn on the SCIF in my office. If the Spanish diplomatic goons appear, Tori and I will take them into the conference room. Go!" Dillon complied as Boop walked in. "Boop, you have the stuff to turn Tori back to normal?"

"You know it!" Boop smiled.

"Get her back to normal and replace the nameplates with real ones. Might as well make Carla, Rodrigo, and the Spanish government look like fools if they try to nail us."

"How screwed are we if this goes sideways?" I asked with a wince. Jason held his hand above his head. "Great, second day on the job and I'm going down the tubes with you!"

"Go big or go home; it's how this team rolls!" Jason smiled as I laughed. What a way to go!

After my natural color returned to my head, I went up and joined Jason in the conference room. There, we spoke with Dillon in Jason's office. Inside the conference room, his assistant, Polly Richardson, operated the conference keyboard. A woman of Navy distinction; she's a semi-retired Reserve Chief Petty Officer with skills that kept the office management in sync with NCIS-Chicago. Her mocha skin and light brown eyes framed her smile beautifully.

She nodded to me as our conference with Jason's office continued, "Anyway, we're gearing up for the Spanish government to come in here and cause a stink due to the Title Eighteen we dropped on Rodrigo's pointed little head. So, you guys are staying in my office under the SCIF until we deal with this issue."

Jennifer nodded. *"This is why you sent Dillon in here; to keep them from accusing him of a political or international incident. Jason, I spoke with Dillon after I visited Maria at the hospital an hour ago. She has an issue with Rodrigo due to his age and Carla's...lack of male experience. I told her about Dillon's incident last spring with the Russians and...about Pete's unannounced visit. He walked in and she read him the riot act about the Title Eighteen and threatened to divorce him if he ever came near us again. Both Pete and Carla are in trouble!"*

"More Pete than Carla I'm assuming?" Jason asked with a sly smile.

"That's putting it mildly, but Carla's been told by her mother to cool it on hanging out with Rodrigo until this Title Eighteen nonsense is sorted out. Carla's not in the mood to listen to anyone anymore. Why is that?"

"Mom, I think I know why." Dillon sighed heavily as he continued, *"Carla's upset I've moved on and won't pine after her like some lovesick puppy. Tori helped with that as her cover of Gina Torelli. Carla got under my skin, and she thinks I'll just stop living unless it's to express love for her. Apparently, I grew up in everyone else's eyes...except hers. She wants to relive high school...I don't!"*

Jennifer shook her head. *"And to think I was worried about Tori dating him! Was I ever wrong! Do I need to haul Carla into the station downtown and give her my version of* Scared Straight?"

"No Jen; that'll just irritate her more. Let me continue to play up my romantic interest in Dillon as Gina. I'll tell her I dyed my hair so I can blend in with the college crowd." At least I hoped my bluff would work. "Then again, I might just tell her who I really am. Her little ad hoc surveillance mission blew my cover. And by doing so, put all our lives at risk!"

"And that's why the Title Eighteen was served on Carla, Pete, and Rodrigo. Don't these guys get the point Dad?" Gracie asked. I guess when family security became an issue; the Vaughn children had equal say concerning family matters. *"Dad, I had another thought; if Carla blew Tori's cover...will that fall under the Obstruction of a Federal Investigation statute?"*

"Not unless her intention was to directly harm Tori's operation. She would likely be guilty of reckless endangerment than obstruction. Only a Q and A would satisfy that curiosity sweetheart." Jason quoted the actual law, but that only works if in a courtroom or interrogation.

I shook my head. "Maybe she needs a *Scared Straight* moment with me or someone to stop her nonsense, Jace." Then I offered, "We need to know just how...involved she is in this case."

"Maybe coming clean and informing her and Pete of what's at stake, might just straighten both of them up. One point of contingency: you and Dillon will have to continue to lie about the truth of your relationship...for security reasons."

I nodded as Dillon chimed in, *"Considering to some, our relationship might be questionable anyway, I agree. Looks like dating's on hold until we nail these chumps gorgeous!"*

I smiled and nodded. "Remember when I told you I thrive on competition?" Dillon nodded. "In this case, I know I'm the winner before the match is fought. And knowing that; turns me loose to engage in a full-court press to discover Carla's true motives."

After I concluded my little plan, Gracie beamed. *"I love it when a pro athlete installs basketball terms to thwart a bunch of bad guys!"* We all laughed as I prepared for my Q and A with Carla and Asst. Chief Baez.

THIRTEEN

The next morning after TV/Media; Santana and I removed Carla from the TAMU-CC campus and informed Chief Baez to join us at NCIS. We read Carla her rights as she continued to maintain she'd done nothing wrong in the last couple of days. Was she ever in for a reality check. When we arrived, Chief Baez stood and asked, "What the hell did you do young lady?"

"I don't know Papi; honestly I don't know." She looked fearfully into my angry eyes and gulped.

I nodded to Casey who took Carla's arm. "I'll put her in Room One. Who's handling the Q and A?"

"I'll be primary," I said meaning I'll be *Good Cop*. "Agent Court will be secondary," meaning Danny got the role of *bad cop*. "Santana, I need you and the boss in Observation." And I turned to Chief Baez. "Santana, take him with you. He needs to see how deep the hole his daughter has dug for herself."

"I'll handle it," she smiled as Chief Baez went with her.

Jason walked up to me. "You want to take this? I'm curious as to why?"

"Carla wants to face her rival for Dillon. Maybe she needs to see my true nature."

I purposely waited ten minutes before I walked in as Danny waited under the interview security cam. I sat down and arranged my file folders as Carla asked, "Now, do I get your real name...Gina?"

I smiled as I looked over my file. "You still think this is some kind of joke...don't you Carla? You think giving Dillon hell for moving on is the best method of closure for you to move on with a suspected drug trafficker?" I looked into Carla's eyes and her pupil dilated. *Genuine surprise; maybe she didn't know about her boyfriend's activities.* "I take it by the look on your face; you either knew or were suckered by a handsome Spanish Toreador?"

"I certainly didn't know!" Carla's smugness remained as Court walked over and stood over Carla menacingly. "Excuse me Agent...?"

"Court, FBI Liaison Danny Court. I guess it's time for you to come clean...my friend." He smiled menacingly again as I nodded.

I stared right into Carla's eyes. "I am NCIS Special Agent Tori Blanton. And your little...impromptu tail of me and young Mr. Vaughn has been researched by the Spanish government and as a result, jeopardized an undercover operation to discover the source of a new supply of crystal methamphetamines. A supply smuggled off of a US aircraft carrier which was attacked by the Sicilian Mafia from the Island of Malta three months ago. A supply that the basic chemical composition elements originate from a mountain region outside of Madrid, Spain." I let that knowledge settle on Carla's brain as I took a breath. "Coincidentally, a supply that appeared at TAMU-CC the week you enrolled in classes with the young Toreador Rodrigo Aponte-Sosa. A supply, that's already, claimed its first victim." I placed a photo of the late Donovan Corey of Dillon's Organic Chemistry class. "He died yesterday afternoon at the hospital."

Carla cried as Danny leaned in. "If you know something, tell us now!"

"I don't know anything! I just wanted to make Dillon jealous...that's all!" Finally, the truth came out. It was all a game, but a game that put the lives of our agents in danger, and Dillon.

"And tailing him to the south gate of NAS Corpus Christi; what about that?" Danny asked.

"Rodrigo felt...following him would unnerve Dillon to where he would quit going to class. He's very territorial in his protection of my honor. Any ex...suitors in his opinion, have no business breathing the same air as us." Carla calmed down some after my initial barrage of questions. But I believe she realized we were no longer playing a game. Hunting down this speed supplier was a deadly game of cat and mouse, and it was a game I intended on winning. "What will happen now?"

"We're not done yet. I need to ask you about these men." I laid out the photos of the men Rodrigo met with yesterday. "Do you know their names or how they're connected with Senor Sosa?"

Carla pointed to the security men. "These three work for Rodrigo's father, Ambassador Alejandro Aponte-Sosa. He's the Spanish trade emissary to the EU. This man is his maternal uncle Don Fernando de la Cruz. He owns Spain's largest pharmaceutical company. And he owns land in the mountain regions near Madrid." Then Carla's eyes lit up and her tears dried with anger. "You, you don't think?"

"That your boyfriend's involved in a crystal meth ring that someone on our side of the pond pipelined here to the US? It's possible, but it's also possible he's an innocent dupe like you are. I have to ask one more question. The thread you use to stitch together your clothing creations; who supplied it?"

"Don Fernando. He owns textiles as well as clothing manufacturing."

I suddenly was blessed with inspiration. "What exactly did Don Fernando supply you with to create your designs, Carla?"

She shook her head in utter shock. "Everything; materials, thread, even the sizing to keep the fashions from wrinkling."

"Sizing?" Danny asked with a blank stare.

"Liquid starch for dresses and non-denim material. Men never need it for anything Danny."

"Gee, thanks for the gender profiling!" Danny said sarcastically. Then he added, "Carla, you have any samples from your designs you feel…aren't up to your standards as a clothing artist?"

I watched as Carla's impish smile returned. She knew exactly what we wanted to do. "Actually, I have two or three samples of dresses and evening jackets that I don't care for at all. I have no problem parting with them. They were unsolicited ideas from Rodrigo's aunt; who fancies herself as a fashionista."

Even better, one of his relatives who got on poor Carla's nerves. "Okay, I'm going to have Agents Collins and Ortiz, since your family knows them, escort you where you're keeping your design samples and retrieve them. We'll write you a receipt for those items and provide you with a federal court order for the design samples."

"How could I have been so…naïve to think some young, handsome Spanish gentleman could actually fall in love with me? Do I have the words *young and foolish* written on my forehead Agent Blanton?"

"Not *young and foolish*, but you were naïve to think Rodrigo wasn't as or more clever than you. Sometimes, we learn those lessons the hard way."

"Well, I sure as hell learned this one the hard way." Then Carla looked at me with lost eyes. "You think...Dillon will ever forgive me for the trouble I've caused?"

I looked at her for the longest time as Casey and Lena came in and replaced Danny. "Forgive you; safe bet he will. The real question is will he ever trust you again? Dillon has to have all the variables before he can solve that equation. So I can't speak to the trust issue or lack thereof."

She nodded as Casey gently took her arm. "Come on kiddo; let's go get those design samples."

Once I exit the interview room, Jason exited with Chief Baez in tow. "Care to tell me why I can't accompany my daughter to her apartment?"

"First, you're not a federal agent; second, you're an Ingleside Assistant Police Chief and not a chief on this side of the bay. And finally, if I cut you and Carla slack during a federal investigation, I lose my job. And after the stunts your family's pulled in the last six months; you're damned lucky I haven't asked Chief Forsyth for your badge and your ass on a silver platter!"

"All right Jason I get it. I've acted unprofessionally and I'm guilty of being a Grade A asshole! Carla's my only daughter!"

"And you think Dillon, or we didn't understand that she was *that* precious to you?" I stopped and watched as Baez took in a sharp, deep breath. "I'm fortunate, I'll admit that. I have only the one son and the one daughter, but I also have the right to protect my children. But Jen and I, we have to let Dillon grow up now and make his own decisions. Some will be good, some bad. But he knows what doesn't kill him, will make him stronger; as you already know."

"That's certainly true," I said as I passed them in the hall on my way to the squad room.

Before I rounded the corner, I heard Chief Baez comment. "She's a hard ass in the same vein as you Vaughn."

"Oh, I've mellowed in the last twenty-five years. Blanton's much worse than I am!" I peeked around the corner and caught Jason winking at me. Yay, he really, really likes me!

Thirty minutes later, Carla returned with Casey and Lena with one blue cotton dress and two cotton-polyester jackets; one yellow and green, and one red and blue. Casey handed Carla a receipt. "You understand; if these garments contain what we suspect…we won't be returning them."

"I understand Agent Collins; even if you don't find what you're looking for, destroy them. I won't be taken in by a handsome face anymore." I saw the sad, humiliation in her eyes as Chief Baez put his arm around her. Father and daughter left as our case was about to pick up steam.

FOURTEEN

Thursday, we picked up surveillance as Dillon attended his other morning classes. This morning, I was in the van with Boop and Casey. I wore one of my TAMU-CC Maintenance and Facilities green polo shirts with khaki trousers and black work boots. Both my cohorts wore blue City of Corpus Christi light-weight coveralls with tan work boots. "Hey Boop, there's Dillon. And look at this; isn't that Rodrigo with his uncle Don Fernando?"

Boop zoomed in on the computer lab. "Yes, looks as if they're waiting for him. All units, all units; computer lab. Circle the wagons with Shadow Wolf...now!" I donned my vest and checked my Sig to make sure I had a full clip. "Casey, go with Tori! Go, go!"

When we arrived at the computer lab, Jason and Jennifer met with Dillon. As Rodrigo and Don Fernando stepped forward, we hung back as Dillon nodded to us. Jason and Jennifer's badges shined from their belts as their jackets were pulled back to expose the deadly weapons both knew how to use with deadly precision. "Vaughn!" Rodrigo stepped forward with his uncle in tow and with a hurried gait as Dillon turned and clenched his fists... prepared for battle. "You took Carlotta from me! I will destroy you pero!"

Dillon laughed, "Really; the man who can't handle a man's handshake, and you declare you will destroy me; how? Are you going to talk me to death; peon?" My Castilian dialect was current as Rodrigo called Dillon a dog, and Dillon called Rodrigo something worse...a peasant. And due to the pedigree, Rodrigo originates, Dillon, calling him a peasant was equal to calling him a zero. Rodrigo rushed Dillon full of rage as Dillon perfectly executed a deep-arm drag take-down and stood quickly in a fighting stance as Don Fernando removed a silver Beretta nine millimeter pistol. But as he raised the weapon, it fell from his hand as bloodshot from the shooting hand.

I scanned over and witnessed the smoking barrel of Jennifer's black Glock service pistol. "You try that again, and you return to Madrid in a steel box Don Fernando! Stand down gentlemen!" We took a visual inventory as members of Don Fernando's security detail stepped forward with weapons drawn. "I said stand down now!"

When one of the Spanish guards raised his black Beretta; Jason fired and shot the man between the eyes. "Okay, one more time and this time the federal agent gives the orders. Drop those weapons or Chief Vaughn and I drop you...now gentlemen!" Weapons dropped by the remaining four men as federal agents rushed up and arrested them as well as Don Fernando. Jason and Jennifer stopped the pending fight between Dillon and Rodrigo. Jason arrested Rodrigo on the spot. "You're under arrest for assault young man. You have the right to remain silent..." As Jason read Rodrigo his rights and finished, then he asked. "You have any weapons or sharp objects such as knives or needles on your person?"

"Go to hell!" Jason and Dillon shook their heads as Rodrigo ranted further. "She discovered crystal meth properties on the clothing she designed. It was the perfect setup...all she had to do was create and sell her clothing! But you had to ruin it all!"

"I didn't ruin a thing for you. You, Rodrigo, you lied to her, used her to bring illegal controlled substances into this country. If she broke it off, that's on you amigo...not me." Then he walked up and stood nose to nose with the diplomatically protected Spanish brat. "You're lucky it wasn't Carla's father that arrested you; he'd killed you slowly and methodically. He hates anyone who makes his family look like fools. He may not like me, but he hates your guts right now. And that's motive enough for him to rip you apart."

"So where is this padre who loves his little Carlotta; huh? Tell me, where is this Pero Tejano?" Then Dillon stepped aside to where Ingleside Asst. Police Chief Pedro "Pete" Baez stood and smiled like a hungry cougar. I watched with an evil glint in my eye as Baez slowly walked up and stood next to Dillon.

"Hiya Chief; you didn't happen to get an invite from my mother, did you?"

"Oh no I didn't get the invite from Chief Vaughn; but Agent Vaughn felt if trouble brewed up over on this side of the bay, I might want to...observe Task Force Corpus Christi in action. And based on how it closed both of these cases; very entertaining!"

Dillon smiled. "It demonstrates the philosophy of warriors who believe in the teachings of Arthasastra: the enemy of my enemy...is my friend. I'll let Chief Baez explain it to you." Dillon nodded to Baez and left.

"Mijo; allow me to explain it to you this way. The King and Queen of Spain will hold tribunals against the corrupt police officials and those of your family's businesses. And I met the head of Spain's Interpol office in Paris at an international police conference last year. I called him at Agent Vaughn's request. Your student visa will be revoked, and you and your uncle will return to Madrid...as international narcotics dealers...the illegal type."

"I...loved Carlotta, Senor. I would have shamed young Senor Vaughn for you."

"And you felt I would benefit from your what, benevolence mijo? In my family boy, honesty is the definition of honor. You, little peon, have dishonored my daughter by your deception. But I prefer the political, suicidal method of interdiction; yours and your family's Rodrigo. Enjoy your flight back home!"

"You heard the Chief people...move them out!" Jason smiled as he nodded to Baez and Dillon shook hands with Carla's father. "Excuse me gentlemen; mind clearing off my LZ please?"

Dillon smiled as did Baez, "Copy that...boss!" Dillon smiled as Jason shook his head. Dillon looked at Baez. "If I never pick on my father in that manner, he'll think I never loved him at all."

Baez nodded as he witnessed Carla as she spoke with Zach Miller. "Dillon; you know that kid?"

"We're in a study group together for Penal Codes of US Law. His maternal grandparents are the Angelinos of Ingleside."

Baez turned his head in surprise. I think the man finally found a pick for a son-in-law. "As in the owners of *Stefano's Italian Grill*? Is he Ana Maria Miller's boy? Wow, what a small world."

"He found out about Rodrigo and phoned in a tip. That's why TFCC called you. He not only has a great personality, but he knows all his grandparents' recipes by heart. I know he told me he'd love to cook for Carla and her family sometime soon."

"Dad...meet Zach; Zach, this is my father Pete Baez. Dad's the Ingleside Asst. Police Chief." Carla smiled proudly as Zach shook hands with Baez. I slid up next to Dillon and watched with him. Carla turned and smiled. "I think Zach's a keeper Dillon!"

"Good for you; just watch that cheesy garlic bread; I think there's cayenne in it!"

"Wait...hold on buddy, how do you know about Zach's cayenne ingredient to his garlic bread?" Of course, I had to ask; he knows Zach's give-it-kick ingredient for his garlic bread...how?

"That study group Zach and I belong to; he brings us food most of the time. And he added the cayenne pepper to spice it up a bit. I think his grandmother calls it Zach's Spicy Garlic Bread on her menu." Imagine that, add one little ingredient to an Italian meal, and you get a menu item named after you. Maybe Dillon and I can come up with a barbecue sauce that will make us a fortune. It might be nice to retire before I'm thirty.

Carla and Zach walked over to us as Chief Baez left to return across the bay. I noticed Carla's arm around Zach's, and both smiled. "Hey Dillon," Zach extended his hand. "Nice moves bro; you're sure you don't want to suit up and play Safety or something for the football team?"

I watched as Dillon shook his head. "I tried years ago to play in the Pop-Warner leagues. I hurt a couple of kids because they called me...half-breed. Next to any other racial slur towards an Oriental, Hispanic or Black; calling someone half-breed is just as bad. So I chose other...athletic endeavors and excelled at cross-country track."

"But he tore his ACL and MCL our sophomore year in high school. The tears were so bad; he wasn't allowed to run cross-country anymore." Carla added. "Dillon and I didn't start dating until the summer between sophomore and junior years." Then Carla looked directly into my eyes. "Are you and Dillon for real? I mean...is your relationship...real?"

I looked at Dillon as he smiled. I looked back and did what I always do…tell the truth. "We told the Vaughns…our relationship was on hold until this case was resolved and…looks like it is." Then Carla nodded solemnly. "What?"

"I wanted to say…thanks for the reality check yesterday; and your real name."

"My real name wasn't the reason you and I got cross-ways; remember?"

"I do, but Tori Blanton fits you better than Gina Torelli."

Zach almost jumped out of his skin when he heard my name. "Oh my god, I never thought I'd be standing this close to one-half of the *American Angels!*" Dillon and I buried our heads in laughter as Carla's jaw dropped wide open. "Wait…if you're Tori Blanton, then Professor Wriggle is…!"

Carla completed Zach's sentence. "Santana Garvin; she was so convincing as Professor Wriggle."

"As part of some of her old covers, Santana's taught at all levels of education. For an old DEA cover once, she taught Kindergarten and had more fun singing and being silly with a bunch of five-year-olds." That was her last cover prior to Malta; but Dillon, Carla, and Zach didn't need to know that. Then Jason and Jennifer walked over. "Yes sir?"

"Boop and Casey wrote the primary reports as to this case getting closed. All I need from you and Dillon is your signatures and the paperwork's done." I signed the paperwork as did Dillon. "Okay, the case is officially closed; as is part of the Malta case and we still have the Dixie Mafia to deal with."

"Wait, I thought when Bass went down as my sister did, that case went closed as well?" Jason shook his head. "What happened?"

Jennifer walked up. "Bass reneged; said she made the statements under duress."

"She confessed; we have her on tape confessing to blowing our op in Malta; why is it still open?" Yes, I'm now pissed off! I knew that fibby harpy would pull this stunt and try to weasel her way out of it. "I'm sorry. Okay, what do we do?"

"You take a break; like you said you needed to do." Jennifer nodded.

FIFTEEN

"Take a break? Jason, Jennifer; are you kidding me?" Okay, after what I've been through of late; probably not the best question to ask and in my current state of mind. However, given Bass did everything to destroy this case from the get-go; I'm still beyond angry.

"Tori..." Jennifer began as Jason held up his hand. "Right; you'll handle it." Jennifer reached over and kissed Dillon on the cheek. "Stay close to her; I think you're more of a stabilizing force to her than you realize."

"Hey...Mom? Thanks for watching my six out there."

"You're my son and currently, a paid intern with NCIS. Welcome to the family business!" As Jennifer turned to leave, she smiled at me. "Agent Blanton; you know how much my son...loves you?"

"I have a pretty good idea...Chief."

"Good," Jennifer looked into my eyes and smiled. "If he can help you remain calm, cool, and collected; you can help him cut loose and enjoy life a little more?"

I smiled impishly I'm sure. "Oh, I think I can tap into...Dillon Vaughn's wild side? Besides, I'm guessing the wildest thing he's done so far was kill the Russian Mobster in the spring."

"There have been wilder moments, but I'll save those stories when we're alone." Well, well; my handsome new boyfriend has stories. I might enjoy...interrogating him. "So, any secrets other than what I already know?"

"Patience, my love, patience; we have time. Besides, I need to apologize to your father...again." As I turned to Jason, he shook his head. "I don't?"

Jason nodded. "I expected you to react in that manner. Tori, you feel you have to finish every case; Garner taught you that mentality. But he's never served on federal task forces where he's dealt with multiple agencies across the board. Or if he did, he insisted on being in charge.

82

"Me, I'm the honcho because more often than not, I can liaison with the FBI or ATF or another agency who needs to utilize our resources. That means if FBI Director McBride calls me and has knowledge of case-related information for Corpus Christi; I defer to Danny Court and he will send SSA Cole what's required for us to handle the issue. Same with Leah and the Director of ATF. Suffice to say this is true: you and Santana…you're not alone; not anymore. This is your home and we're your family. As long as you be straight with us on what's going on; we'll back you all the way to DC if necessary. So, please…I'm asking nicely; take some time to relax. Go get into a wrestling match, go fishing, but do something else other than this job for a minimum of three days. You earned it!"

Dillon and I decided to spend the upcoming weekend at the Vaughn family beach house in Port Aransas. We walked into the office so I could sign a voluntary leave form and sign out. When Boop recognized my mini-vacation destination, I knew I was in trouble. "Wait…hold up young Mademoiselle Blanton. Did I read this correctly; you're going to Vaughn Island Resort?"

"Yes…Dillon invited me." When I said this, all four women who probably known Dillon at different stages of our young lives; rose from their desks and converged on mine. Santana stood by my side which forced everyone to halt in their tracks. "I take it by my invite to the Vaughn beach house; I've transgressed some sacred protocol involving the Vaughn family?"

"No, they just think you have since one-half of this 'adoptive aunts' club has known Dillon since birth. And the other half hung around and cheered him up after Carla left for Spain." Jason said as he entered the squad room. "So ladies, is there an issue with Tori dating my son?"

"If…Tori makes him happy; there is no issue boss," Boop said. She smiled her devilish smile at me for the second time in as many weeks. "If you break his heart, Tori?"

"Just make sure you exercise proper judgment when you decide to… end me should that ever happen. If not, remember what I did to my own family…Boop!" Then Jason noticed my own feral smile as the *Rosa del Diavolo*. "And just so we're clear on that note: have Casey and Lena look my most recent personnel file notes. They might find those notes colorful reading!" I grabbed my backpack and stormed off to the elevator. Boy, do I need a break!

Thursday afternoon hadn't reached 1500 Hours before Dillon and I arrived at the Vaughn beach house in Port Aransas.

Earlier in the day, Jennifer drove my navy Ford Fusion to the beach house and returned to Corpus Christi via chopper. The house was located on Sea Breeze Lane with a four-garage ground floor setup. The two-floor structure had a sea blue color with what looked like a large living area on the top floor. "Wow, this is what I call a beach house!"

"You might want to park your car in that far garage to the left. That way the salt air from the Gulf won't damage the paint job." Dillon smiled. His smile started to grow on me.

As I got out, I noticed my car was already in the garage Dillon indicated. "I thought your mom left my car out."

"Did you only have one set of keys for it?" I didn't; so it makes me wonder, who was here to park my car in the garage. As we carried our bags up to the main floor, Dillon looked around and slowly removed his Walther PPK and called out. "Aunt Kat; you here?"

"Da Nephew, I am here!" the woman with a thin Russian accent emerged from the hallway. Dillon's aunt didn't seem much older than us with dark brown hair, Jennifer's hazel green eyes, and pouty lips. She had a much fuller figure than Dillon's mother and wore a red, long-sleeve tee with *Bartoni's Gulf Coast Deli and Souvenir Shop* across the chest. Her tanned legs accented her white shorts as Katerina Svetlana Petrov grabbed my carry-on bag from my shoulder. "Your mother described your new girl-friend as a rare beauty from North Carolina. But even I recognize *American Angel* Tori Blanton." She held out her hand and introduced herself as I shook it. "I'm very pleased to meet you as well Tori."

"Same here Katerina. So, were you staying the weekend as well?"

"Oh no, I'm not staying. My sister told me Dillon's truck needed a LOFR service." I looked at Dillon confused. Obviously, I'm not that me-chanically inclined.

"LOFR stands for Lube, Oil, Filters, and Tire Rotation. Every three to five thousand miles, it's a good idea to lube the chassis, check all the filters and rotate your tires so the ware evens out. We can check your car when we get back to town." A man who; cooked, cleaned, was mechanically inclined and studied to be a law enforcement officer. Added to the fact he loved me; I've found my dream man! Now, if Boop and the other girls in the office wouldn't give me the *dead woman* look from their eyes, life would be perfect...for the moment. "Thanks for getting my truck back to Tommy, Aunt Kat."

"It pains me to say this Dillon, but I'm more sure of your closeness to Tori than I am about Thomas and Gracie. They are way too young."

I heard the concern in Kat's voice. Although I never met Tom and Ellen Engle's son Tommy, I knew the concern for Gracie where her relationship with Tommy was concerned. I sat there and contemplated how my own life was shaped by my past as a teenager. Would I have had a boy in my life like Gracie, or an ex like Dillon had with Carla? I lost so much as learning how to cope with such issues when Mom was killed. I guess I went a little crazy when I cut into my older siblings; I sort of grew up too, too fast. I guess my thinking face was on as Kat gently shook me. "Tori, are you okay?"

"I'm...fine Kat. Hearing you voice your concerns over Gracie's love for Tommy, sort of reminded me of...what I lost at her age. Mostly innocence for the world; my virtue's still intact. How I'll never know. I dated little in high school and I started college at seventeen." I sighed. I never took time to think or deal with this underlying issue I had; about growing up too fast. Maybe, that's why the Baez family was so, scared of Dillon and his family. They feared Dillon grew up too fast for their daughter. Perhaps he had. "Remember when I told you last weekend, I hadn't dated much?" Dillon looked at me and nodded. "Perhaps...that's why Chief Baez thought you were not right for Carla; he thought you grew up too fast. Maybe that's what my dad feared I did...grew up too fast."

"Perhaps we did; maybe we're not as grown up as we think we are." To hear Dillon say those words eased my tension a little. I saw Kat nod in agreement as we sat around, staring at one another. "I forgot, I left sandwiches for us out in the truck."

As Dillon got up, I followed him. "I'll go with you; I can check to see if the perimeter's secure."

"Seriously?" Dillon asked as I gave him a low stare. "Okay, okay; check it."

When we exited the house and reached the truck, a black Chevy sedan rounded the corner. It stopped suddenly and out popped my brothers Tad and Junior. *Oh shit; they made bail!* "Dillon, get down!" Both raised two Mac Ten submachine guns and began spraying bullets our direction. "Kat; call TFCC! Tell them Code Red, repeat Code Red!"

"Think your bros found out you were dating the kid of a cop?" Dillon smiled as the spray of bullets continued. "Okay Agent Blanton, on three; one, two, three!" We rose as my brothers reloaded and fired our own spray of lead as they ducked behind their doors. "I think they have an armored car!"

Then Kat emerged from the front door and shot a Remington 870 Express Tactical Shotgun. I didn't realize it, but the balls in those cartridges were titanium. *Hot damn, she has armor-piercing shells!*

I heard screams of pure pain coming from the Chevy as my brother Tad fell to the side. Junior slammed the doors shut and peeled out. Yep, when the ship started to sink, the rats deserted the craft with haste. Tad laid on the ground bleeding as I walked up with my Sig pointed at his head. "Kat, call for a medevac; he's wounded!"

SIXTEEN

Fifteen minutes later, EMS loaded up my eldest brother onto a chopper and flew him to Christus-Spohn Hospital in Corpus Christi. A moment later, another chopper landed behind the beach house and the Vaughns emerged. Port Aransas Police Sgt. Gilbert Montez took our statements as Jason and Jennifer walked up. "Jason, Jen; I take it you spoke with Chief Fitzgerald?"

Jason shook Montez's hand. "We did Gil; I thought my son and his new love were coming here for a nice, quiet, weekend. Care to tell me what happened?"

"Tad and Junior followed either me and Dillon or Jennifer here when she dropped my car off; no other way that could've happened." I hated to say that; my brothers weren't that smart to use GPS from a satellite and a laptop. One of them put a tracker on Dillon's truck or my car. "We need to check both vehicles."

"Dillon and I will check over his truck," Jason nodded to Jennifer as she and pulled my car out of the garage and began to look it over. I checked under the left front fender. I dislodged a small, black metallic box.

"I found it!"

Lightning and Leah showed up in a mobile command vehicle to take possession of the tracker and analyze it. Lightning wore one of his blue t-shirts with funny writing. This one said *SEALs do it over Sea, Air, and Land!* I looked over at Leah and shook my head. "He found out I was upset with you and Dillon being here for the weekend. He wore that in honor of your budding relationship!"

"Agent McCoy!" Jennifer yelled, "If you have reservations about my son's love life, direct those concerns to him or me at present thank you!"

"No Chief!" I yelled. I just hit my last nerve with the adoptive aunts club!

"If ATF Special Agent McCoy has a problem with me, have her meet out of the beach in fifteen mikes; and we'll settle this issue once and for all! I've put up with Garner's bullshit, Bass's bullshit, and IG Thorn's bullshit; it stops now!" I stormed out the back and walked briskly towards Port Aransas beach Road. I survived multiple firearms attacks this week and all Leah and Boop could do, was prattle on about the last time Dillon's heart was broken.

In a period of four days, I went from trusted teammate to villainous mob princess because I dared to love my boss's son. I stopped short of the dune that overlooked the beach beyond. All I could do was cry and scream as the waves broke onto the shoreline. I turned and through my tears, I saw Dillon running towards me. He yelled, "Tori get down!" When I saw him draw his Walther, I hit the ground. Instantly, he fired and when I looked up, my brother Junior flew back against the dune. Blood poured from Junior's chest as Dillon rushed up to me. "Lightning traced the GPS on the tracker to a scarab floating a mile offshore. A zodiac from the craft approached the shoreline with a single occupant. I'm glad you were in a listening mood."

"Junior," I said as we ran over to his limp body. "Why, why do this twice in one day?"

Junior bled all over his dark blazer and blue jeans. His beard frothy with blood as he coughed and wheezed. "You're a dirty federal whore; just like our mother. But when we killed her, it wasn't to punisher her, but you. You wanted to be just...like her."

"So you thought there were only two traitors to the Dixie Mafia, huh big brother? I got some truth to lay on your dying ass." He looked at me as if I had told him St. Peter was about to give him a free pass through the Pearly Gates. "You're right; Mom was undercover FBI...until you three killed her. Did you ever wonder where she got her information to bury the top guys at the time?" He coughed as he laid there dying. "Dad was her Confidential Informant! They married to protect her cover. They loved each other that much dumb ass! So you committed Matricide for the good of your bosses. All you did was make Dad hate you more! He was glad I became a cop!" Junior coughed some more and reached for his Beretta nine millimeter pistol. I put the sole of my tennis shoe over his wrist. I applied enough pressure to prevent his grab for the gun. "Oh, no you don't big brother; you're not getting that chance again!"

"Medevac's on the way back here!" I heard the shrill of Leah's voice over the waves. She saw Junior bleeding from a chest wound and Dillon's Walther in his hand. "I'm guessing Agent Blanton forgot her badge, weapon and her good sense when she ran out of the beach house?"

"Unlike some, who choose to provoke people into making mistakes hoping to learn or get hurt by them…Agent McCoy?" Dillon glared right into Leah's eyes. She realized she lost a great deal of respect in his eyes for not respecting his decisions. She's a mother, like Jennifer, and she forgot Dillon's learning to fly. And in doing so, must learn to make his own course corrections in life. But in her eyes, I crossed an unwritten boundary I chose to ignore. A boundary I didn't even know existed. "Anything you'd like to add…Aunt Leah?" Leah looked down and she knew…Dillon challenged her own judgment in how she handled this situation.

"Fine, I stay out of your love life. However, Mr. Vaughn, the federal agent you planned on sharing an amorous weekend with, is part of this federal task force and if you compromise her effectiveness in any way, shape, or form; she's rendered ineffective and a liability to this team!"

"Everything okay here?" Jason asked as he walked up. Dillon and I stared at Leah as she kept her angry eyes locked on me. "Okay, if I have to ask again, someone's getting fired!"

"Fine, since there is a fear I'll be compromised and rendered ineffective as well as a liability to this team, I will speak up!" Leah's eyes went from anger to pure terror as I finally melted down! "That little rant, Agent Vaughn, is the reason Agents Garcia, Leah McCoy, Collins, and Ortiz are *still* concerned about my relationship with your son." There I did something I told myself I might get fired for doing; yelling in my boss's face. Leah smiled, but an angry glare from Jason forced her to return quickly to the beach house. "Keep my badge and weapon sir; if you decide I'm worthy to continue as a team member, I'll retrieve them Monday morning. For now, I'll leave and go get a room here in town." I turned to Dillon with tears in my eyes. "I'm…sorry. I didn't know…I'd cause this kind of trouble…

being in love with you." I turned quickly and went back to the beach house, retrieved my bags and my car, and left.

I reserved the room at the Plantation Suites and Conference Center. I used an old cover credit card no one could flag, and I paid for my room with cash. I took the battery out of my cell phone prior to leaving the beach house. I wanted solitude, privacy, and no encroachment from those I call… friend. I walked from my hotel suite to a local Pizza Hut to get a pie and a pitcher of beer. I polished off a salad, a supreme pizza, and the pitcher of beer. I wasn't totally drunk, but I had a good buzz from the beer and the food. I walked in, locked the door, stripped down to my undies, curled up and cried myself to sleep.

When I woke up the next morning, Friday, I went into the dining room for breakfast. I found the one person who might be able to find me in all of Corpus Christi…Santana. She wore her white beach comer outfit of a white floppy hat, long-sleeve white tee, white Capri pants, and sandals. Santana gave me this disappointed smirk when she felt I was running away from the world. "You always take your battery out of your cell phone when you're mad at someone. You always to get a pizza, salad and a pitcher of beer to gorge and drown your sorrows. And although Lightning doesn't have all your old cover info to track the credit card purchases, I do. Plus, the place you chose to hideout; not exactly a dive if you get my drift girlfriend."

"I wasn't in the mood to stay at a chain hotel and have someone else from the office show up in Kevlar with automatic weapons pointed at me." Santana nodded and understood what I meant; I wanted to keep from killing any of my coworkers who had issues with my social life… meaning Dillon. "I don't know San; maybe…coming here was a mistake after all."

"Well, how about a real distraction; which might lead to a tag-team match the following weekend in Houston."

I smiled and leaned forward. "Tell me more!"

We returned to Corpus Christi and met with a recent hiring for a local wrestling promotion in Texas. "Mickey Solo; I'm with Talent Relations. Our newest female tag-team champions, Caged Women, have publicly called you girls out. The CEO of the company wants the *American Angels* to come in following their next match and hand them a beat-down...felony style."

I smiled impishly at Santana and Mickey, "Just like a Kimora Twins in Tokyo." I sat there and looked into the eyes of this new promoter/talent relations manager. His thin build and a light blue suit made me pity the poor man. Then I remembered, Mickey Solo was once a top cruiserweight in line for a championship until he broke his back in a skiing accident in Vail, Colorado. Well, at least he found a way to remain connected to the business. "What did Santana tell you already Mickey?"

"She said something about...violent stress relief?" I looked at my tag team partner who grinned like a possum.

"Tell your boss...Bopper Harris, we'll do it!" Santana smiled as did Mickey. "See you tonight!"

"Should I tell Caged Women you're here?"

Santana answered, "No, let it be a surprise. They want to surprise us by calling us out, we'll surprise them by replying in person!"

We left the American Bank Center prior to the event tonight. Just as we made it to the parking lot, Dillon appeared and waved. *The one person I didn't need to see this weekend!* Santana leaned in. "Just wave and we'll try to dash off as quickly as possible." After she said that, Jason and Jennifer appeared and waved. "What the hell; what are the odds?"

I shook my head and laughed, "San my old friend, I learned this week; when one is associated with the Vaughn family, some veils of mystery are ripped apart and no longer exist!"

SEVENTEEN

"Well, well; what brings you two here?" Jennifer asked.

"We're about to go get a workout in prior to the event tonight," I lied. Santana and I always worked out to remain in ring shape, but no sense in telling the Vaughns that...right? "Some women's tag team has called us out; thinking we won't show up...you might say. Why are you guys here... getting tickets for tonight?"

"Dillon wanted to attend the matches tonight and Jason wanted to go as well. I came along because for some reason; they thought some wrestlers might make a stop for publicity photos." Jennifer groaned as Dillon laughed. "You...two aren't here for that are you?"

"No, no publicity photos right now. We needed to know what the setup was before we returned tonight. Besides, you gave Tori and I both the weekend off Jason." Jason smiled and nodded. Something told me Santana lied as part of some conspiracy to find and ascertain my overall well-being. "Anyway, we need to go limber up to get ready for tonight."

"Really?" Dillon asked as Jason gently grabbed his shoulder. "Okay, okay...look for me tonight?"

"I will," I smiled and kissed Dillon's cheek. "Go by and see Mickey Solo. Tell your dad to tell him, he needs extra seats for the match tonight; ringside facing the stage where the performers enter the ring. Tell your dad I want your adoptive aunts, all of them, present at the matches tonight. They need to see me and Santana, cut loose!"

Later on that night, Texas Gulf Coast Wrestling landed at the American Bank Center in Corpus Christi. The main event that night, the Women's Tag-Team Championship would be decided between the challengers: Legion of Love vs. Caged Women.

As the championship started, Santana and I heard the call from the TV/pay-per-view crew. I gave Dillon a tablet to watch the live feed.

"This Marty Calder with the Menace, Mike Petrovsky; coming to you live from the American Bank Center in Corpus Christi, Texas. And Menace, we have a wild championship match for tonight." Calder wore a black tuxedo with red bowtie and green waistcoat as part of his attire. His salt n pepper hair denoted his years as a wrestling announcer.

The retired wrestler who sat next to him wore a white do-rag over his bald head and offset the gold ring in his nostrils and blinding gold blazer he wore over a blue velvet shirt. Mike Petrovsky was someone Jason told me he remembered from his days as a SEAL but never pictured the former Navy Chief Petty Officer as a wrestler. *"You got that right Calder; it's gonna be a nasty night for the goody-to-shoes Legion of Love's Mandy Love and Dizzy Dana. They have crossed into a fight-to-survive prison environment with Caged Women's Twyla Black and Tanya Tate. Caged Women have held the tag titles for a record 285 days. That's longer than the record set by Santana Garvin and Tori Blanton the American Angels in Japan."*

"For weeks, Caged Women heard rumors the Angels returned to the U.S. after a brief sabbatical to heal from the post-match beat-down Black and Tate gave them in Tokyo a year and a half ago."

A year and a half ago; about the time the Malta op began! Dillon watched as Jason leaned over. "What are those knuckleheads Calder and Petrovsky talking about?"

"About the Angels rumored to have returned home and Caged Women calling them out to fight. Didn't you say Tori and Santana inherited that Maltese operation from two other agents?"

"They did; they had to lose or forfeit their tag team championship prior to their departure to Malta. Why are you asking?" I could almost hear father and son discussing the case and little did we know, we'd come face-to-face with the real traitor who blew our op.

We watched the live coverage with Mickey in his office at the arena. "Black and Tate know someone's coming to jack them up; we didn't tell them it would be you two!"

Santana smiled at Mickey, "There's a reason why we wore star-spangled tank tops, blue jeans, and black Justin Roper boots Mick; Black and Tate need a beat-down, we'll give them one."

Caged Women won in convincing fashion. They totally dominated Legion of Love from the opening bell and nailed them with their patented maneuver, the drive-by jam. It's a leg drop from the top rope with the other team member holding the one opponent to be pinned. There are times I wonder how Santana and I survived our title match against them in Japan. Santana and I grabbed a pair of old black service batons Jennifer loaned us from her private LEO equipment collection. We crept up from each side of the stage as Twyla Black began her rant. "Well, Sista Tawny looks like another team bit the dust. Too bad it wasn't those soft, weak, American Angels Garvin and Blanton."

"Yeah," Tate smiled as she looked into Dillon's eyes. "I think one has an admirer here!"

"Woo wee…ain't he a cutie pie?" Dillon laughed at Twyla Black in her long, dark hair, white jumpsuit, and black wrestling boots. "You laughing at me boy?"

Dillon smiled like a sadistic cat playing with a mouse as Santana and I quietly rolled into the ring. The crowd slowly stood and roared as Tanya Tate screamed, "Shut the hell up you bunch of worthless fools! That little peckerwood on the front row has no right, no right to laugh at us!" Then we tapped them both on the shoulders of their white jumpsuits Tate's black hair swished as she turned her head and I hit her right between the eyes with my right fist handling the handle of the baton. Black turned to get plastered in the face full of wood from Santana as we commenced with the beat down.

We beat their faces black and blue as Santana and I picked them up, Irish-whipped them across the ring and landed two high crescent kicks to the sides of their heads. Black and Tate reeled from the attack as I grabbed each of them in turn and applied my *Whirly-girly* version of the DDT. I locked their arms behind them and dropped them flat on their faces. Then Santana put them closely side-by-side and executed a *Shining Press* moon sault and landed in their middles with hers. Both rolled out and held their heads as we climbed to the middle ropes and raised our hands above us.

The crowd roared with cheers as I got down and demanded Petrovsky hand me a mic. I looked directly at the shocked and rattled Tanya Tate. "Hey girls, we hear you've been looking for us! Look no further...we're baaaack!" The cheers resounded into the rafters of the American Bank Center. I looked at the crowd and saw Dillon as he clapped and smiled. "Excuse me, sir," Dillon pointed at his chest. "Yes, you; were you the one those two hussies were hitting on a moment ago?" He nodded and I turned to smile sadistically at my future opponents. "Would one of you nice folks in security, please help that handsome young stranger up here please?"

The crowd screamed and cheered as the security guys helped Dillon over the guardrail and he slid under the top ring rope. Santana took the mic and spoke as I embraced Dillon. "While my partner's getting the loving the so-called champs hoped to have gotten from that good-looking fellow here with us, I wanted to let you girls know; your reign of terror over this women's division, is over!" The crowd cheered as I looked over and saw Jennifer hold her thumb up in approval. Santana continued our promo. "As you know, when a team like Caged Women, puts us, allegedly on the shelf; we implement a Three "R" comeback. The first 'R' is Retribution. Well, based on how the bruising is coming along, I think Twyla and Tanya get the point!" Some of the crowd laughed as she continued, "'R' number two is Redemption. You see, we've been busy doing other things preparing for our return to action. One of them is doing what we do when not in the square circle...be law enforcement officers." The cheers continued as Santana smiled. "Someone blew an undercover operation some time back; almost killed my partner over there. And ever since then, as in the movie *Braveheart*, she hasn't been right...in the head!

"So that brings us to the final 'R' in the three 'R' plan; Resolution. Tori, mind breaking away from that handsome, young, Texas Stud, to explain the rules of engagement to our opponents please?"

I kissed Dillon passionately, even in front of the ladies of TFCC, and the crowd roared with cat-calls and wolf-whistles. "Hold that thought Lover, I'll be right back!" I said into the mic as I turned my attention to Caged Women. "Ladies, three match stipulations have been met by Big Bopper. One, the champion's privilege has been removed!" The crowd cheered as

Caged Women stomped their feet like spoiled children. "You try to get disqualified or counted out, you lose the titles."

The crowd cheered again as I shook my finger. "Oh, no ladies…it gets worse! Your…attorney or manager, that little East L.A. hussy Chi-Chi Gonzales; she's banned from ringside!" The crowd cheered as their manager, a light-brown haired Hispanic female walked out with a mic and interrupted me.

"No, no, no Senorita; you have no right to come in here and demand such alterations to this match!"

"Oh, Chi-Chi mia amiga; as I said before I started naming off the changes, you and your clients had no say at all. This brings me to my final word on this match. Texas Gulf Coast Wrestling PPV, Houston, Texas, the Toyota Center; Gulf Coast War; Caged Women vs. the American Angels for the Women's Tag-Team Championship; a Texas Tornado Rules match!"

The crowd roared as Black and Tate shook their heads "no" in reverent fear. "Yes girls, that means you double-team one of us, we'll all be mixing it up for most of that match. Bind up your wounds, fix your faces, pray to God, the Devil whoever will listen, because a legion of angels, led by us, will destroy you one week from Saturday!" Our opponents ran off into the back as the crowd cheered us on as I returned to my in-ring distraction… Dillon. "Now…handsome, may I have the pleasure of your name? For the rest of this fine crowd here with us tonight?"

"I'm Dillon Vaughn." When all the young ladies in the crowd went wild, I realized just how well the Vaughn family was connected to this city.

"I'm guessing by all the other young ladies cheering, you have some… connection to this town?"

"I…have a special connection to NAS Corpus Christi as well as the Corpus Christi Police Department."

"Then I can only say, as a cop myself; this bears investigating!" The crowd roared!

EIGHTEEN

I returned with Dillon to the beach house after a little question of, 'Would you like a night in heaven with an American Angel?' The crowd roared as I exited the ring with Dillon. Jason and Jennifer whispered to Boop and Leah to remind them to lay off about our dating relationship…or else!

Caged Women walked up to Mickey Solo and complained about us and the impromptu throw-down tonight. He cautiously reminded them of our Tokyo beat-down they gave us a year and a half prior and told them they were due for a dose of their own medicine. The moaning and groaning stopped as we prepared for our championship match in Houston the next weekend.

But, before I get ahead of myself…the beach house, and Dillon. To make sure no one followed us, Jason and Jennifer drove us, and we returned to find Dillon's truck parked in the driveway. Jason looked around, "We all will do a perimeter sweep as well as an internal sweep of the house; including the house security system."

"Why the house security system?" Apparently, I've missed something in the last day or two.

"Although Lightning will respect our privacy; Leah and Boop might not." Dillon smiled.

"Meaning they will tap into the security system to spy on, and then berate me Monday morning?" Jason nodded to my query as I bowed my head and counted to ten; something I haven't done since I worked for Garner in DC. When I raised my head, Jason nodded again. The Team Building hand-to-hand re-qualifications will become interesting Monday afternoon at the gym. Jason and Jennifer checked the outer perimeter while Dillon and I checked inside.

After the ground floor and outside were cleared, Dillon checked the security system. "Okay, one line of code under the Command prompt and…"

The screen suddenly went dead. "Dad, has the system ever done this before?"

"No, it's never done that before." Jason dialed his cell phone and got Lightning on the other end. "Hey buddy, Dillon attempted that code you taught him to spy on spies in our security system; and as soon as he hit 'enter', the screen and system went dead." Jason nodded as he motioned Jennifer to remove the network cables from the server tower and the wireless router. Then the computer kicked back on. "Inform your wife, she has until Monday morning at 0800 to restore the original security settings for the beach house. Failure to do so will result in her transfer to the Corpus Christi ATF office and a new liaison will replace her. As a caveat, I will simply request Agent Garcia's personal effects and inform her husband as to her termination. I thank you sir; enjoy your weekend." Jason pushed *end* on his phone and smiled. "Your weekend is spy-free...enjoy it!"

I went over and threw my arms around Jason; then Jennifer. She hugged me back and asked, "What was that for Tori?"

"That...was to thank the both of you for allowing me to be someone other than a cop, or a wrestler where Dillon is concerned. You see, no one's ever let me drop all that and just be me...for a short time." And I meant every word.

Jennifer smiled as did Jason. "No Tori; thank you for allowing us and Dillon some normalcy in our lives." I never thought I could provide normalcy for anyone, much less for myself. "With my job and Jen's we're always a target for someone's scope; regardless, who it is, someone's always trying to take us out. When you and Dillon decided to have a relationship, you helped us deal with something...normal as part of life. And as unfortunate as the situation is, Boop and Leah's questions concerning your budding romance are also...normal."

I nodded and understood now; they simply extended their concern because Dillon hadn't left home...technically. It was an unwritten rule of TFCC to look after each one's families and each family member. Apparently, in their attempt to let Dillon grow up, Jason and Jennifer forgot to tell the remaining original members of TFCC to let Dillon...grow up. Or, let him make relationship decisions, and they felt I was intruding since I was the newbie. So, I asked, "Jason, other than what we need to clean up, we have any other active cases at present?"

"No, why do you ask?"

"May I meet with you, Monday, prior to the workday starting? I need to...evaluate my overall effectiveness so far."

"Fair enough, but you'll need this!" Jason handed me my ID wallet with all my NCIS credentials and my badge. "And how are you planning on getting to work that morning?"

"Tori and I will be back at her cover apartment complex Sunday afternoon. It's roughly four-and-a-half to five miles from those apartments to the NCIS office on Station. She might run to work."

"Let me know for sure after you get back."

"No need for that Jason." I protested.

"Like hell there is Tori!" Even Jennifer gave Jason a look of shock. "Something I'm trying to remind you of, regardless of some negative attitudes in the squad room, is you're still part of a much larger team."

"I realize that; what I was about to tell you is Santana lives a building over from me at my normal place. She can bring my gear to work as well as my workout clothes for hand-to-hand re-qualification that morning."

Jason nodded and chuckled. Jennifer gave him a peck on the cheek. "You see; you can relax and play "honcho" without making special trips to assist. Now, since she's offered us her suite at the Plantation, may we go please?"

"Yes dear," Jason groaned as he looked at Dillon. "Yes, I still love her; and yes, she still is the queen of the castle. However, she remembers who is king once the door to the bedchamber closes." He looked at Jennifer who frowned at him. "Need I remind you of that fact...your Majesty?"

Jennifer shook her head. "No...Sire, I am well aware of who is king, queen and crown prince! And the prince will watch over *this* keep until Sunday afternoon!" She stepped over to Dillon and kissed his right cheek. "You two have fun!" Then Jason and Jennifer left.

I kissed Dillon as we received a courtesy call from Lightning. "Good evening sir!"

"Hey Dillon, did you reconnect the network cables yet?"

"No, Dad said to leave it alone…why?"

"*I need you guys to grab your stuff and let's get you two someplace else!*"

"Okay, we'll do it now!" Dillon pushed *end* on his phone and said, "Grab the bags; there's a problem."

"What's wrong?" Something Dillon told me last Friday night when I first got here. 'If I'm ever told to vacate my home, apartment, or the beach house; something was wrong, and I'd find out later'. "Security feed picked something up prior to our return?"

"Probably," Dillon said as we cleared out and went over his truck; under the hood, by the gas tank, around the tires, and under the dashboard.

I found one device and called Port Aransas Police. CCPD's Bomb Squad flew in by chopper and disabled the explosive device. They checked the house and found another device attached to the newly installed Hibachi grill's gas line. Dillon slowly shook his head as Jason and Jennifer returned. "Dad, are you two sure this qualifies as…reality?"

"No, this isn't reality…this is targeted. And I really, really hate being targeted!" When other members of TFCC arrived, Jason motioned Lightning to approach. "You have the surveillance feed?"

"Yeah right here," Lightning said as I watched Jason's eyes. When Jason looked up at me, he nodded me to join them. I walked over as Lightning turned the tablet to me. "You recognize either of those guys?"

I watched the surveillance footage recognized booth of the Dixie Mafia goons from Nashville. "The red-haired lummox is Billy Joe Tulane; he's a swamp rat over by Shreveport. The fat, bald one is David Farrell; he's from Lexington, KY. Both are freelance hitters for Joe Don Clayton out of Charlotte."

"And if I miss my guess; your mom's notes from her undercover assignment, indicted and convicted him of violating the RICO act." Santana always boiled down a threat to brass tacks. "I'm sorry Tori."

"No skin off your nose San; these jerks are after me and my dad. I need to find Teddy!"

"Not to worry; Teddy's safe…I made sure." I turned as Leah nodded to me.

And before I could go and yell in Leah's face, Boop cut me off and held up her hands. "Whoa Champ; hold your horses. We do come in peace... Honest Injuns here!" Then Jason's brow furled downward as Boop gulped, "You know what I mean boss!"

"If I didn't give you hell for that phrase Boop, you'd think I didn't love ya like a sister anymore." Jason walked over as Dillon held me in a hug to keep me from losing my job. "You mind if I take over on the hug? I promise to return her in better spirits." Dillon eyed his father suspiciously; then begrudgingly gave up the hug to Jason. He took me in his arms and whispered, "How are you holding up kiddo?"

"I'm about to crater here." Then the frustration hit me, and I cried and didn't stop until Boop and Leah walked over.

"The tall red-headed agent has something she'd like to say, provided you're willing to listen?"

I shrugged my shoulders as Jason backed off and both Leah and Boop embraced me. Leah spoke where only Boop and I could hear her. "I screwed up and I admit it. I, not Dillon, caused you to be distracted, compromised, and I became a liability by making you one by mistake. I won't do that, ever again." I waited because Leah had more to say. I've learned with a senior federal agent has a point to make, to wait and listen. In this case, I'm glad I did. "Tori, a lot has been made concerning your youth. It's both a blessing and a curse. It's a blessing in the respect to you can do things those mature agents used to do, and maybe can't anymore. You have incredible instincts and you anticipate some information that's needed. But the curse is; you yelled at an IG while he conducted your shooting review. You disrespected your SAC due to those actions, and you made decisions in the heat of the moment; which almost on one occasion got you killed. And I don't want you getting killed over, in my opinion, a stupid argument. You're too valuable to lose over that nonsense baby." Leah embraced me. "I have two daughters who one day, may want to be cops. And I did something, if you were one of them, would in all likelihood, get them killed. You understand?" I nodded.

Boop continued to console me as Dillon and his parents spoke with others about the safety factor of the beach house. "Listen to me kiddo; we love

Dillon, but we love you too. I guess it was difficult for us to see Dillon, fall in love with someone we would work with daily. Then Jason reminded us oh not so gently this morning; as we got our asses reamed out by him and Dillon both, we were young once, fell in love and got married as well as had babies. And we made rookie agent mistakes as a result. We were extremely lucky we weren't killed due to some of our decisions. I guess what we're trying to say is; be in love, but keep your head in the game when you're playing in the law enforcement sandbox, okay?"

"Copy that ladies," I beamed as they hugged me with smiles. Okay, we're all friends and sisters again…for the most part. "So Leah, would it be against protocol to ask where you stashed my poor pop?"

"No, but just in case any more of your brother's playmates hit town and are watching; might be better to take you rather than tell you. And, we can play a little shell game on them at the same time." I like shell games, especially when I won't be directly involved. Crooks hate this because they need at least three cars to tail the shells.

NINETEEN

Saturday morning, we borrowed three black Land Rovers from Hampton Investigations-Corpus Christi. And the three drivers contracted to assist in this little maneuver were three of the top folks at the company: CEO Joe Hampton, a Marine from Jason's military era of Desert Storm and Bosnia; CCPD Police Captain Pamela Hampton, Joe's wife and one hell of a cop I might add; and a cute-as-a-button Marine Corps Captain Laquita Boggs.

Joe had a short haircut, not as short as Jason's, but it was business-like as he wore a blue long-sleeve Oxford dress shirt, blue jeans, and tan boots. Pam wore a similar outfit and it complimented her sandy blonde hair and chocolate brown eyes. Laquita's short stature made you almost want to pick her up to hug her. She was only two inches shorter than Santana and I, but her professional attitude matched that of a fearless tigress for a petite black woman. Add to the face all three of these folks were active or discharged Marines made my anxiety disappear.

I peeked in all three vehicles and three mannequins resembling me sat beside each driver in the front seat. Laquita let her arms rest on the driver's side window. "So, you're the NCIS Agent/Pro Wrestler with the Dixie Mob dad who went straight?"

"Sounds like a mad, mad soap opera doesn't it Captain Boggs?" I smiled and shook my head.

"Whoa, whoa there girlfriend; if I'm doing this, according to Joe, for a friend, there is no 'captain' this or 'agent' that." Then she stuck out her right hand. "Call me Quid!"

I smiled and shook her hand. "Pleased to meet you Quid; Tori!" Joe and Pam exited their rides and met us at Quid's. "I'm really glad you guys are helping out."

Joe smiled as Pam nodded. "Well, when Jason and Jen told us what needed to happen, we called Quid to assist." Pam's sly smile brought a smile to my own face. "We'll run around town with your triplets and hopefully catch the Dixie goons in the cross-fire."

"Well, if anyone can get those curs to run around in circles, it's safe to say a couple of Chi-town girls with Texas' top PI can handle it," I say that, but do I actually believe we can pull this stunt off? Only time will tell.

"You worried about something Tori?" Joe asked. Being the fact he's one of Jason Vaughn's contemporaries from a military and law enforcement standpoint; I'd expect him or Pam to notice the anxiety on my face.

I shrugged my shoulders; which meant I had one too many answers to that question. And none of them brought me any peace. "Too many to name Joe: my dad, Dixie Mafia with my brothers, trying to be a good teammate for TFCC, and Dillon…"

"Dillon?" Pam asked with shock in her voice, "How did Dillon become one of your worries?" Then I looked longingly into Pam's eyes and hers widened as her mouth contracted into an "O". "Oh my god, you're in love with him!"

"What?" Joe asked surprised.

"Whoa, time out playas; Tori…you and Dillon…boo?" I nodded sadly, "Oh my lord; no wonder you're so worried. How many attempts to take you out; while he's been in proximity?"

"Three," I said without hesitation, "Twice on Thursday by each of my brothers Tad and Junior; then two bombs set at the beach house yesterday by two heavy Dixie Mafia hitters. I'm starting to feel like I'm cursed."

"And as I said, you're not cursed, but targeted. And this will help take some of the heat off," Jason said as he fist-bumped Joe and hugged Pam as well as Quid. "Thank you, Hamptons for returning the Vette so we could pull this off."

"Thank you for loaning it to us in January," Pam smiled as I just looked at her. "Oh, Jason forgot to tell you, you and Dillon will go visit your dad in a nice…Vette."

"As in an actual…Chevy Corvette…Vette?" Why would anyone be surprised a twenty-one-year-old federal agent would ask that question? I mean seriously; the next thing someone will tell me was Jason was actually a rich guy from Texas who has worldwide financial interests. "What; you expected me to know that?"

Jason smiled, with a bit of disappointment in his eyes. "I thought you did a Level Three background check on me, Tori. Are you telling me you didn't know about my refurbished 1966 Chevy Corvette Convertible? Or the fact I have multiple international financial interests…Agent Blanton?"

Well, now I know; I am working for the Corpus Christi, Texas version of *Daddy Warbucks*. I smiled my *Rosa del Diavolo* smile as I walked up and stood, what would be considered nose-to-nose with my boss. "When I looked at your file from this agency as well as the Navy; I only wanted professional and family background sir; not your entire life story! I wanted to reserve…discovery of those things in social, and not business or law enforcement settings…sir!" Then I looked at the *Three Amigos* of drivers with my so-called triplets. "I'll go over and get ready to ride," then I looked to Jason with extreme anger in my eyes, "so I don't punch my boss in the nose and lose my job!" I smiled sweetly and walked away.

I walked over to a beautiful, candy apple red two-seat Corvette in which Dillon sat in the driver's seat. He got out in a nice red polo shirt with blue jeans and black sneakers. "Are you okay?"

He embraced me as I took a whiff of his aftershave. "Wow, *Polo* by Ralph Lauren, I'm deeply honored."

"Back on point; are you okay?" Dillon asked again.

"I'm a little scared and a little angry. I think I just got suckered by a seasoned Special Agent in Charge." I told Dillon about my exchange with his father due to what Jason thought, was my apparent lack of study on his life. "So, what do you think?"

Dillon smiled. "I think whatever Boop and Leah said to you, just took. You showed some poise he hoped you'd show. Most young agents when my dad pulls a stunt like that do take a swing at punching him in the nose. You chose to walk away and remind him neither of you knows each other that well yet. To him and the team, you've grown up some in the last couple of days." And then he held me closer. "And I'm glad you have too. I don't want to say goodbye now that I've gotten to know you…and love you."

"No worries darlin'; I'm not going anywhere yet. At least until the Good Lord calls me home." There was always the possibility I could get killed in the line of duty. Hence why I told Dillon what I told him. Having been raised in a Christian home all my short twenty-one years, I'm not arrogant enough to believe I'll live forever. I made a profession of faith two years ago and was baptized in a Florida church, but I have moved on several times since then.

The romantic moment faded as Jason walked up. "Okay lovebirds, you two ready to do this?"

"Locked and loaded Pop!"

"Ready, willing, and able boss!" I said as Jennifer gazed my way and shook her head as she turned around. "What?"

"You say that while still hugging Chief Vaughn's son? Seriously?"

"Okay," I said with a lazy look in my eyes. "I get it; she's concerned or scared. You think I'm not? These guys are after me…thank you!"

Jennifer walked up and gently slapped Jason on his arm. "Quit yakking and let's go!"

Dillon and I waited by a hand-held unit in the Vette as Jason called out to the Hampton units. *"Night Wolf to Three Amigos; start your runs!"*

"Hampton One headed to Lady Lex," Joe said as he headed out through Ingleside. *"Night Wolf, confirm if El Jefe with cop shop's on board?"*

"Both bosses are on board; called about fifteen minutes ago."

"Hampton Two headed down 361 towards JFK Causeway." Pam's voice all business as she headed out. We were parked in Corpus Christi near the NAS south gate not too far from Quid's bungalow.

Then Quid started out. *"Corps Girl on the move. Shadow Wolf, on my six until cut-off then proceed to objective…over!"*

"Copy that Corps Girl," Dillon said as he started the Vette's engine. The roar of the 327 horse powered engine scared three cats and a grackle as we pull into traffic. As Quid continued on Waldron Road, Dillon and I took the JFK Causeway and headed to Corpus Christi. We caught Pam's Rover out of the corner of my eye as she passed us. She continued en route to Corpus Christi as we took a detour to Rodd Field Road.

Dillon turned left and continued for several miles until we turned off on Saratoga Blvd and came across JerZee's Sports Bar. We turned into the parking lot and checked the time. "Time for the bar to open up," I said as we walked in. It was a standard bar and grill multiple screens with ESPN, Fox Sports, and a few news channels. I scanned the room and recognized two people from Charlotte who knew my family. I sent Jason a text. *JerZee's Sports Bar send backup now!* Moments later, CCPD SWAT and Major Case Detective Sgt. Sasha Hassan entered. I nodded to her as we proceeded to the north back table by the bar. A dirty blonde-haired woman with a gray pantsuit and a man in a dark suit looked up. "Stay seated Clayton!"

TWENTY

SWAT officers leveled P-90 assault weapons at Joe Don Clayton and his on-again-off-again girlfriend Wynona Campbell. I sat down as both glared into my eyes. "Not surprising you two would scope out all the sports bars in the area. Tell me, did you find Teddy, or were you hoping for me to walk in and lead you to him?" Wynona's blue eyes dropped as she rubbed her forehead. "So, that was your brilliant plan huh? Sasha?" Sgt. Hassan walked up and smiled. "Would you have Chief Lester's office over at CCPD run the licenses on this place? I have a sneaking suspicion you'll find it part of a conglomerate owned by Nashville Sports Unlimited, owned by Mr. Joe Don Clayton here."

"You do, Detective, and your family will suffer for your discharge of your duties." Clayton smiled as Sasha turned, glared and then smiled her own little, sinister grin. Clayton and Wynona suddenly looked at me with startled eyes. "Why, why is she staring at me with that smile?"

"Oh, I'm sure Sgt. Hassan would be ecstatic to explain that grin, but first things first. Lt. Harper?" A cute, red-headed SWAT officer walked up and nodded. "Would you take Ms. Campbell outside and read her the Miranda warning please?"

"My pleasure Agent Blanton; Ms. Campbell, step this way please?" Lt. Harper smiled as Wynona got up and started toward the door.

Wynona looked over at Dillon and smiled as she turned her head back to me. "Boyfriend...Little Tori?"

"Driver...consultant with NCIS. Grandmother's a CIA hottie from the Cold-War. Never met the woman, but she was one of our country's best spies and leg-breakers. Rethink any threat you might voice Wynona; his family's more lethal than anyone you employ. Just go outside, shut up and listen to your legal options please?"

She left as Clayton looked at me and spoke in his gravelly voice again. "I would've thought you'd roll over and just die...after your little beat-down in Tokyo; or…your blown operation off of Italy." Clayton smiled like a weasel.

Then Sasha's phone rang. "Hassan, yes Aunt Sharon?" Her sinister smile deepened. "You don't say…I'll relay the news to Agent Blanton. And what about the other part of our trap? Sprung two more spots huh? Awesome, okay bye!" Sasha pushed *end* on her phone and smiled. "Good news, your suspicions are right on the money. Mr. Clayton does own this bar and I'm betting his manager's behind the bar, calling in reinforcements. Would you like me to deploy SWAT outside and wait for said reinforcements?"

"Make sure the staff leaves with your officers Sgt. Hassan; I want my conversation with Mr. Clayton to remain private. Should he…attempt to leave or use the snub-nosed thirty-eight in his right boot; inform Agent Vaughn the new IG Inspector might be interviewing me for another fatality?" Sasha nodded as the bar staff all exited with SWAT. Sasha left soon after as Dillon remained on guard at the front door. "Just the three of us now Uncle Joe Don; and I do use that term with extreme sarcasm."

"You always were a snooty little bitch like your mother Tori. Giving the order to your older brothers and sister to kill her; the highlight of my life. I let them kill your stepfather and step-siblings as a bonus." I sat there with a stone, cold gaze in my eyes. Then Clayton pointed with a feral smile of his own. "There, there it is; that cold, heartless incarnation of your brothers and sister. The kind of person that fits into our organization. But…you're a…Navy cop. You have to play by the rules…don't ya lil' cutie pie?"

Just then, Jason walked in with a Hispanic female an inch taller than me and wearing a smartly-tailored light gray skirt suit with black blouse and pumps. Her long dark hair flowed behind her as the brown eyes of US Asst. Dist. Attn. Antonia Melendez handed Joe Don Clayton a federal search warrant. The Marshals who accompanied her began to go through the bar and grill. "Mr. Clayton, do you have a son named Theodore who works for you here in Corpus Christi?"

Clayton smiled. "He handles all my network support concerns for all my business dealings here in Corpus Christi. Why do you ask…Counselor?"

"Agent Vaughn; how will you handle Theo Clayton?" Jason motioned to me. "Agent Blanton?"

"Call Captain Boggs and have her execute Operation: Jack-up!" Sasha looked at Jason's shocked expression as I looked up to my boss and nodded. "The purpose is to disrupt command and control of the Dixie Mafia's criminal enterprise here in Corpus Christi."

"But using Jack-up? I hope Quid led them somewhere where no one will see a stinger missile launched from a shoulder tube."

"Disrupt command and control, huh, Jace?" Melendez gave me a low stare.

"Dixie Mafia uses choppers to maintain command and control while expanding." I continued, "Unfortunately if we don't knock out the primary command and control tech, another will assume the duties immediately." I placed my Sig on the table and cocked back the hammer. "Hand over your phone, Joe Don." When he started to use his thumbs, I kicked his shin under the table. He dropped his phone and Sasha retrieved it. I recognized what he tried to do. "Sasha, send this text; tell him I'm dead and he can pursue the red Corvette at the bar. That will lead him to Teddy Blanton."

"What does that do for us?" Sasha asked and I smiled. She smiled and knew what I did; found a way to jack-up Theo without killing him. "Okay, I sent the text and he says, 'that wasn't the plan'." Damn, my bluff was called.

I looked at Jason and he nodded. He called while we attempted to bluff Theo. Then Jason received a call. "Vaughn? Yes Quid?" I heard him sigh heavily. I know now what happened...Quid fired the stinger and killed the pilot and all the occupants. "I see, I'll let Mr. Clayton and Agent Blanton know...thanks and good work." Jason pushed *end* on his phone. "Five minutes ago, southwest of the Barney Davis Reservoir, a blue chopper belonging to Nashville Sports Unlimited, went down in the water. All hands lost," Jason eyed the now seething Joe Don Clayton as his tears matched his angry breaths. "How does it feel Mr. Clayton, how does it feel to lose someone you love due to your own, criminal enterprise?"

"Empty," Clayton said quietly as he glared into my eyes. "I hope you and Teddy rot in hell for this bitch!" The Marshals cuffed Clayton and led him away while they read him his rights.

Leah and Boop walked in with Jennifer in tow. "We saw Joe Don Clayton being led away by the Marshals; way to go Tori!"

I nodded with tears in my eyes. "It was a team effort; I didn't do this alone; I had my family behind me." I walked up and embraced Leah and Boop. "This family!"

"Amen little sister," Leah smiled as she fully embraced me.

"Copy that kiddo!" Boop cried as she Leah let go and Boop gave me a big bear hug. "You showed us more poise and guts in this past week, than anyone who's come through here in the last five years. Even in the face of us getting in yours about Dillon, you still have stepped up in ways someone your age would never do. And it all started, when you and Santana gave those Caged Women hussies that beat-down last night."

"That was us...being angry; we were able to do something we needed to do in that business...return the favor for Tokyo." No one who has never laced up a pair of wrestling boots, or put on wrestling tights, or put in the time training, would understand the anger Santana and I experienced for that week we spent in Tokyo General Hospital. And why it forced me to heal for a year as a federal agent to slowly work back into the ring as an undercover assignment. Now, I know we were set up, by the Dixie Mafia, to lose to Caged Women, and not by the promoter's whims, but a crime syndicate's. "Sisters, Santana and I need to make an arrest at that match in Houston."

"We heard the wire; my question is why wait for a week from today?" Leah asked as I looked deeply into her eyes and smiled a feral, evil smile. Then she understood. "It's not just the arrest; you and Santana want to take what's most precious to those girls, their titles. Then they're so dejected, they won't know why US Marshals are putting them in cuffs."

Boop smiled. "It's not about breaking their bodies; you girls already did that. It's about breaking their wills, even their spirits to compete. You do that, either by pin-fall or submission; you have them beat."

"You two suffered; it's their time to suffer," Leah smiled, and she agreed with us. "How do you do it?"

"That's why Santana and I requested those stipulations prior to signing that temp contract. The promotion knows we're doing this as a favor for an old friend from Japan. What the promotion doesn't know is why they'll be arrested after they get back to the locker room area. That's where Santana and I will need your help; yours and Boop's Leah."

"You take the belts; we take credit for the mob-induced assault post-match. The problem we'll have is obtaining what we need from the Japanese promotion." Leah sighed, "We might need to go through the State Department."

"That promotion has offices in Los Angeles. Have either NCIS or the FBI in L.A. go over and request it in an assault case regarding a fan from the U.S." I smiled. "They don't need to know the people who need it are me and Santana."

"Okay, I'll ask Jason to put in a request with NCIS-LA to get what you need. It might take a day or two though." Leah said with a sideways glance.

I smiled. "A day or two's all we need!"

Dillon and I caught a ride on a pontoon-geared chopper headed about two miles off the coast of Port Aransas.

Santana, Jason, and Jennifer accompanied us to what appeared to be a sixty-foot yacht with two deep-sea fishing seats on the top bridge of the ship. I looked at the stern of the yacht and the name *Raven Witch II* displayed in dark black lettering. Then I remembered the yacht was a private, corporate charter owned by DMD International out of Port Aransas. Jason yelled, "Clayton and his organization would never have found Teddy. The folks at DMD Security owe us a lifetime of favors, after a fashion!"

"How well do you guys know the family?" Santana asked. "I heard once of a commandeered, British commercial frigate in the early 1700's bearing the same name."

"You a pirate at heart Santana?" Jennifer yelled and smiled.

Santana smiled. "My dad knew this old Navy Chief Warrant Officer from Vietnam who once found the wreck off of the coast of Jamaica near Montego Bay! He dove it once, but the wreck was picked clean of its treasures save one small chest."

"Did the man tell you what was in the chest?" Jason asked. Something told me Jason knew of the chest and its contents, or what he suspected was the contents.

"Former Navy Chief Warrant Officer Marko Devane willed it to me for some reason. I have no idea why. He and my father were really close as neighbors. He was one of my dad's fans when he used to wrestle in Florida."

"You said this CWO's name was Devane?" Jason asked as Santana nodded. Jason looked at the pilot, "Bobby, radio *Raven Witch II*. Inform Dr. Matthews only three of us will be coming aboard. I'll explain when we land."

The pilot nodded as he closed the channel to radio the yacht. Jason looked at us. "CWO Devane is the descendant of an old Russian priest from the late seventeenth century. He has a distant cousin at the Vatican in Rome serving as a cardinal. It might be a long, awaited peace-offering for two long-feuding families."

"If that's what I think it is, won't Arthur be upset you didn't call him first?" Jennifer cited a possible...issue.

"He wants to keep the peace as much as we do; his version is the extermination of one family. David wants to build bridges where he can!"

This Ping-Pong conversation left me dizzy as Santana sat back and smiled. "How valuable is that chest Jace?"

"To those you're about to meet...priceless!"

TWENTY-ONE

We landed fifty yards from the stern of the *Raven Witch II*. A zodiac sped from the aft section of the yacht and carried a man I had only read about in medical journals. His long, light brown hair blew like a lion's mane in the wind and salt air as Dr. David Matthews approached. He tossed a line from the zodiac and stood on his knees. "Well, it's about time you got out here brother!" Both laughed as they shook hands. "And I'm guessing the young lady sticking her head out is Teddy's daughter Tori. Dr. David Matthews."

"Pleased to meet you, Dr. Matthews," I said as I shook his hand. My lord, he has a strong grip; must work out. "I wanted to thank you for letting my dad hang out on your yacht."

"Not a problem; now, who's staying and who's going? Nikki wanted to plan for lunch."

"Doc, this is my partner...Santana Garvin; she has something back in Corpus Christi...that might belong to your wife's family...the Dubois."

"Is it something that can wait? We're planning on putting into port in three hours." Dr. Matthews smiled. Everyone nodded. Looks like we're all going aboard. "Great, I'll have the pilot here radio back to add...five places for lunch!" Something tells me my life just wandered into the *Weird Zone!*

The yellow zodiac rubber boat came to rest at the stern of *Raven Witch II* as a sturdy older female caught the towline and pulled us closer. I marveled at this woman's upper body strength as Dr. Matthews and Jason hopped out to tie off the zodiac to pull aboard later. Jason yelled in French, "Permission de monter à bord du capitaine? (Translation: Permission to come aboard Captain?)"

The woman answered in French, "Permission accordée commandant Vaughn! (Translation: Permission granted Commander Vaughn!). And welcome aboard my friends. I am your hostess Dominique Dubois Matthews."

"Thanks, Nikki; this young lady is Teddy's daughter Tori, and the new CCPD Liaison for TFCC Sgt. Santana Garvin."

"Ah, I'm pleased to meet you ladies. When Teddy told me his daughter Tori, was one-half of wrestling's most popular tag team, the *American Angels*, my twins Sean and Katie almost went into orbit. In fact, Katie worked really hard to imitate your ring costumes and to honor Santana by posing as her mini-me." We turned to find a sixteen-year-old brunette with one of our star-spangled costumes with a red, white and blue halter, red bottoms, red wrestling boots and Santana's signature blue bandana in her hair. Her dark brown eyes sparkled as her smile radiated the cabin. Dominique turned, "Ladies, this is my youngest daughter Katie. Katie, meet Tori Blanton and Santana Garvin."

Katie tumbled over to us like Santana would do when she was introduced to a match. She hugged me first and almost took Santana's breath away when Katie hugged her. "Wow, you could bear hug a walrus with those arms, Katie!"

"I'm sorry Miss Garvin; I sometimes don't know my own strength. I'll be gentler with you." The girl's smile didn't do her joy justice. Then a young man walked out from the galley.

He shared his sister's raven locks but had David's bluish green eyes and infectious smile. "This is Katie's twin brother, my son Sean. Sean, meet your so-called wrestling sweethearts, Santana Garvin and Tori Blanton; the *American Angels*." Sean stood motionless; terrified he had been ratted out by his mother. "Oh come, come darling; no need to be shy. Come over here!"

Sean stepped up slowly. I guess if I were a sixteen-year-old teenage boy with raging hormones and my two favorite female superstar wrestlers were visiting, I'd be a little in awe or shy to be around them. "Hi...Sean, I'm pleased to meet you." I held out my arms and gently hugged him. Although he embraced me back, it was strong yet gentle.

"I'm...pleased to meet you too...Tori." Sean eked out as he spoke. Wow, he really was shy...or nervous. "Excuse me for a moment." I released the hug as he left and returned with a poster. "I made this for you guys. We plan on going to Houston for the matches next weekend."

The marker artwork resembling Santana and I was extraordinary. He captured our souls and smiles with great artistic precision. Sean had a talent for art that rivaled his sister's design talents for clothing and costumes.

And the poster's caption made my day. *Heaven will Reign Supreme– American Angels are back!*

I almost cried as Santana put her arms around my shoulders. "Sean, this is a beautiful poster. You took a great deal of time and effort to create a ...a thing of beauty."

"I actually made two: one for the matches, and one...for you two to sign...maybe?" Sean smiled sheepishly as Santana and I nodded and signed the one he'd keep with white-inked Sharpie.

Then Dr. Matthews returned, "Lunch is ready if y'all will follow me?" I often wondered what sort of lunch cuisine the super-rich...dined on while at sea.

We went forward to the dining area as I saw a large Hibachi grill where shark steaks sizzled. I watched the familiar chef flip them over as they browned, and he looked up and smiled. Yes, my dad did the cooking and was quite shocked when I looked to our hostess. Madame Matthews smiled. "Teddy insisted on pulling his own weight on this voyage. So, I put him in charge of the galley!"

I smiled and looked at my smiling father. "You realize putting him in charge of the galley, is like putting a sea rat in charge of the onboard fridge right Madame?"

Dr. Matthews smiled. "At least when we told him the contents of the onboard fridge and freezer, he suggested a menu while at sea. It's been a delicious sea-faring adventure."

"I can imagine." I sort of said that under my breath. Don't get me wrong, my dad's a phenomenal cook either on a kitchen stove or a grill. But some of his marinades...well; he's way too much a vegan at heart. The man needed to cut down on some of his spicy ingredients. Of course, he gave me a low stare as I shook my head. "Cut down on the cayenne pepper slices a bit."

"All I do is roast them on top of the fillets, so the juices naturally have a spicy tang to them," Dad said as he flashed me his wicked grin. From the time I was ten, he tried getting me to tolerate spicy cooking. I think I inherited my mother's stomach; not enough cast-iron on my insides to tolerate that mix. But he's my dad and I discovered…I love the old coot! "Okay, okay…I'll put some A-1 Steak sauce on two of these for you."

"Thanks, Pop; you're a prince of the grill masters!" He blew me a kiss as we went into the yacht's massive dining room. The two massive tables seated around ten guests per table and made it a party; for even the crew were family to the Matthews family. "I love this version of ship's mess Madame."

"Oh please, Tori; call me Nikki. That goes for you as well Santana. And no need to call David Doctor; you can call him David…or Doc. Why he smiles at 'Doc' I have no idea…" If I had to guess, he liked being called 'Doc' because he earned the title. However, David and Dominique seemed more appropriate for my future memoirs. Yes, I do plan on writing memoirs someday…just not now. I smiled as Dominique looked at me oddly, "What?"

I shook my head and smiled again. "A little reflection, like confession, is good for the soul; my mom used to tell me that when I was a teenager. I never knew what she was trying to tell me, until now Nikki." We sat down to dine as David offered a prayer for the meal. After grace was spoken, we dug into our fillets. Dad was good to his word. My shark steak was smothered with A-1 Steak Sauce. The baked potatoes with sour cream and cheese added to the steamed mix vegetables and the gluten-free dinner rolls.

Dad sat next to me and Dillon sat to my left. Funny thing about Teddy, I never told him about any of my relationships. Primarily because most of the guys I've dated were wrestlers and interested in bedroom wrestling more than ring-wrestling. Fortunately, I never had sex with those knuckleheads. But with Dillon, I don't know. For some reason, the urge to…couple with him was stronger than with anyone I've known to date. Dad looked at me and nodded to Dillon. "So, college man from TAMU-CC?"

"Yes and…he's Jason's son." As soon as I said that, Teddy choked and almost needed a Heimlich maneuver performed. "Take it easy. Nothing's happened yet. We're still trying to get time alone, but Karma hates me at the moment."

"He does know what I used to do for a living…right?" Dad asked with a grin. His way of reminding me to not move too fast.

"Yes, he knows; my whole team knows Dad!" I whispered it but Dillon heard me. "What?"

"Excuse me…Tori," Dillon leaned back as did my dad and extended his hand. "Dillon Vaughn; pleased to be reacquainted with you, Mr. Blanton."

"Ah yes, we met first at the Pizza State on Monday night, right?" Dillon nodded as I looked at Dominique as she mouthed *you and Dillon?* I nodded and bowed my head. When I looked up, she smiled and gave me a thumbs up. "Those are some good pies at that joint. Now, I do have one question; how long with you and my daughter?"

"We met last Friday, and I agreed to assist in helping her sell her cover as a new student to TAMU-CC. It was suggested due to an ex-girlfriend of mine returning to the area; with a young Spaniard who we discover duped her into an international criminal conspiracy." Dillon took a breath and continued.

"However, I didn't know how special she was to me until I spoke with her after your eldest daughter's death. My condolences sir."

"Thank you, Dillon. That means a great deal coming from you." Then my dad looked at me. "You know, you could do worse than Dillon, but I doubt you could do any better than Dillon. He's a great young man with a bright future ahead of him. And with you in his life, I see it getting even brighter; for both of you. And should you make this…permanent, you have my blessing…both of you."

"Thanks…Dad." I couldn't say it any other way. I have a wonderful life, part-time entertainment job, full-time government job, Dad, boyfriend, and…a family that supports me. Maybe Karma decided to cut me a break… for once. Then I saw Dominique bring in two bottles of what appeared to be champagne. "Oh, what's this Nikki?"

"When our family gets to witness young love budding with promise, it's a cause for celebration. So, we have champagne from my private stock." The generosity of DMD's family of owners was legendary when they knew you or grown to love you. I'm guessing Dad's loved.

"More for me, or love for my father? I ask because I'm guessing you found out the Dixie Mafia's business holdings as well as the syndicate, is falling like dominoes stacked to make a pretty design. Your family is known for its generosity; especially when you make friends you want to protect or keep them from harming themselves. And yes Nikki, there is a difference."

"David, would you open these please?" David nodded as he put the bottles in a corkscrew. Dominique sat down and faced me. "Now, Tori, why would you say that?"

I couldn't contain my cop's intuition. "Anyone who knows, or who has heard of my father, knows of his culinary talents as a classically-trained chef. They also know he's a vegan; which means he'll only grill shark steaks for family. That's why I razzed him about it." Then I leaned in to ask. "Did someone you know; you love within your mansion in Las Colinas… retire recently?"

Then I saw what appeared to be…sadness in Dominique's eyes. She did lose a member of her family. The staff of her homes was also considered family to her. "Yes, our chef…Marion Harris, went home last Friday night after preparing a tasty supper…and I was notified…by DPD. He died in his sleep."

I got up and walked around the table and embraced the matriarch of the Matthews family. "My condolences Madame; you loved him like family. No one can blame you for your mourning." She smiled weakly at me and accepted my loving embrace. "Were you…interviewing my father?"

"In a way, I was. In a way, I offered him…my protection from those who would try to harm him…or even you. You see Tori; your father did me a kindness some years ago…that saved my life. I told him I owed him a debt and the marker was good for a lifetime; even if he passed it on to you."

TWENTY-TWO

While everyone else gathered around Santana as she told of our Japanese adventures, I sat out at the stern of the yacht and spoke further with Dominique. By now, we'd all traded our business attire for relaxing swimsuits or sweats, deck shoes or sandals, and sipped on our favorite beverages. I sipped a customary glass of champagne and switched to a diet soda. Dominique and I watched as the Gulf of Mexico slipped into the distance as the *Raven Witch II* made for port in Port Aransas. "So, you've known my family for a long time I take it?"

"I have; I was at your parent's wedding, and present for the birth of each of their children. However, you were your mother's life-change baby. One minute, she thought it was menopause; the next, her doctor told her she was pregnant. Ha, your father fainted on the exam room floor."

I had to laugh; my dad the tough guy fainted the moment he discovered I was coming along. "I wish I had a video of that…he had to have been beside himself."

"Ah, but no one was more joyful when you were born than Teddy Blanton. Your siblings loved you…at first. Then when everyone needed to make a choice of a path of life, your mother stood between you and your older siblings and said, 'Her path will be different; as will her life!'."

"Did you know my mom was undercover for the FBI, and my dad was her CI?" I asked because since she was present at each child's birth and my folks' wedding; she might have known.

To my surprise, Dominique shook her head. "No, I never knew that part; not until Teddy told me after Charli and your step-family died. He asked me to use my security consulting firm to keep your step-grandmother Hattie Wayne and you safe. I know you felt you had to grow up fast and take charge of your life early, but to be this…driven and purposeful at twenty-one? Even I didn't see this coming."

"Weren't women in the seventeenth up to the nineteenth centuries getting married and having families as early as fourteen years of age?"

"Some earlier; it also depended on arranged marriages between patriarchs of families either common or aristocrat. I did some research years ago on the Dubois family of France. The original matriarch of my family; according to my research, I was named after her and her origins were from a small island off the coast of Greece. Apparently, a young and dashing Vicomte from the mountain region of France fell in love with this goddess of the Aegean Sea, married her and they returned to France. They married in the year 1670, had two older children and the son I come from, Pierre, was born in early 1695; the year of the Chateau Dubois Massacre." I listened intently as Dominique told of her family's origins. The manner in which she told it, one would imagine she built a time machine and relived every detail of the original Dominique Marie Dubois' life. Then Dominique smiled a quirky, but melancholy grin. "I'm sorry Tori; I'm being a silly old woman."

"No, it's not silly to relive those memories; if something good comes from it." Dominique's shocked expression permeated the moment of sunshine. "How did I know?"

"Yes...that's exactly the question," Dominique said as David and Dillon joined us. "She figured me out!"

Dillon sat there and chuckled. "I told both of you; the more you try to hide something, the more she pays attention. And how you present your stories makes her pay attention. Did you two forget my dad wrote a five-minute profiling course for NCIS agents at FLETC?"

David smiled. "Tori picked up little ticks and vocal patterns to draw the right conclusion to the truth."

"Wasn't just that David; I was still awake and watching from Granny's kitchen when Dominique and Granny sat out on the porch sipping Cooking Sherry. Except, she called herself Marie Nicollet Devereaux; or Nikki for short." Dominique's smile shortened to a half-smile as David nodded with a satisfied grin. Dillon reached down and kissed my right cheek. "I'm sorry if I ruined this wonderful moment Nikki."

"You didn't ruin a thing, Tori. In fact, your whole first name is Victoria; which means in Latin...Victory. Your mother named you that because you were a fighter. She had you with no drugs and you came out kicking feet first. Your first cry was a primal scream and Charli laughed. She looked at Teddy and laughed, 'Hey Daddy, your baby girl's declaring a victorious birth of her!' Then she named you Victoria Dominique Blanton."

Wow, I was named after my maternal grandmother by the same name and one of richest women in the world. "However, I like calling you Tori. It seems…to fit you well."

"And since I don't know why or how you became…immortal, there's nothing I can confirm or deny. Besides, who would believe me?" It's not like I know enough to say much on the subject. As I asked, who would believe me? "Plus we just met. For all I know, you're just a crazy old rich lady with a French accent who lives in Dallas."

"There is something to be said for plausible deniability Agent Blanton," Dillon smiled as did David and Dominique. "And once I talk to my father, he might let me spill the beans about our Comanche family."

"It's an interesting story for the ages; much like ours Tori. And the day I met Jason three years ago at the Flying V Ranch in Snyder, Texas, was the day our families became closer, had a few scrapes, but we managed to repair most of the fences." David made the two family stories sound like the feud between the Hatfields and McCoys. Well, I'm glad to know them as well as Jason and Jennifer Vaughn. "We're about fifteen minutes out from making port. You guys might want to change into something for public visual agreement?"

"I thought young women in bikinis were visually agreeable David?" I smiled as I remember how I looked in this red floral two-piece swimsuit and Dillon nodded. He liked my attire.

"It figures; I'm trying to keep normal people on this yacht from having massive coronaries and Tori wants to cause heart failure!" David shook his head with a mock frown as Dillon motioned to me to head into the guest cabins to change. Oh well, it wasn't like I'd cause too much heart failure since I have a large A cup or a small B cup bra size.

We returned to the mid-deck of the yacht as Dominique's pilot docked the yacht in the Port Aransas marina. We disembarked to our vehicles as members of TFCC met us for transportation. Lightning smiled. "Ahoy there mates; nice to see you guys survived your time at sea!" David and Dominique blew raspberries at Lightning as Leah, Boop, and Boop's husband Lt, Manuel Garcia smiled as well. "See, I brought the old Master Chief with me. Jen made him an officer though!"

"Is he still trying to flirt and steal other men's wives from them Lightning?" David laughed as Manny held out his hands and smiled back. "Because I'm telling you right now, my wife doesn't fall for that lame Cubano charm he lays out from time to time!"

"That's because you never let me be alone in conversation long enough for my charm to kick in Doc!" Both laughed as Dillon and I sat back and watched the friendly reunion. Boop never told me how Manny convinced her to marry him. Manny took David's offered hand. "Good to see you old friend."

"You too Manny. Jace looks like everything's in order for the most part."

"Thanks for looking after Teddy Dave; Tori, I think your dad might want a hug and kiss before he travels to Big D?"

Jason's right; so I walked up and gave my dad a hug and a kiss. "You take care of yourself with those folks; you hear me Pop?"

Dad nodded. "I will kiddo; you love that young man right and let me know if…I have to come and walk you down the aisle?" I kissed him again and nodded. "David, Nikki; guess it's time we shoved off."

"Just for Tori's info purposes, did you guys talk to Chief Deputy Marshal Santiago in Corpus?" Jennifer asked.

David nodded. "Here, we thought Tori might want to get to know Teddy's new name." I looked at the Matthews household new employee sheet; Gino Torelli. Huh, Dad used a variation of my cover. Well, looked like Gina will get to meet her father, Gino, after all.

I hugged him one last time and whispered, "Love your name, Signor Torelli!" He smiled, kissed me again and left with David and his family. I sighed, "I was the one…who had to let him go this time…right, Jace?"

"Yes you did Tori, and this will save his life. You returned the favor in this case. And it allows you and Teddy to start fresh; no understood debts hanging over either of you. It's good reason to keep a cover intact huh?" Jason smiled.

"It is; now when I go visit Casa Matthews, Gina Torelli will visit Papa Gino. And that allows Tori to visit Teddy. I like that idea." And I did. But what I liked at the moment was members of TFCC secured the beach house. That means the grounds were checked, all the closets and bedrooms, common rooms, garages, and crawl spaces were checked and double-checked. Hopefully, Dillon and I will have at least one night together and alone.

Dillon walked up and threw his arms around me. "Are you ready to head back to the beach house?"

"I am kind sir; let us be off!" Then as we headed off back, I realized we forgot something. "Don't forget to tell San to bring that chest with her when we go to Houston."

TWENTY-THREE

After a wonderful dinner Jason and Dillon prepared on the Hibachi grill, Jason and Jennifer left and finally...Dillon and I had the beach house all to ourselves. We slipped into our beach attire again as the honk of a horn sounded out front. Dillon peeked out and groaned. I walked up and asked, "Who is it?"

We witnessed four older adults and two younger women emerge from the silver SUV. Dillon groaned again. "Apparently, either Aunt Kat or Gracie cracked! Both sets of my grandparents are here!"

"I take it, no matter what we do; we're doomed to not have a romantic weekend?" I sighed as all six people approached the front door. Then four tires of a four-door silver sedan screeched to a halt and Jason as well as Jennifer dove out and intercepted them. I looked at Dillon and smiled. "Did you happen to change the security codes on the alarm system here?"

"I did," Dillon said as he watched his parents. Both Vaughns in charge of law enforcement entities gave their parents a well-deserved blowing up. "Whoa, Dad's furious with both sets of grandparents."

I heard Jason yell, "I don't care who told you what!" Wow, he was angry.

"Look, son, all we wanted to do was check on Dillon...and maybe... meet the young lady. What harm is there in that?" I'm guessing the taller man who called Jason...son, was Jim Vaughn–owner of the Flying V Ranch in West Texas. The shorter woman with the light brown hair, trying to calm father and son down, was his stepmother Cecilia. Which meant, by the process of elimination, the other couple was Gerald and Grace Moran of Savannah, GA.

Grace was a tall-looking brunette with greenish blue eyes and held a fiery gaze when she was angry. "Exactly, how do you know this young woman is who she says she is? For all we know, she could be an axe-murderer!" Now I'm insulted!

This old hag from the CIA doesn't know me from Adam and threw out an inflammatory accusation like…axe-murderer. I never used any axes to kill anyone. A field knife to leave bloody roses on mob guys' chest…yes, after I broke their necks, but never axes.

"Remember when Dad spoke of the warrior-shaman wolf spirits we carry in our souls?" Dillon asked and I nodded. "If Grandma Grace doesn't calm down, you'll see mine emerge. Just bear with me and don't get scared…please?"

"I promise; as long as you don't eat me alive, I won't get scared!" I smiled as we returned to observing the argument outside.

Gerald spoke next, "We just want to meet her darling." Gerald addressed Jennifer and hoped she'd see his point of view. Then I heard a growl; a ferocious, feral growl. I looked at Dillon, he was normal. I looked at Jason and Gracie, both were normal. When I gazed at Jennifer; she grew a thick mane behind her head and sprouted fangs. All four of Dillon's grandparents jumped back inside the SUV.

"Mom's grown to love you a bunch. She'd never wolf out to silence the grandparents." I'm glad Jennifer loved me that much too. After what I saw, Dillon's wolf had to be majestic!

"All right, all right Jason we get it; we're intruding on a budding love affair." Well, well; seemed as if Lady Cecilia, aka Dillon's Gram, had the coolest head at the moment outside. "What's the harm in meeting her?"

"There's no harm, just not tonight!" We slowly opened the front door as Jason continued, "Look, everyone around here's had a rough week. The last thing we need is for you four to show up unannounced and read Dillon some riot act about his choices in dating or relationships. Do you really think I didn't check this young lady out thoroughly? I knew exactly who I was getting in my office as an agent when I did that background check."

"Oh, that's just lovely; she's one of the TFCC agents to boot!" Grace still didn't get the point. So Dillon and I descended the steps to the front yard. "Well, the lovely young couple joins us. Time to hash this out!" Family members attempted to calm Grace Moran down. But Jennifer's mother wouldn't be dissuaded. When she finally got to me, she reached out with her hand. Dillon stood between us and glared into her eyes. "Dillon, this is for your own good!"

"My...own...good. That's rich coming from you; the woman who attempted to abduct my sister last year due to the Blue Knights trying to kill Mom." Then Dillon shook his head.

"You know if you want a confrontation that badly," he said as I backed up a bit to give myself some operating room, "Be my guest Grandma."

Dillon stepped back as Grace looked deep into my eyes. How much does she really know about me? Is this judgment due to family associations or the fact I dared to love her grandson? I never broke eye-contact and I'm betting my glare unnerved the former Valkyrie. "So, you're the *Rosa del Diavolo?* You look too cute to be that frightening." Aha; she had a supremely arrogant attitude. I simply smiled at her as she became unnerved again. "What?"

"What is a good word and question. The proper one is why; why not honor them?"

"Honor...what, exactly?"

"Why not honor your daughter's wishes, and respect the boundaries she's set for your relationship with your grandchildren?" Grace's frown deepened as she started to step towards me again. "Think very carefully Mrs. Moran. I am a federal agent and I will use deadly force if necessary." When she rushed me, she called my bluff. I performed a deep arm-drag like I did recently on Caged Women. I plopped on Grace's right shoulder and held her arm in a Fujiwara armbar. Grace screamed as I pulled back just enough to keep her under control. "Didn't I tell you to think carefully?"

"You let me up this instant...now!" Despite Grace's orders and protests, I held firm on the armbar until Jennifer walked up with her handcuffs out. "Jennifer, Jennifer Faye what are you doing?"

"You're under arrest Mrs. Moran; the charge is Assault on a Federal Law Enforcement Officer. Need I remind you of the Miranda warning?" Jennifer looked at me and winked. I smiled and kept the armbar applied until Grace was appropriately restrained. Once we were back on our feet, Jennifer glared into her mother's eyes. "As I see it, you have two choices: choice one, I can call Port Aransas PD and speak with Chief Fitzgerald.

We'll see if he can house you for the night in one of his jail cells or choice two; you stay on the *Comanche Warrior* or at a hotel of your choice. By then, your grandson might be in a good enough mood to have us all over for breakfast tomorrow morning. But the one choice all four of you do not have is staying here as chaperones. Both Dillon and the young lady are consenting adults and can make their own choices. So what will it be Mrs. Moran; jail or a choice between the yacht and a hotel suite?"

Grace waffled; then said, "Might as well check out the wine closet on the yacht for the night."

"Excellent choice!" Dillon said as he walked over and opened the rear, passenger side door so Grace could get inside. However, she remained handcuffed. When Grace turned to be released, Dillon shook his head. "Call this a gentle reminder to honor the boundaries set. Grandpa, you may remove the cuffs once she's onboard the yacht."

Gerald Moran smiled. "I shall make sure your grandmother behaves herself. Here," Gerald handed Dillon a set of handcuffs. "Give this set to your mother. Tell her she's raised a fine young man in a son."

"Thank you, sir; I will," Dillon smiled as he kissed Grace on the cheek. "When you decide to behave like someone I can love as well as respect; I'll be more inclusive in the future." Grace smiled weakly as Kat and Gracie loaded into the back of the SUV and buckled inside. Dillon shut the door as Jim started the engine.

Cecilia rolled down her window and took Dillon's extended hand. "You, young sir, have a lovely companion. Do take care of one another?"

"I shall, Chief Superintendent Vaughn." Dillon smiled as Jason slipped him a marina set of keys. "Here, big key allows you access to the dock. The smaller key unlocks the mid-deck party area so you can access the cabins." She smiled and blew him a kiss as I extended the courtesy of a British military salute to Lady Vaughn. She smiled back and returned my salute with a pop of her wrist as Jim pulled out of the driveway and headed to the marina. Dillon let out a big sigh as the pressure-filled situation came to a close. "Thank God that's over!"

Jennifer wiped sweat from her own brow. "I wish our parents would just respect our wishes and not jump at a chance to hop on a plane and come here to surprise us." Then Jennifer reached over and hugged me. "Thank you for using the least violent option when dealing with my mother. You see why Jason and I stay here now?"

"I do; anywhere else would turn into more insane family drama; much like my family." I turned my attention to my beau Dillon. I jumped up into his arms and he kissed me as he caught me. I love it when a man can multitask like that. "So, is that the extent of the family drama?"

"Pretty much," Dillon smiled as he put me down on the ground. "Now, this is where I give you the...out, per se, so you can avoid that insanity in the future. You can run back like a wild woman to Corpus Christi and we can say this was a learning experience as far as dating one another is concerned." I looked at him and shook my head. "Didn't do enough to scare you off?"

"You didn't even come close to running me off Mister!" I pulled him to me and put my arms around his neck.

"I have not endured every little miscue and pitfall of the last two days, to simply quit on you now. The moment I laid eyes on you, I said to myself, 'Tori girl, that's the kind of guy you need in your life. One who's fearless, driven with purpose; someone who can bring balance to your life'. And you have, more than even your own family realizes. You didn't just extend my life Thursday night my dear; you changed it...for the better."

"If you can stand the heat in this family's kitchen; you're definitely a keeper Tori Blanton. So folks," Dillon looked to Jason and Jennifer. "What happens next?"

"We're going to go back to the suite and enjoy ourselves," Jason smiled. "Nikki left us a bottle of her champagne and I believe your mother's dying to take advantage of me!"

"Right...as if!" Jennifer laughed as she twirled the handcuffs on her left forefinger. "I might let you use this tonight Agent Vaughn." Then I saw a wicked grin etch across Jennifer's face.

"Okay, please go so I don't get any horrid images of seeing you two naked?"

Jennifer held out her hands at Dillon's observation. "What?"

"He's trying to say without being rude, Mom is that the image of his parents enjoying a coupling of their own, sort of...grosses him out. Primarily because he's now an adult male."

"Oh...right; the day I've dreaded for years has finally come. It's not cool or socially acceptable to discuss our sexual escapades in front of our grown or near-grown children." Jennifer said stoically as Jason nodded. "Good; gives me something to torture him with when my grandchildren are born!" Jennifer kissed Dillon on the cheek, patted him on the shoulder, and returned to their car.

Jason shook his head as he put his arm around Dillon. "Remember I told you one day, I'd welcome you to my hell?"

"I just walked right through the gate and got burned...didn't I Dad?"

"Big-time buddy!" Jason laughed as did Dillon. "We'll see you to-morrow morning son. Good night Tori." Jason got into the car and he and Jennifer left.

"Shall we Miss Blanton?" Dillon asked me as he extended his arm.

"Yes sir Mr. Vaughn; let's shall!"

TWENTY-FOUR

"Now, shall we go back up and enjoy a leisurely soak in the tub? I might need to shave tonight." Dillon said, but I kissed him and shook my head. "No, you don't want me to shave?"

"Shaving is acceptable; just not you doing it. I know; it makes you nervous to have someone else do it. But, I did it a few times for Teddy when he was hurt and couldn't use his arms. My step-grandfather owned a barber shop and Grandma Hattie taught me." Dillon still gave me a nervous look. "Every time I gave Dad one of those shaves, I never nicked or cut him. He got a clean, smooth, close shave every time. I promise you, Lover, I won't harm your handsome face. And in return, I'll um, let you practice placing me in protective custody...Mr. Vaughn."

Dillon grinned like the Devil. "You have a deal Agent Blanton!" Woohoo; it's gonna be a hot night. We went upstairs and I stropped my straight razor for Dillon's romantic shave.

Sunday morning and I awoke all smiles. Dillon went into the bathroom and I heard the shower going. My phone sat on its charger all night and I turned it on. No missed calls, but a call came in from Jason. "Good morning Jace."

"Good morning Tori; I tried calling Dillon. Is he in the shower?"

"Let me go check." I walked over while I threw a Carolina Panthers night shirt Dillon bought me as a welcome home gift. I saw his naked backside scrubbing away. "Yes, he's in the shower. What's up?" Dillon turned and gave me a *what* look. I mouthed *your dad* and he smiled and nodded.

"We just got up and are getting ready to come over. We should be there in forty-five minutes. Is there anything we need to pick up?"

"We kind of used the apple juice to celebrate our...alone time? We need another bottle."

131

Yes, we didn't have any booze, but we drank up the apple juice. "I believe that's all we need. Dillon cleaned up from our dessert romp last night."

"Okay, we'll stop by and pick up some apple juice. See you in forty-five!" I pushed *end* on my phone as Dillon got out. I told him what Jason said. He nodded and I took my shower.

I walked in fully dressed as Dillon handed me a cup of coffee. My hair, still wet from my shower, stayed wrapped in a towel as I sported a brown Oso Grill long-sleeve tee, blue jeans, and my blue tennis shoes. Dillon wore a green *Bartoni's Gulf Coast Deli and Souvenir Shop* long-sleeve tee, tan cargo pants and black tennis shoes. "Anything I can do to help?"

"Here," Dillon handed me a card with the house security code on it. "Unlock the security system so Dad can get in without any trouble."

"Not a problem." I went to the door and as I was about to put in the code, the grandparents arrived with Gracie and Kat. "Your grandparents, sister and aunt have arrived!"

"Might as well let them in; we tortured them enough last night." Dillon laughed as he got a call. "Gramp, are you guys outside?"

"No, the SUV was stolen!" He looked at me and shook his head violently. I left the alarm keypad alone.

"Call Dad and then Port Aransas PD and get them here now!" He stopped cooking and pulled out the Remington 870 Tactical Express shotgun and pitched me his Walther PPK. "The door gets shot out, shoot at anything moving into the house, from any direction!"

"Copy that!" My heart pounded as I watched the door. And when I noticed the outer door to the beach, my older brother Tad stood grinning at me like a possum. That meant Junior was coming through the front door with another friend from the Dixie Mafia. "Oh shit Dillon, we're surrounded!" Then just as Junior kicked in the door, I fired my Sig and the Walther. Junior flew over the balcony as Tad kicked in the back beach door. The boom of the shotgun sent Tad flying down below the beach house as two more men attempted to enter. I never saw these guys before. Had to have been local muscle my brothers picked up for this job. "Drop them gents or get dropped!"

The man's accent was from Georgia, or was it Mississippi? "You may have shot Junior and Tad, but we were told to keep coming until you were dead bitch!"

Then the one ally I didn't expect cocked the hammer of a Lady's Smith and Wesson five-shot automatic back and pointed it in the man's right ear.

"The young lady said, 'Drop it!' If you don't, I'll drop you. Besides, calling my grandson's girlfriend a bitch…shows extremely poor manners young man!" Grace Moran smiled as Gerald and Jim came up the back with Tad between them. "Dillon, you might want to help your grandfathers. I think that fella's pretty stout for them to handle." I slumped down and passed out.

I woke up a half-hour later and looked up into the eyes of a pretty brunette with a white cowboy hat, light-blue Oxford ladies blouse, dark jeans, and boots. A star within a circle was over her left chest as she spoke. "Welcome back Agent Blanton; I'm Texas Ranger Valerie Stanton. Looks like you just survived an ambush most Old West outlaws would find to be their best work; if they lived to tell the tale that is. How are you feeling?"

"Like someone shot me purely as a reflex," I said that and looked over over my left shoulder. Blood slowly seeped through my t-shirt as I took in a labored breath. "I think someone needs to get me to a hospital." And I passed out again!

I awoke to the smell of antiseptic and a bright light in my hospital room. I looked over to my left and found my arm receiving generous amounts of fluids to replenish what my body lost during surgery. Then I looked to my right and found a crowd of people who waited for me to return to consciousness. Among them were my dad Teddy and Dillon. Dad held my right hand. "Hey there honeybee; good to know you're still with me!" I nodded slightly due to the morphine.

"Hey beautiful," Dillon smiled as Dad got up and let Dillon sit with me for a moment. "I didn't see you had a hole in your shoulder. I would have had Dad call in a medevac. I'm glad you're still with me too."

"Ditto for all of us Tori," Jason said as the other members of TFCC gathered around my hospital bed. "You and Dillon almost single-handedly took out the Dixie Mafia crew. The one Grace caught was the only survivor." I closed my eyes. I couldn't tell if my tears were those of mourning or relief. It's when I started to wail, I knew I was mourning them; all three of them: Tad, Junior, and Tessa. Gently, Dillon helped me sit up as I cried on his shoulder. Jason patted me on the back. "Good, get it all out kiddo; you earned a good cry after the week you've had."

"I'll stay with her Agent Vaughn," Dillon said as he continued to hold me. "We've become incredibly close this past week."

"And although there was spirited protest before last weekend kicked into gear, those protests have ceased." Leah smiled.

"And the infirmed agent demonstrated a poise and determination that personifies the spirit of NCIS and TFCC. I'm proud to call her my colleague."

"In fact, SEC-NAV and Director Darrow are on vid-conference for you Tori." Lightning smiled widely.

"Me; why would he want to speak with me?"

"Apparently, someone around here believes you performed an act of extreme bravery. In doing so, caught the attention of SEC-DEF (Secretary of Defense). SEC-DEF couldn't be on due to a briefing at the White House, but asked SEC-NAV and Director Darrow to read the citation." Jason smiled as he handed me a tablet. Then the familiar images of NCIS Director Vincent Darrow and Secretary of the Navy Elise Marcum appeared on the screen. "You're on sir, ma'am!"

Darrow spoke first, "*This is becoming a habit with you Agent Blanton. The more you do, the more extraordinary your results. So much, in fact, DC has taken a serious interest in your young career. So every move you've made since Monday has been followed by me, SEC-NAV here and SEC-DEF. In fact, Secretary Marcum sent you a special commendation from the Office of the Secretary of Defense...Madame Secretary?*"

"*Thank you, Vince. Well Tori, I recently found out your full name is Victoria Dominique Blanton; and that name ended up sounding off lots of bells and whistles on the beltway. Especially when the Spanish government and Interpol, confirmed the De la Cruz family set up the in-laws for a crystal methamphetamine operation. The deaths on the Abe Lincoln, from Malta, your match in Tokyo; all connected to business interests related to the Dixie Mafia."* Joe Don Clayton set me and my family, up for a major fall; only I didn't bite. So he took everything or tried to take everything from me. *"Because of your ferocious tenacity in working all these cases at once; you set a record for the most cases closed in one reporting period. That's outstanding work, Tori. So, on behalf of the President of the United States, and the Secretary of Defense, we are honored to present you with Secretary of Defense Medal of Valor. Congratulations, NCIS Special Agent Victoria Dominique Blanton!"*

Jason placed the medal around my neck as Dad reached over and kissed one cheek and Dillon the other.

"Madame Secretary, please extend my appreciation to SEC-DEF and the President for honoring me with this award. I wanted to say this as a way of how much I appreciate this honor. I quote Raymond Chandler: 'Down these mean streets a man must go, who himself is not mean, who is neither tarnished nor afraid.' That was his definition of a hero. I have been mean, and I have been tarnished, but others have come along and repaired my armor, stitched up my cape and made sure my weapons of heroism work properly."

TWENTY-FIVE

After we said our goodbyes, Teddy received pictures of my presentation of the Medal of Valor. David texted him crying because he was so proud of my accomplishment. He even said Mom was smiling down from Heaven; knowing her baby girl did well. I spent another day in the hospital and was checked over by a sports medicine specialist. She indicated I could still wrestle in Saturday's event in Houston.

So, Santana and I worked out at the gym in the basement at NCIS on station. After we finished, showered and a rub-down from Casey and Lena, we returned to the squad room where Boop caught us. "Hey, FBI caught up with and sent Bass back to us! You guys want to observe Danny and Leah question her?"

An evil glint in my eye formed as Santana smiled the same way. Santana nodded. "Count us in!"

We sat in Observation with Jason as Danny and Leah questioned former FBI Agent Rhonda Bass. Rhonda looked a little rough after a week. Her hair was frizzy, she had dark bags under her eyes, and her clothes looked like rumpled burlap. Definitely not her week!

Lightning observed the recording equipment as we listened and watched. Danny asked, *"Just so we're clear Miss Bass..."*

"That's Agent Bass...Agent Court!" I have to say this for Rhonda, she hasn't lost her charm or lack thereof. *"I'm challenging the OPR* (FBI's Office of Professional Responsibility) *ruling concerning my status. Therefore, my correct title is still Agent."*

Leah set her straight. *"You may be an agent to him, being he's FBI. But to me, you're nothing more than a spoiled, traitorous bitch who should hang for getting sailors killed on an operation you had nothing to do with... Miss Bass!"*

Bass forgot someone handcuffed her to the iron eye on the interrogation table. Leah resumed questioning. *"You claimed in our squad room prior to any...physical confrontation, that you held a marker on late NCIS Agent-Afloat Dumont Talbot. In which you betrayed the international task force and got two agents of allied nations killed. Nations who want to prosecute and hang you for those crimes Miss Bass. If it were left up to me, I'd send you to a black site somewhere in the world and ask to see how much more betrayal's in your lying eyes!"* Leah left the room and came in here to us. "I don't believe her; she really thinks she did nothing wrong."

I looked at Santana and smiled. Then I said, "Maybe the wrong bad cop is in there with Danny." Leah looked at me and smiled. "Perhaps, it's not about a bad cop or demented cop; maybe sadistic cop's in order."

"Please explain...Agent Blanton?" Jason asked as Leah folded her arms. She knew what I was thinking. But how do you get someone like Bass to cop to her original confession? Answer; you send in someone who recently won a major commendation for her law enforcement endeavors and get her to sign an attorney waiver.

"I go in with an attorney waiver...and my new lapel pin."

I walked in wearing my new Dubois-tailored bullet-proof navy pantsuit with my Medal of Valor lapel pin on my left jacket lapel. In my hand was a nice, fresh attorney waiver to see if Rhonda Bass would be fool enough to sign. Danny smiled at me. "Why Agent Blanton, what brings you in here?" Danny looked back at Bass and all the color washed out from her face.

"Oh, I came in here because Agent McCoy is on 'parent duty' in case one of her girls has an emergency at school. And her daughter Katherine was in the nurse's office with some stomach bug. So, as her replacement, I need to follow procedure." I pulled out the attorney waiver and kept it in my hand on the outside of the case folder. "You were made aware of your Miranda rights?" She nodded. "And in the same manner, you are well aware you can retain counsel during this interview?" Again, she nodded. "Would you like an attorney present?"

"I see no need for it." Bass smiled.

I put the attorney waiver flat on the table. "Would you please sign this waiver; to refuse to have counsel during this interview?"

"Sure, why not? I have nothing to hide." And as predicted, she signed it. In came Boop who collected it and left again. She noticed the lapel pin. "I see someone's wearing a new decoration. Who did you pay off to get that?"

I smiled and sat down. The sadistic cop angle was working like a charm. "It's a copy of the actual SEC-DEF Medal of Valor awarded to me on Tuesday afternoon. Of course, I took a bullet Sunday morning to get it, but it all worked out. My remaining siblings are dead, due to some idiot's constant abuse of power in getting them released. Some idiot, whose husband the DEA discovered, got undercover FBI Special Agent Charlene Faye Tolliver, killed." I laid my mother's last picture, prior to her death, in front of Bass. "Killed by her own children, not me, but my older siblings on the info supplied by a dirty DEA agent named Allan Bass!"

I slammed his picture down as Bass almost broke out of her restraints. "You're lying! Allan would never do that! He loved his job and respected his supervision; he'd never do that!"

"Oh, and he'd never, ever get involved in drugs or get a habit from a controlled substance either; or would he? To maintain his cover?" I laid down a document Bass picked up and read. "That is a Toxicology report done during Allan's autopsy. It showed based on continual use; he was an addict for most of that year. And that he got most of his team killed as well. The Dixie Mafia kept him protected and in seclusion during all those busts going south. He betrayed everyone, Rhonda. You, my mother, his team; and his sins... somehow through your own bitterness, betrayed and almost got me killed multiple times in the last eight months. Did you know; my own father... was my mother's confidential informant?" By now, Bass's tears flowed as she shook her head violently. Yes, the sadistic cop angle worked too well. "My mother made sure I was with my grandmother Hattie Wayne, and I was guarded by people more dangerous than the Dixie Mafia at the time."

"Why?" Bass asked through her tears.

"She discovered someone close to the case betrayed her. She and my dad decided to divorce, and she got custody of me. When she found out my sibs were closing in, she sent me to Granny Hattie. Then she and the only stable family I had in years were brutally killed to send me and Teddy a message. The message: mess with us, you die too!" I'd thrown a nasty combination of pitches to get Bass to drop her insanity. But I had one change-up she needed to see. "You tried to screw me, because of my last name only! My folks made sure I never, ever fell into the Dixie Mob's influence. And between two idiotic government agents named Bass, my father and I are the only ones left! So, here are your options as I see them: you confess, write it down and testify in court against Dixie Mafia. Two, you maintain this insanity. By maintaining this insanity, we present the A-USA with this evidence, your meltdown at NCIS, the fact you falsified orders to spring my brothers to come after us again, and you go on trial for the biggest charge on the books; treason. That automatically guarantees you, if convicted, life in prison or the death penalty. And to add to your continuing stress levels, you have five minutes to decide on the rest of your miserable life. See you in eternity Rhonda."

As I made my way out the door, Bass cried out, "All right, all right; I'll allocute!" She sobbed as I looked at Danny and nodded. Then, in one moment of weakness, I walked back over to Bass and handed her a handkerchief to dry her eyes. She looked up and frowned, "You're a cold bitch, Blanton."

Then I bent down into Bass's face. "If I am as cold as you claim, it's because you helped in creating me…Rhonda; you and your bastard husband!" I stood up and walked out.

I returned to Observation and hugged myself as I walked inside. I sat down and attempted to decompress from what I just did. Boop knelt down beside me with her blue eyes shining with joy. "Good work kiddo, you got her!"

Then I looked into Boop's eyes. I felt drained by the whole interrogation. "But…at what price Boop? She did this because she thought I was part of all that…mess with her husband. She dug her graves of revenge and planned on burying us both. I wouldn't let her. However, I won't have any vengeful family trying to kill me anymore."

Leah smiled as she patted my shoulder. "There is always a bright side Tori. Now, you have one more square to fill and all this mess will be cleaned up. And the nice part; you get to be as physical as you want, and you won't be suspended for it!"

I emphasized my response. "Yay yes! I will have a bunch of fun Saturday night!"

I walked over to my desk as Danny and the rest of the team returned to the squad room. I took off the lapel pin and began typing up my final report on the Malta case. Lightning returned as he typed up his interrogation report. "Hey, Tori, nice work on that interrogation technique."

"Actually Lightning, I don't think that was me. I think that was the Tori Blanton who was still imprisoned on Malta. I detoured by the ladies room so I could splash water on my face. I looked in the mirror and…I saw *Rosa del Diavolo* in my eyes, and that bitch scared me to death." I shivered, and I have never shivered before. I stopped typing my report and saved it. "Excuse me; I need to go see Doc Wise."

I went down the hall to where our analysts resided and knocked on Dr. Wise's door. "Come!" She ordered as I opened her door. Her glasses were on the end of her nose and then she looked up. "Tori please come in." Then I remembered she wanted me to call her Amanda. Amanda got up and smiled as she greeted me. "Have a seat on my little sofa." I smiled and sat down. "Well, you've had an eventful week. And you were awarded SEC-DEF's Medal of Valor."

"That's…not why I'm here Amanda. I faced Bass in interrogation thirty minutes ago."

Amanda sighed, "Probably not the healthiest choice given what's already happened. What made you come see me?"

"I saw her…in the mirror in the ladies room Amanda. I saw my own darkness…I saw the Devil's Rose in my eyes!" Immediately, Amanda embraced me. She sensed what I saw, scared the hell out of me. "She scared even me; is that normal?"

"I faced my own dark half once; looked her square in the mirror, and I think I dealt with it by having coffee and toast with her." I sat up and glared at her like she was nuts. "I'm kidding!"

TWENTY-SIX

"Damn it Doc I'm not!" I shot up off her sofa and almost ran out of her office. "How the hell am I supposed to do my job now? She...she's been the edge I've needed...for so long. And now she suddenly scares me? What do I do?" Then a knock came at her door.

"Who is it? I'm in a session at the moment!" Amanda yelled.

"It's Vaughn Mandy; I wanted to check on Tori. See if she was okay?"

Amanda looked at me and asked, "Did you say something about this in the squad room?" I nodded. "Okay, I'm going to suggest...we let him in. Tori, I think he can help you more than you realize. Maybe, even more, than I can." I relented and nodded. "Come on in Jason!"

Jason walked in and he only wore his white dress shirt, no blazer, no tie with his tan khakis and maroon loafers. He walked over, turned one of high-back, brown leather chairs to face us and sat down. "How are you feeling young lady?"

I cleared my throat. "I don't know. I stopped off at the ladies room on my way back to my desk. I needed to splash water on my face and cool off after Bass's interrogation. Then I saw my own darkness, the Devil's Rose, staring back at me. And...she smiled an evil, sadistic grin. She scared me, Jason." Tears leaked from Jason's eyes as he wiped them away and nodded. "So, that is normal...right?" Jason nodded again. "How, how do I deal with her now?"

Jason thought for a moment; looked into Amanda's eyes and somehow, both agreed he needed to take it from here. "Each of us has a darkness that only the light can scatter. You remember the analogy of the dogs or in my case, the wolves?" I shook my head with a blank stare. He chuckled because he realized he just lost me. "Okay, we each have two sides of our personality; one good or from the light. The other...evil or dark. The one we feed the most will rule over our emotions, personality, and how we view life." I nodded and understood. "I can tell you, from personal experience; having to choose between those two bastards in my own soul, saddens me some days. But, when surveying the situation, you have to choose which one to feed for your own survival. Now's the time to feed the white wolf; the good person inside you Tori. Let her out and let her run free! Love my son; go take those title belts Saturday from Caged Women. Show Dillon... that loving, young woman he dares to love daily. You do that; the good person I met last Friday her first day, will shine through."

"I'll do that." I have to admit, I felt much better in Amanda's office than I did the first time. I guess having Jason there eased my tension more for some reason. "It's time I went back to my desk and finished my paperwork."

I returned to my desk and saw Lightning as he gazed my direction. I walked over as Leah stood beside me. "Thanks for your concern. Jason was a big help just a moment ago."

He held up his hands. "I'm just glad everything's worked out for now. Keep up the good work Tori. And...kick those hussy's asses Saturday night!"

"Ditto partner!" Danny smiled as did the rest of the team.

"How's the team this afternoon?" Jason asked as he walked into the squad room. He put on his blue-striped tie again as we all looked at him and smiled. "By the smiles on all your faces, I'd say you're in good spirits; especially our latest hero?" Everyone yelled and clapped as I stood and took my bows. "And she's humble as well!" Laughter broke out as Jason calmed us down. "Get your final reports ready and email them to me. I will add my addendums to them and brief Asst. Dir. Vale tonight. He suggested we take four days off and help Santana and Tori...prepare for their championship tag match in Houston on Saturday! After you finish your reports, you're all invited to my place for another team cookout tomorrow at noon. Blanton, Court, and Garvin; your turn to provide the booze for the party!"

"Oh, goody; I have the perfect plan for that!" Santana smiled as she punched up a few keys on her computer. "Garrett's Restaurant accepts online orders for parties; including beverages. And he has a special on five-gallon kegs; a price cut from two-hundred twenty-five dollars to one-hundred fifty. So, you and Tori have a Sam Grant to donate Danny?"

"You guys caught me right between paydays." Ouch hate to hear that! "After my bills to get moved down here, I had to get my truck inspected and tagged as newly transplanted Texas resident." I felt for Danny. I know how hard it is to leave your home behind to accept a new position. However, he mentioned something significant. "I did manage to get a ticket for the event in Houston. And Jason agreed to let me catch a flight with them up to Houston Saturday night."

"And the next US. Govt. payday is Friday," Santana smiled as she looked at me. Of course, she knew I kept extra cash on me for emergencies. And Danny's plight, in our opinion, qualified as an emergency. Well, maybe not, but it's a good reason to spot him fifty bucks for team-building...right? I handed Santana a Ben Franklin and covered the keg. "Thank you, Miss Blanton!"

"I'll make it up to you Tori...promise!" I know what you're thinking; I had an FBI agent over a barrel and in a perfect position to spank him good.

But I can't do that to a nice guy like Danny; regardless whether he's FBI or not. "I have a solution: you have a nephew who claims to be our biggest fan in New Jersey...right?"

"Yeah, told me himself...why?"

"TGCW, the promotion, carries goody boxes for young fans your nephew's age. We can set up the box with all of our merchandise, signed photos, a DVD of the first three seasons of the promotion, and...two signed t-shirts; he can give to a fellow fan. And that particular box runs twenty dollars. You buy that, pay to ship it to your nephew; I'll call it even."

Danny walked over and we bumped fists. "You're a good egg, Blanton!"

"No matter whether it is fried, scrambled, poached or in omelets; all good ways to cook eggs!" I laughed as did the rest of the room as we finished up our reports and emailed them to Jason.

My new, regular place at the Sendera Bay Point Apartments sat in close proximity of TAMU-CC, NAS-Corpus Christi, and Crossroads Yoga where Santana and I decided to get some stretching in prior to a good night's sleep. Santana also lived in the complex and we both joined Crossroads the Saturday morning after we arrived. We walked into the pink and white building to attend a late, evening class for the busy workers of our fair city.

We pulled out our yoga mats and began stretching awaiting our yoga instructor to start class. I wore a dark gray tank top and matching yoga pants while Santana wore a navy tank top with red yoga shorts. What can I say, the woman enjoyed showing off her legs.

Our instructor came in and said, "All right everyone, let's start with a basic child's pose!"

TWENTY-SEVEN

Wednesday evening turned into night as we drove up in front of my building. Santana and I started car-pooling to keep expenses under control. We did the same thing when we were active on Indie Wrestling circuit. Since my beautiful navy Ford Fusion was still listed as evidence at the last beach house crime scene, we drove everywhere in Santana's Chevy Colorado pickup. You get two southern girls together; you never knew what might happen. Santana didn't mind parking in front of my building; since she lived one building over from me. "Well, here we are Tori-girl; home sweet home…for now!"

We both laughed as I sighed. "I think we should have been using yoga to relax the moment we arrived here in Corpus San. But before I realized that, I fell in love with our boss's son. And the funny part, I wasn't even looking for a boyfriend yet. Then, he walked in with both of those cases of beer and…I got lost in his eyes."

"And so it begins…"

"What?"

"The…oh San, he's adorable, a perfect gentleman, love of my life; the kind of man I want to marry…spiel. And even though you've only known him for a week, there was a difference."

"And what was so different this time with Dillon?"

"You never spent the night with any of the other guys before Tori. Added to the fact, none of them would have gone to the extreme to help you sell an undercover personality; maybe…Dillon's the real deal. I firmly believe…you really are in love this time!"

Oh wow, Santana finally said what I've been trying to figure out since my night with Dillon; I am in love with him! Somewhere between last Friday and today, I actually crossed over from flirtatious dating and general relationship mayhem into…I love him and want to keep him in my life.

145

Okay, Tori, take it easy girl; you're in love and now that you have him, you need to take it easy for a bit. "Okay, I agree…I love Dillon and it's a really, lusty version of love and I guess he and I need to slow down a bit. I don't believe it; he and I…did we really do that?"

"I think you did." Santana smiled her goofy grin when I think I made a really stupid mistake in the ring. "But Tori, I saw you every time someone mentions Dillon's name around you. Your smile lights up a room, your voice goes raspy, and you close your eyes and smile wider. Sweetie if that's not love, I don't want to know the truth about love."

"Problem is; Agent Blanton wouldn't know the truth if it came up and bit her on the ass!" I turned and pointed my Sig at the source of that gravelly voice. Santana leveled her Glock at the same source who was in his mid to late sixties. His salt n pepper hair, cropped close to his head, resembled a Marine Corps non-commissioned officer as did his cruel hazel eyes. His cheeks full of laugh lines though the man hardly cracked a smile. NCIS Supervisory Special Agent Jerrod Garner stood before us.

He wore a plain, green jacket with a tan brush-popper shirt with blue jeans and tan hiking boots. "Santana Garvin meet my training agent; a former pain-in-the-ass Marine Corps Gunny named Jerry Garner. Garner, this is former DEA agent Santana Garvin. She's now a detective."

"I would walk over and shake your hand, but Agent Blanton's pointing her Sig at me."

"Well, based on what I've heard about you Agent Garner; her pointing a gun at you is a reflexive safety precaution." Then Santana holstered her Glock. "And I was told if you ever appeared in Corpus Christi without notifying the NCIS office here, I was to call SAC Vaughn immediately."

"Vaughn give you that order Garvin?" Garner snarled at her.

"Nope; Chief Vaughn gave me that standing order. She's my boss downtown at CCPD." Santana whipped out her phone and called Jason. Apparently, Jennifer answered. "Hey Jen, tell Jace Garner's here in Corpus. Yes, he's standing outside the building and…Tori's got her Sig on him." A few moments passed as Santana nodded. "Okay, I'll let her know. See you later Jen…bye." Santana ended the call and announced, "Jason received word Garner came here to look you up. Someone else took the call and gave him your address…by mistake. The agent has since been admonished not to do that again and Jason will be here in two minutes."

And exactly two minutes later, Jason pulled up and Jennifer was with him. Hmm, I think she took a chopper and met him at NCIS. I heard she did that when she wanted to give her protective detail a break for a time. I love her tan business pantsuit with light brown boots. "Santana, you call CCPD yet?"

"No time Chief; he appeared out of nowhere. Agent Blanton drew on him the moment she turned to face him." I never told Santana Garner used to be a Force Recon Marine…from Desert Storm.

"Agent Garner has a bad habit of sneaking up on people; especially those who are his allies. I almost shot him with a SOCOM .45 pistol in Bosnia once. His major and I were at Annapolis together and he came close to ripping the stripes off of Garner's BDUs." I never heard of Jason being so angry, he'd want to shoot anyone on purpose. However, where Garner's concerned, I'd shot him in Bosnia. "And he loved doing it to NCIS agents he trained. That's why over seventy percent of the agents he trained, complained after they left DC or the agency. So, with Blanton belonging to that number, why are you here Agent Garner?"

"I heard she was shot; I came here to check on her. Is that a crime Agent Vaughn?" Oh yeah; Garner, out of the goodness of his heart, came here to check on me because I almost died. And yet, when I shot my sister and my brother recently, he never even bothered to call and check. No, he was probably in MTAC in DC when I received the Medal of Valor and wanted his own version of…validation.

"So, let me get this straight; you coming here had nothing to do with the fact I received the SEC-DEF Medal of Valor…Agent Garner?" I finally holstered my Sig and folded my arms across my chest.

"I simply came here to check on an agent I trained to see if she's okay or not."

"You know, if I were the average newbie agent, I might believe that line of bullshit. However, I'm a Garner-trained agent who was refined by working with Jason Vaughn. And before then…survived a botched op in the Med due to a less than sane FBI agent who threw us under the bus. Where was your mentor-like concern then…Jerry?"

"I made some mistakes…"

"Some…mistakes? Try driving away seventy out of every one-hundred agents you've trained in the last twenty years! Mistakes; how about acting like some sawed-off jerk because you were asked to retire from the Corps because you lost your marbles. I'm fine; no need for you to stay… go home!"

But Garner's too damned stubborn for his own good. "I want you back on my team."

I smiled; then let out what I called my maniacal laugh. And I laughed until I finally calmed down. "Jerry, Jerry, Jerry; what the hell makes you think I'd come back to DC and work for a sexist, disrespectful, overbearing jerk like you? All you would do is put me on a desk because you don't think I can handle myself. And that's not what I signed on to do at NCIS. So, go get back in your rental car, go back to the airport and fly home. You're not needed here!"

When I turned my back to leave, Garner reached out to pull my hair back. And he yelled, "Don't you dare sass me you ungrateful little bitch!"

Santana dropped to one knee and punched Garner in the balls. Garner let out a scream that caused a few stray dogs in the neighborhood to howl from their own pain. Garner's knees hit the pavement and I threw a right cross to his jaw. He dropped like a lead balloon and turned over on his belly. Then I jumped on his back and cuffed his hands behind his back. Jason spoke, "NCIS Special Agent Jerrod Garner; you are under arrest. The charges: assault on a federal agent, violating agency wellness policy procedures, unauthorized absence; that came from Director Darrow, and last but certainly not least disturbing the peace–specifically NCIS Agent Victoria Dominique Blanton's."

Then two light blue Ford Crown Victoria sedans drove up. An older, but gorgeous Hispanic female walked overdressed to the nines in a black cocktail, spaghetti strapped dress with black peep-toe high heels. Leave it to me, a fashionista, to notice the shoes. She walked up and hugged Jennifer. Then she stepped over to us. "Good evening ladies, I am Chief Deputy US Marshal Lydia Santiago. I see you have someone in the federal lock-up here in the area?"

"Yes ma'am," I said as I rose off of Garner's back. "I'm NCIS Special Agent Blanton and this CCPD Detective Sgt. Santana Garvin."

We shook hands and Santiago looked down. "Ah, Agent Garner from DC. Too bad!"

"You know Garner?" I asked as my shock registered with Santana as well.

"Yes, unfortunately, I do Agent Blanton; I was part of the Virginia Fugitive Retrieval Squad when NCIS ended up with a hostage situation involving a fugitive we pursued. It happened to be late NCIS Special Agent Caitlin Thomas. She lived that day, but Garner killed my fugitive with a sniper shot; after getting a green light from the FBI." I met the lady Santiago mentioned, as TFCC Senior Analyst Kate Belmont Talbot; wife of CCPD Asst. Chief of Detectives, Grady Talbot. Santiago resumed our conversation. "What are the charges?"

Jason stepped up and confirmed the charges. "Assault on a Federal Agent, namely Blanton; Violation of NCIS Wellness Police procedures, Unauthorized Absence, and finally Disturbing the Peace; Agent Blanton's to be precise."

Santiago motioned to the second sedan. Two burly, but handsome Deputy Marshals exited the vehicle dressed in their Fugitive Retrieval Kevlar. "Okay boys, read Agent Garner his rights, take his badge and weapon, and secure him for transport to the federal lock-up."

"I will remember this Blanton; I swear to you I will!" The Marshal who drove Santiago walked up as the other two escorted and placed Garner into their vehicle and left.

Also a handsome rogue; I wonder if Chief Santiago collected handsome males for her office and even hired female Marshals. This new man's name was Jim Slater and Santana's smile widened when Deputy Marshal Slater smiled at her. I cleared my throat. "Um…Sgt. Garvin; you're drooling!"

"What? Oh, my apologies!" I had trouble containing my giggles with Jennifer and Santiago as poor Santana blushed at Slater. She extended her hand. "CCPD Sgt. Santana Garvin; pleased to meet you."

"Deputy US Marshal Jim Slater; pleasure's all mine Sgt. Garvin." Love is in the air!

TWENTY-EIGHT

After Slater and Santana exchanged phone numbers, he and Santiago left to make sure Garner was processed at the federal lock-up. What a week! "Hey, partner; have you recovered from you apparent connection with Deputy Jim?" I laughed as Santana continued to blush. In the last three years I've known her from our tours wrestling, she never reacted with flushed cheeks. I found it cute in my tag team partner.

"I need to go upstairs and get some water," Santana smiled nervously. "Or a cold shower?" The pained expression on her face told me her girly parts were flying beyond the stratosphere at the moment. I guess she and I have both denied ourselves the company of the male gender for too long. "Okay, I'm calming down now. Jace, what were you guys talking about while I was…hypnotized by the handsome Deputy Marshal Slater?"

"Jason and Jen suggested we stay with them and they would fly us into Houston Friday afternoon. I take it from your…prolonged hypnosis, that you will have a plus one tomorrow for the cookout?"

"Yes and I ordered an upgrade to a ten-gallon keg from Garrett. I believe Dillon will be delivering it on a drink dolly tomorrow." Santana smiled as I frowned. "What?"

"Oh, I guess my lack of maturity is showing through now." I sighed; Dillon had to work that morning to help Rudy Garrett make those deliveries of catered food and beverages. But the last stop he had was Jason's house. And that meant Rudy would pay him and leave him there. So, my sad sigh was quickly replaced by happy thoughts of my plus one's short workday. "This is what it is meant by the quote, 'Absence makes the heart grow fonder'. Now I know how Dillon felt when my work week picked up speed." Then Jennifer put her arm around my waist. "Jen, did you ever deal with this when Jason was a shore cop?"

I felt her take in a deep breath. "As a shore cop, he was normally home every night. It's when he became an NCIS agent; those times we weren't working in the same city, made me miss him the most. Then I transferred to Savannah PD and became my father's SIU captain. After Jason did some teaching at the Iraqi National Police Academy, he told Darrow, who was Director of NCIS back then, to make sure he honored his promise to Jason and let him stay close to us. Jason commuted to NAS Glynco, GA to teach Probies for NCIS. He'd stay for a month to teach his class; then come back to Savannah for two months. The NCIS Asst. Director, a woman named Morton, had a hell of a time trying to get him back into field work and he refused to do so; until Leo Vale became Asst. Director for the Central Region. Then Jason became the SAC when the office was across the bay in Ingleside."

"Then you became, at some point CCPD Police Chief and after that, NCIS moved the offices on to NAS Corpus Christi. I'll bet that saved a bunch of time and money for the commute." I asked. "So, you do know how I feel."

"Sugar, I've known how you felt from the moment I met you and you met Dillon. I have been you and Dillon's been both me and Jason." Jennifer put her other arm around me in a comforting hug. "Love is funny; some only stay for a short time; and some...stay longer."

"My mother once told me; if you can talk to your love about anything at all, you'll have a love that poets and songwriters will express envy for you. You and Jason have been married for what; twenty-three years?" Jennifer nodded. "And your relationship started out like ours?"

"Same types of distractions and interruptions; mostly friendly ones, but generally the same type of timeline. Married Jason three months after I met him. Our parents thought we were both crazy. And yet, here we are... twenty-three years later; still in love even after two kids and two careers."

"I want a love like that; one that defines patience, kindness, thoughtfulness, and goodness. And knowing that part of the struggle; is fighting to keep those core values of love in place at all times." Funny how a few words from a member of the Vaughn family can help a person get back on track. Then Santana returned from her apartment. I didn't even notice she left. "I need to go pack?"

"Unless you plan on wearing what you're currently wearing to Houston, and to wrestle in the match?" Santana smiled sweetly. Yes, she's gone to the land of a smart ass. But I've been there and back with her several times. I nodded and went upstairs to pack.

When I returned Jason, Jennifer and Santana waited and then Dillon drove up. He nodded to Jason and those three left us in the parking lot. He got out of the Vette. Have I mentioned I love that car? Dillon walked around and opened the trunk of the Vette and put my luggage in and shut the lid. Then he turned to me and kissed me, "Going my way cutie-pie?"

"This little pick-me-up in the Vette was by design, wasn't it Lover?"

Dillon took me in his arms and gently twirled me around. "Yes ma'am, it was by design. And I missed you too this week. I hear I missed some excitement a moment ago."

"You missed me and Santana arresting my ex-boss at NCIS...Jerry Garner!"

"According to Dad, I probably didn't miss much. However, I'd love to have seen the take-down by you and Santana. Did he do anything against the rules?"

I mockingly cried crocodile tears. "That mean ole' man pulled my hair!"

And in mocking response, Dillon frowned deeply, "I'll kill that old bastard!"

"Nice to know you love me that much!" I kissed him and we left to go to his parent's house.

When we arrived at Jason and Jennifer's house, Gracie came running out of the house. Immediately after I got out of the Vette, Gracie tackled me with a bear hug. "My Tori!"

"Hey there girlfriend, how was school today?" I asked. Oh my god, I sound like her guardian sister!

"I aced all my tests; I doubled my workout weight in strength training and...I increased my vertical leap by two inches!" I saw that her lean muscle mass increased by a full percentage point and for Gracie's metabolism, that said a bunch. "How's your shoulder feeling?"

"Fully healed, and a full range of motion; I'll be ready for Saturday in Houston kiddo. You keep your grades up and some college recruiter will find a blue-chip point guard for a Division I school." Gracie worked hard at her basketball game, according to Jennifer. My mom always maintained that if you strive for the best in everything; schoolwork, athletics, even student government; you will achieve every goal you set for yourself. What I love about this young lady, she has no hang-ups to force her to grow up too quick. In a way, I envy her; in a way, I'm glad to know her. I look and I saw a beautiful spirit in a lady tigers hoodie and matching sweatpants.

"Tori, mind if I ask you something?"

"Of course Gracie...what is it?" A felt a lump in my throat. I feared her question; mainly because she saw me as a baby-face pro-wrestler. She's still working on the concept I'm an agent who works for her father...first.

"How much do you love Dillon?" Yes, that's the question I feared her asking. "I ask because Dad talked about your last...incident at the beach house..." Gracie tried to be tough for me, but her tears flowed, and she collapsed into my arms.

I held her firm and gently lifted her chin. "Hey, look at me Tiger!" She smiled through her tears. You call a kid a tough name, they always smiled. "Am I still here?" Gracie nodded. "Are the bad guys dead or in jail now?" Again, Gracie nodded. "Then unless God decides to punch my ticket to Heaven to work crime scenes for him; I'm here to stay. You read me, Gracie Vaughn?"

She hugged me tightly. So tightly, I felt like she was putting a sleeper hold on me. "Copy that Agent Tori Blanton!" As I continued to hug Gracie, I caught Jennifer as she leaned against the frame of the front door. She smiled and mouthed *thank you*. I winked back at her as Gracie finally let me breathe. "Dad felt pizza from Authentic New York Pizza was a good idea for supper. He ordered two extra-large Supremes, one extra-large Veggie Delight, and one extra-large barbecue chicken. What would you like me to save for you?"

I smiled as Gracie smiled back. "One of each; and I mean no extra supreme slices...okay?"

"Got ya covered Tori," Gracie smiled as she skipped into the house past Jennifer.

Dillon eyed her curiously as I kissed him on the cheek. "Your mom wants a talk with me, it's okay. I've been expecting this one."

"You sure?"

"I'm sure. The chief has some concerns she needs to air out with me. And probably…I need to listen, and we can compare notes later." Dillon gave me a sideways glance; primarily because of issues he and Jennifer had concerning his life a year ago. "Hey you, trust me. We're good here." This time, Dillon kissed me on the lips and went inside past Jennifer. He stopped and gave her the same sideways glance. She held up her hands in surrender; then Dillon kissed his mother on the cheek and went inside. I met Jennifer at the door as she shook her head. "I'm sorry about that. I told him we needed to talk and it was okay. I guess he's developing selective hearing in my case."

Jennifer shook her head and giggled. Then she looked at me with her warm smile. "Welcome to my hell, Tori!" We laughed as walked arm-in-arm inside the house.

Jennifer and I sat down on the sofa as Gracie brought each of us a paper plate piled with delicious pizza. She left us alone as Jennifer resumed the conversation. "You're right; I am concerned. I've been concerned the entire week. With that said, you have done some impressive work over the week and you've had some bumps in the road to overcome. And you have responded like a LEO twice your age and experience. To some; that's an outstanding trait. To others, it scares the hell out of them Tori. My problem is…I've grown to love you as if you're part of my family. Dillon falling in love with you concerns me like everyone else. But you've made some smart decisions, Dillon as well, and that's why Jason and I fought so hard for you two to have that romantic evening. So you can realize where you two are and what you need to do from here."

I sat there stunned as I bit into my supreme slice. "That's not how I pictured this conversation progressing."

Jennifer and I sat there and dined on our pizza as Jason brought us a couple of long-necks. Jennifer went on to explain that how I dealt with Garner, both of my shooting incidents, and Jason; had positive influences on the team and those officers she's spoken within the last week. My gentle handling of Gracie's concerns about Dillon's heart and my own safety, told Jennifer my capabilities extended well beyond my years or experience. "Okay, you said this wasn't how you pictured this conversation going. What did you think I was going to ask you?"

TWENTY-NINE

"I thought you were going to ask me to break up with or slow things down with Dillon; which I already intended on speaking with him on that concern. Actually, I thought it would be about my two shooting incidents as well as getting shot myself. And the fact Dillon shot and killed my brother Tad to keep me alive. He didn't need…to be involved in either case, but there he was…watching my back when someone else should've done that." I shook my head as I tried to articulate my pride as well my own fears for someone I loved. Then Jennifer smiled. "What?"

"Tori; although all those points are concerns of mine for you and Dillon, it's all water under the bridge at this point. You two love each other, and you two need to work that out."

"Okay, point taken!" We both laughed as I realized she supported us no matter which direction we chose. "Okay Chief, where do you see Dillon and I headed?" I know I asked her to predict where we were going in our relationship. I had a good idea, but I desired her thoughts and I wanted confirmation if she and I thought the same way.

Jennifer sighed as we noticed Jason and Dillon stealing glances our way. "I see Dillon putting an engagement ring on your finger; then a wedding band, and then informing us we are about to be grandparents." *Booyah! We're on the same wavelength!* "I selfishly see that because…I believe I'm ready for that phase in my life. Jason and I have contemplated about retirement the last couple of years. "It might be nice to have a daughter or son-in-law, with a grandchild or two to bounce on our knees and babysit while the parents go and protect life, limb, and property."

"You know what's scary, I just expect it at any time, and I don't know what I'd say if he sprung it on me now Jen.

And I thoroughly enjoyed our romantic night and the cuddling after; I actually enjoyed the cuddling more." Oh man, I'm getting deep with my future mother-in-law? Did I just think that? Jeez, I really did grow up too fast! "How do you think Dillon will react to that thought?"

"Why don't you ask him?" Jennifer asked me as Dillon walked over and joined us. "Hi, babe!"

"Good evening ladies; what's on tap for conversation?" Dillon smiled as I took his hand and held it. "Was this topic about me or our relationship?"

"Both...actually." I looked at Jennifer who smiled and her eyes widened with guilt. "Your mom and I came to the same conclusion that we were both concerned about how last week ended and how this week started. We need to talk about...throttling back a bit?"

"And this, dear ones, is where Chief Vaughn takes a page out of Snaggle Puss's playbook by saying, 'Exit; stage left!'." Dillon demonstrated his gentleman-like demeanor and stood with Jennifer. And then he kissed her on the cheek. "What was that for dear?"

"I'm saying thank you...for being a good mom and letting me...us, discuss this on our own." Then Jennifer sighed, kissed him back, winked at me, and joined Jason in the dining area. Dillon sat back down and asked, "Okay, we were about to talk about slowing down a bit in our relationship."

"Yes, I kind of want to slow down, from the sexual aspect. I enjoyed the cuddling a bunch after...we made love. I guess, I want more of the non-sexual touching, kisses, conversation, and just knowing you're there. Am I even saying, that right?" I shook my head and felt as if I lost my pee-picking mind.

Then Dillon smiled and nodded. "After everything that's happened, I was going to suggest we spend more time not...having sex. We still have our studies or professions that we must honor, but we can still have each other too. I like those differences between us and everyone else does too. I also, like those common interests that brought us together." Then he sighed, "And...I still need to formally introduce you to my grandparents. You've smiled and nodded, but that's not enough. Something else happened when you at Corpus Christi Medical Center, my grandmother, Grace Moran, saw your spirit and what you did. She realized I loved you that much to shoot someone to keep you alive. And she asked me, 'Who is she to you?' I told her you are someone I love. Whether she accepted the answer or not, I loved you."

He defended me to her; the legendary CIA agent he called Grandma, and she realized I wasn't going anywhere or did I want to leave him… alone. "So, we need to at least…get on the right foot with one another?"

Dillon nodded his head from side to side. "She knows I'm not changing my mind about you. She also realizes she's not going to win that battle. So, my other grandparents reminded her that each generation grows up and makes their own decisions. My parents glared into her eyes and made her realize, she'd be sacrificed to secure our choices regardless of her personal views. We're going to try the breakfast-thing tomorrow morning, again!"

"I see." I looked around and found Santana talking with Gracie and Jennifer. Then I saw Jason on the phone; presumably speaking with his father and stepmother to come over tomorrow morning. "I think; I'd love to meet your grandparents and…even members of your Comanche family too!"

"Oh, you're in luck then!" As soon as Dillon said that, the horror-filled fears came to light. "My Comanche grandmother, Dr. Rachel Wolf, is coming to Houston to watch you wrestle. I showed her your pic from your earlier Indie wrestling work, and she told me she was a fan!" Oh my lord, my boyfriend's Comanche grandma was a fan; Heaven help me! "TGCW also contracted her to be the official fight doc that night."

"Oh boy; you didn't tell her…about our night…in Port Aransas, did you?" The last thing I wanted the one grandparent I haven't met yet, was for her to cultivate a need to scalp me!

"I…didn't lie, but I tell her we agreed to use protection and to make sure every…subsequent round, protection was used. I also told her we might decide to hold off on any future…romps until we've spent more time talking and just settling into a non-sexual relationship routine. Grandma Rachel thought that was the best idea she heard."

"Good; I'd hate to think she would want to scalp me before she's met me. Next time you talk to Grandma Rachel; tell her thanks for her support, and…I love her already!"

THIRTY

Santana took Dillon's old room upstairs as Dillon and I slept in TAMU-CC Islanders tank tops and matching green shorts. We cuddled and fell asleep in the ground-floor guest room so we wouldn't be disturbed by anyone. In the same light, we wouldn't disturb anyone else if we suddenly had the urge…to make-love. When we awoke Thursday morning, our bed clothes were still on, but we were intertwined with one another as Jason knocked and came inside. "Good morning you lovely people! Breakfast will be ready in an hour as well as Dillon's grandparents arriving. Besides, you need to get to work with Rudy Mister!"

I looked at my clock on my phone. "Dear God, it's 0530!" I sighed as I kissed Dillon several times on the cheek. "C'mon babe; time to rise and then shine when the sun pops out!"

Slowly, Dillon rose from his peaceful slumber. "Walk me to the bathroom so I can shower to wake up please?"

"Want me to use just the cold water?" I asked impishly.

Dillon's eyes popped open and he immediately sat up. "You do that; I'll pull you in with me!"

"Oh no buddy, I prefer my showers warm and steamy. Go, I'll save a cup of coffee."

He kissed me and smiled. "I'll be out in a little while."

When Dillon got up and went into the bathroom, Jason nodded. "Yeah, you two will work it out; no problem!" He left me so I could get dressed. I decided since the weather cooled down a bit, I'd wear jeans, my green Islanders long-sleeve white tee, and my black sneakers.

I walked out after making up the bed and walked into Jennifer's kitchen to a cup of coffee from Gracie. "Good morning Tori!" Gracie hugged me as she handed me the mug.

The slogan *Angels Rock* proudly displayed as I saw Santana complete her sou chef chores of chopping up veggies for Vaughn's Famous Omelet Surprise. "Looks good huh?"

"Sure does; how can I help gang?"

"Help me with my grandparents when they arrive? Aunt Kat's had a rough time wrangling them the last couple of days!" Gracie gave me a low stare. I guess putting Grace in the Fujiwara armbar sort of calmed her down a bit.

"You're asking me to help ride herd on your grandparents. Gracie, I only had one grandma growing up sweetie; I don't know how wrangle grandfathers!" I looked over at Jennifer and winked at her. She chuckled as she mixed up fresh apple and orange juice for breakfast. "Besides, I have to run your brother to work after breakfast. So, you're doing the wrangling kiddo."

"Oh great!"

"Here…Gracie, go ahead and have some breakfast." Jennifer smiled as she handed Gracie a plate of freshly cooked omelet, two biscuits and a glass of orange juice. Dillon walked up as Jennifer handed him a breakfast plate and I handed him a cup of coffee. "Now that's teamwork!" The Vaughns have all dressed in long-sleeve tees of various colors as well as jeans and tennis shoes of assorted colors. "How many deliveries for you and Rudy Dillon?"

"We have five, but they're so spread out, we left the one here for very last. That way Rudy can pay me, in cash, drop me off and not see me again until Tuesday night!" Dillon and I continued our noshing until we were ready for him to go to work.

Then the doorbell rang. "I'll get it!" Gracie yelled as she walked, peeked outside and then let in both sets of grandparents as well as Kat. "Hello everybody!"

Gracie greeted each of them in turn as Dillon took his turns with hugs, kisses and well wishes from family. "Okay, before we head off to take me to work, this is Tori. We wanted to introduce her to you in this setting so it would be calm, cool, and collected."

"I agree; this is a much better setting," Grace smiled as she let her dark hair flowing behind her. "I'm pleased to meet you the right way, Tori."

"Same here Grace; and I love your green and white wind suit. Dillon get that for you?"

"He did actually," Cecilia said as she walked up and hugged me next. "He got all his grandparents some variation of the TAMU-CC color scheme we love wearing them."

Cecilia's hazel brown eyes smiled at me as she spoke. "Yes, my grandson found a lovely young lady." When Grace's husband Gerald walked up, Cecilia gave me a playful smirk. "However my dear, be careful around that old bald-headed reprobate. Just because he's a retired Chief of Police, he believes that gives him carte blanche authority to steal hugs and kisses from Dillon's girlfriends!"

He turned to face her with his nose pointed slightly upward. "Madam, I invite you to keep a civil tongue in that feminine mouth of yours!" Then he faced and hugged me. "I'm Gerald; pleased to meet you, Tori."

"Same here Chief; I'm deeply honored to be included in your infamous banter with Cecil." We both laughed as Jim reached over and hugged me next. "Pleased to meet you too!"

"Same here Tori; when you get the chance, have Dillon bring you out to our ranch in Snyder. I think you'll find our desert sagebrush quite stunning from the top of the mesa bowl." Dillon told me how the Flying V was surrounded by four mesas which were situated in a bowl-like landscape a mile in either direction from the house.

"Dillon showed me photos of your ranch Jim. That's someplace where Jason grew up. He also told me of his Comanche family. Is it true that Jason's uncle Ray and you were in Vietnam together?"

"We were and Jason was still very small at the time." Then I sensed Jim was about to tell me something significant. "At the time, we all thought my ex-wife was dying of cancer, Jason too. Three years ago, he found her on the reservation up in Lawton, OK serving as a doctor for the clinic and the reservation hospital. Jason spent a great deal of time and effort rebuilding that relationship. Cecil's been a little jealous; but after hearing what Rachel did to…protect her son and me at the time, she stopped being jealous and encouraged mother and son to reconnect."

"Sounds like a fine woman I'll get to meet Saturday in Houston." Then Dillon looked at me and tapped his watch. "Time to take Young Mr. Vaughn to work. Good talk Jim."

And as I left, Jim Vaughn nodded. "Good talk; Devil's Rose."

I dropped off Dillon at *Garrett's Restaurant and Catering*, picked up Santana at Jason's; then we went to the Police Impound Lot off of Greenwood Drive. An obese lot attendant who wore police coveralls and a badge stepped out to greet us. His bald head reflected the sun well enough and he smiled with a stogie between his teeth. "Morning ladies, how may I help you today?"

Santana made the introductions. "Sgt. Santana Garvin and this is NCIS Agent Blanton. We're here with this affidavit to release from the lot a navy Ford Fusion license plate number David–X-ray–David five-three-zero-three." I handed him my license and my registration as well as a copy of my insurance.

"You're the owner of the vehicle, Agent Blanton?" I nodded. "Sorry, we released that vehicle an hour ago."

"What?"

"Yeah, some older guy with short hair. Looked like a grizzled old Marine to me!" *Damn you, Garner!* I turned and glared into Marvin's blue eyes and I believe he saw his tombstones in mine. "I take it this guy's not a friend of yours...Agent Blanton?"

"No Marvin, he's not!" I dial Jason's home phone. "Boss, impound released my car...to Garner!"

I heard Jason sigh on the other end, *"Not a shocker there; Marcum and Darrow are here with him. He drove it over to Rudy's place; the same spot you dropped Dillon off at an hour ago."*

I held back my frustrated tears; I guess Karma's in bed with Garner. She's sure as hell pissed at me at the moment. "Okay, I'll go over there; and I'll give SEC-NAV, Darrow, and Garner each...five minutes to convince me why I should leave the only true home I've had in the last ten years!"

Then what Jason said next made me smile again. *"Then you'll have this family at your back when you walk in there!"*

When we all arrived, none of the TFCC agents were present. But I realized what Jason meant by *this family*. He meant Dillon's immediate family and his grandparents. I love working for Jason! "Ready to do this kid?"

"Let's do this gang!" I said as we all walked in the front door of Garrett's over on West Commerce. When Secretary Marcum, Director Darrow, and Garner turned to face me; they realized they were about to suffer a Custer-like defeat at Little Big Horn. The color washed from Garner's face as Jennifer stood right next to me. Apparently, the haunting image of Caitlin Thomas froze him where he sat. Okay, one down two to go. I sat down in front of Marcum.

She quickly said, "I didn't invite you to sit down Agent Blanton."

"Fine," I said as I removed my pancake holster and my NCIS badge. "I can see that based on the presence of all three of you here; these are my options: one, I can accept whatever insane offer you have, and I call it insane because you plan on having me work with Garner.

"Option two; I refuse in which you fire me. So, I'm going to give you the option now, Madame Secretary…take my creds and I go resign effective immediately, or I pick them up and leave. But there is no way in hell I will ever work for or with Jerrod Garner, ever again in this lifetime!"

Santana watched Garner open his jacket and immediately, drew her Glock and pointed it at Garner's head. "Make a move jarhead; I'll drop you where you sit!" Garner slowly set his Sig on the bar and stepped away from it. "Good boy Devil Dog!"

"That begs me to ask the Devil Dog a question: who called Bass, who called Talbot, which blew Blanton's op in Malta?" Garner rose and rushed Jason. Jason flipped Garner onto the bar and drove his lock-blade hunting knife through Garner's right hand. "Who blew the op?" Jason yelled the question as he began to twist Garner's neck. "I'll snap it Gunny; then I'll scalp you. You know I have a standing Alpha dash Twelve to eliminate traitors on site! So, last time…who blew Blanton's op in Malta?"

"Mike…Petrovsky!" The Menace Mike Petrovsky; he did this, why?

THIRTY-ONE

"Jason, keep him there!" My bad wolf wanted to come out and play. But before I went over to torture my former boss and idiotic mentor of NCIS, I slowly stood and asked, "Which of you knew this…little tidbit of information?"

"I never knew," Darrow said without hesitation. When I looked at Marcum, she shook her head.

So, only Garner knew why and why he tried to get me reassigned. I walked over as Jason stepped aside. He released Garner's neck as I began to handcuff Garner spread-eagled over the three-foot diameter of the restaurant bar. I turned and looked to Grace and Cecilia. "Either of you has something resembling a tattoo needle or a scalpel? I feel like carving a rose tattoo on Mr. Garner's chest."

Cecilia smiled. "Oh, I have a surgical needle in my emergency med-kit; will that suffice?"

"Is it in a plain, sterile wrapper?"

"Of course darling!"

"Perfect!"

"Okay, okay…joke's over!" Darrow said as the grandparent's club drew their side arms.

"Vince, I believe that's their way of saying *sit down and shut up!*" Then Marcum looked over at me. "I'm assuming whatever I was going to say, would have no weight at the moment?"

"Not unless it is to say Agent Blanton; you found a good team and you need to stay here. No ma'am, no weight whatsoever."

"And we'd have advised her against taking any job near the DC Beltway Elise," Grace smiled. "You know how crooked politics is in that town. She puts up with enough considering how Cecil and I wanted to give her fits for dating our grandson.

And if she's willing to resign to prove that point; you'd lose the argument anyway. So, why not let her stay where she is and where she's most effective?"

"Good point," Marcum said as I turned and looked into her eyes. She smiled. "Continue your inquiry, Agent Blanton."

"Yes, ma'am!"

"Are you crazy?" Garner yelled as I dropped my face to his nose and waved the surgical needle. "Okay, okay I'm sorry Tori. I wanted you on my team because we were joining the protective detail for Marcum."

"Okay, that explains your selfish motives the last twenty-four hours; but not Petrovsky...spill!"

"All right; Petrovsky's a mobile recruiter and trainer for the CIA Farm!"

"Explains all my hell back in '91 Vince." Jason smiled. Then he leaned down. "Spill the rest Devil Dog!"

"All your recruitment; the *Committee* and Callaway; that was all Petrovsky. When he couldn't get you, he went after someone almost like you!"

"Me!"

"Yes, Tori." Jason's almost whispered response was loud enough for me to hear. He pounded his fist near Garner's head and the old Marine flinched as if his life depended on it. Which it probably did. "When did he start after Tori?"

"When he found out Charlene Tolliver was undercover for the FBI!" I stepped back; the horror obviously displayed across my face. I almost stepped on Santana's right foot. She stopped and embraced me. "After your mother was killed, his plan: if he could get you young enough, naïve enough, he could train you and make you the perfect weapon. But your mother and father made other arrangements."

I found my voice again. "With the Matthews family and DMD Security."

"Petrovsky realized the moment DMD's people emerged as your protection, he couldn't get at you then. So he waited until you became a wrestler. Then he arranged your tag-team title debacle in Tokyo." My tears flowed as Garner continued. "But the beating just engrained your resolve. Then you went to FLETC and became an NCIS Agent. He called me, told me to work you like a dog and treat you as badly as I could within the regulations. Petrovsky thought after six months under my wing, you run kicking and screaming to the Farm in Langley."

"And I chose to be an Agent-Afloat instead." My voice seemed lost as Grace reached over and took me into her arms. I guess after hearing all of this, she felt I needed the comfort of a grandmother's embrace. "Then he used both husband and wife Bass to blow Malta and tried to get me killed."

"When he found out you were here, he tipped off the Dixie Mafia; the rest you know."

"And if you don't write all this down an allocute before the special oversight panel Jerry, I'll tie you down to the closest table I can find and let her finish with you!" Darrow whispered. Then Darrow stood erect, "I'd like for you to stay on and finish this Tori."

I smiled; at least Darrow had the good sense to invite me to stay with NCIS and TFCC. "Now that I know how all this jells now sir, I'm going to have so much fun Saturday in Houston."

"What's so fun about pro wrestlers beating the snot out of each other for two bling-filled belts?"

"Did you ever participate in sports when you were younger Director Darrow?"

"I was part of a state high school football championship team," he said as he smiled; then he turned to me and the little light bulb above his head lit up. "I see; like my state championship, it's all about being the best at what you do!"

I smiled like a cat that swallowed a canary. "Petrovsky's premise, like his with Jason all these years, if you're not CIA, you're not the best! I beg to differ: if you're NCIS or TFCC, you have your moments as the best in that moment! Like a pro wrestler; you're the best when you strap that title belt around your waist. You are the best!"

"Jason, I'm temporarily pulling rank! Blanton, kick those bitches asses and knock Petrovsky's teeth out of his head!"

Jason looked at me and nodded. "Aye, aye sir!" Then I asked, "Would you like tickets; you and Secretary Marcum?"

Marcum smiled. "Put me down for four; to be left at the box office by no later than 1400 hours central time."

"Very well and you Director Darrow?"

"I'm unable to attend, but this gift card can buy about four ringside seats for fans who would love to go but can't afford it. Try military members first."

"I shall," I said as I took the VISA gift card.

Then I turned to Jason. "Time for team stuff!"

Jason smiled. "I agree!"

We returned as Dillon arrived at home and Lightning had all the meat grilled for the eats and the fun. Dillon greeted me with a hug and a kiss. "Hey, how was it running all over town?"

Dillon shook his head. "Traffic's murder when you deliver from all over. I really need lunch and something to drink."

I took him by the hand. "Then come with me, my dear. We will feed, liquefy, and otherwise relax you from your multitude of labors."

"Heard you had some labors at Rudy's restaurant. What happened? Dad's been tight-lipped about it."

"Let's just say; we found a common link between us; your dad and I. That color commentator, Petrovsky for TGCW, was once a Navy SEAL for Team Five." I watched as Dillon understood my insinuation. "He was there when all this crap with the CIA started. The moment current CIA Director Scofield announced he had that special license to protect you and the rest of his family, he went looking for someone else, and targeted me."

"You remember when I told you I'd kill Jerry Garner for pulling your hair?"

"Yes?"

"In this case, I'd ask Dad to teach me how to be a sniper; and I'd want to put a bullet between Petrovsky's eyes."

"You do that my dear, the CIA will know who did it. Besides, your dad wouldn't want you getting your handsome hands dirty on something like this." I tried to impress upon Dillon he didn't need to worry, but I am the federal agent girlfriend who works for Daddy. Of course, he's gonna worry. Then I turned his head back to my eyes. "Hey, this is a cookout prior to a supreme victory lap in Houston Saturday night. And if I miss my guess, your parent's plan is to feed me less, make me drink more; so you can see your girlfriend…drunk!"

Dillon smiled. "I'll make sure a root beer gets put in a bottle for every other beer you drink. We'll make sure you're not as buzzed as Dad wants you to be."

"He might get wise to your nefarious scheme Lover."

"Hey, I'm a professional bartender; I told Santana when she upgraded to the ten-gallon keg, buy the brand in the copper-colored keg. It's brown beer!"

My eyes, as well as my mouth, widened with ecstatic joy. "So…this means…?"

"Unless my dear father sees through, as you call it, my nefarious scheme, we're good to go." His eyes lit up like a child who ran rough-shod through a candy store. I love this family, and I'm glad TFCC and the Vaughns consider me part of it. "So, shall we join them, my love?"

"Yes Lover, we shall!"

We ate, drank, and enjoyed ourselves as I pretended to overindulge in spirits. I know, it's brown beer, but humor me for a moment. My boss and possibly, future father-in-law, attempted to get me drunk to observe my general behavior. Dillon's not allowed to drink until he's twenty-one. So, he's made sure I'm not as sloshed as everyone tried to get me. "What's that in your cup?" Santana walked over and took a sip. She looked into my eyes, "Root beer; seriously?"

"Not so loud! I didn't want to get drunk! I'm a nightmare when I get drunk. So, I'm showing them a not-so-scary version of me…drunk. Cover for me or not; I don't care!"

"I wouldn't dare rat you out!" Then Jason walked over as I…accidentally, sloshed my beverage out of my cup. He brought me a regular refill. "Hey Jace; I think the red-hot lover's coming out of her this afternoon."

THIRTY-TWO

Jason nodded as he handed me the beer. He left as I slammed it down and Dillon rushed up with a root beer refill. I looked into his eyes since that last beer made me a little loopy. "Food...please? I need food."

Santana nodded. "Time to satisfy the munchie monster!" Dillon and Santana sat me down at a table filled with hamburgers, hot dogs, grilled chicken breasts and a few kabobs for good measure. I started filling up on food as Leah and Boop walked over. "Hello, ladies."

"Where are her spirits?" Leah asked as if I hadn't had enough to drink. What are they trying to do, unleash *She-Hulk* in me? "I mean, everyone, with the exception of those too young to indulge," her low stare focused on Dillon, "are drinking as well as eating. What gives?"

I looked at Santana and nodded. She pulled out her phone and cued up a video I had her record of me two years ago in Japan...after we got out of the hospital. When both ladies viewed my, drunken, angry and violent state, Boop handed back to Santana. "Oh boy; she does not need to be inebriated. So, how are you managing it while dad's trying to get her malted up?"

"She's still drinking; we're alternating with root beer."

Lightning came over as I continued to down my burgers, potato salad, and pinto beans. When he saw the video, he turned and went back to the grill where Jason held court. Jason took a break and came over to us. "San, let me see that video please?"

"Here you go Jace," Santana cued up the video again. Jason saw me as an angry drunk, tearing up a locker room at the Myoko Dojo where I took my drama classes. He watched with a deadpan expression as I threw fellow students around, teachers, and other dignitaries. It's when he saw a katana in my hands and swinging it like a Samurai or a Ninja; he handed the phone back to Santana and nodded. "You knew?"

169

"Sometimes, someone who drinks in excess; their patterns change. I know your mother has, I know others on this team have, but I needed to know where Tori's concerned; if that pattern had changed to something else." Jason looked at Dillon. "How did you assist in...managing the potential monster you avoided facing...son?"

"That brown beer...is pretty stout in taste. So, Rudy had me saturate it with twenty percent distilled water to soften it up. And as far as Tori's concerned, the brown beer looks a lot like root beer." Jason nodded in understanding. "Dad, sometimes...you do things to test people, much like former Agent Garner, but...your tests...don't injure or hurt anyone; egos aside. You have to understand; I love her enough to stand up to you about this...regardless if you can still kick my ass or not!"

"Wait...hold off fellas," Jennifer walked up as she held a pint of brown beer in her hands. "You...will not...get...violent in my house." When I looked closer, she wasn't staggering drunk yet, but she was close.

"Mom, what are you doing?" Gracie walked over as the grandparents joined us.

"I'm challenging that saucy minx your brother's dating...to a drinking game!" Oh hell!

Jim explained the rules, "The rules are simple; last drinker standing wins! Fifty-dollar minimum bet." I laid a Sam Grant on the table. I had the fifty in my possession after Boop and the others paid me for the bet in the office almost two weeks before. Jennifer smiled like a mama wolf as she laid two twenties and a ten dollar bill on the table.

I don't know how I ended up retching my guts out over near the family compost heap for the family garden, but I wasn't alone. Somehow, Jennifer and I bonded over our ill-fated drinking game and if I remembered correctly, she toppled over first. "Uh, I haven't been that drunk since I met Jason at 1993 Spring Break in Virginia Beach." She looked over at me with pain in her eyes. "How in the hell did you drink me under the table?"

"Dillon helped a little for an hour prior to you making that challenge to keep the peace. I think Gracie was horrified we both polished off that ten-gallon keg!" I saw the look of disappointment in Jennifer's eyes. "Dillon saw an old video of me after I had too much Sake in Japan two years ago. I almost single-handedly tore the dojo apart, killed everyone and demonstrated even a girl like me can have mad ninja skills when she's sauced."

"Ouch; no wonder Dillon did what he did. And why he stood up to his father in that situation. Oh god, I still feel rough. Come on; let's go take a cold shower over in the bathhouse by the pool. I have your other suit in there in case we had a problem like this pop-up."

So Jennifer and I showered and redressed in proper party attire and in a better frame of mind. We laughed, cried and finished sobering up from the experience. I think my experience in Japan taught me, as well as those in the wrestling dojo, my fighting spirit remained. Maybe…that's what Jason wanted to know, was that fighter still inside me? If my contest with Jennifer was an indication, the *Rosa del Diavolo* still existed inside me. "Thanks," I said.

"For what Tori?"

"For showing me…through the drinking game, I can still fight…and not be violent in the struggle." Then I hugged this brave, unapologetic police chief who herself, faced similar challenges in her life.

When she released her embrace, she simply smiled. "You're welcome. You know it's odd; having been married to that man of mine for twenty-three years, I learned a few warrior skills and strategies in that time. The strategies from Sun Tzu's *The Art of War* and Arthasastra's principles of common enemies; those are tools cops at all levels of law enforcement can use as effectively as interrogation techniques, flashlights, side arms, or telescope batons. How you use each of those tools, determines how well you do your job."

"I guess that's why I was so tough on Carla; then on Bass. And eventually, why Jason and I were both tough on Garner. Now, in two days at the Toyota Center in Houston, Jason and I can put the past…to rest." It sounded as if…Jason and I had been on this road together but only met for the first time almost two weeks ago. I probably sounded like some possessive kid with a Barbie doll I couldn't lay down.

But when I looked into Jennifer's eyes, I saw her recognition of my words. She nodded. "I know; Tori, I know all about it. You see, the last time the Matthews family and our family had…difficulties, was last year. Jason made some financial arrangements to assist David's distant Russian cousin–Alexander Sardovsky. When the Russian Mob families threatening those folks, reneged on the deal; Jason sent in some old friends from MI-6 and the CIA to…eliminate those families. Jason turned to David and told him if anyone else was threatened in our family; he'd pay with his eternity on earth. And I reminded Dominique I could end it for her as well. We found out about an impending threat to you. We didn't know who targeted you both.

"In order for David and Dominique to honor a promise they made to David's…family elders fourteen years ago, every piece of mortal-related business minus regular business interests, had to be settled. DMD's protection of you and your father; was the last bit to be had. Dominique begged, pleaded with Jason and me, to help with your situation. When TFCC was allowed to monitor the Malta operation falling apart, Jason saw the opening to help out…someone who was walking down a path he blazed before…yours."

I sat there on the bench outside the bathhouse, stunned by the similarity the paths Jason and I walked. Now, this new mentor and I…get to end the path some CIA mooch tried to force us to walk. "So, the "Menace" Mike Petrovsky committed treason twice; he left Jason behind in Iraq and blew our op in Malta. Here's my problem: he's CIA, reportedly untouchable; how do we get him?"

"Funny thing about Jason's friendship with current CIA Director Martin Scofield, he sent Jason an email with a gift; CIA has disavowed Petrovsky and he's no longer considered…protected by the agency. That means… you and Jason get to put him away for life or watch him get a needle in his arm…for death."

I smiled. "Funny about that Jen, my dark little impish side's smiling big knowing he might…put up a fight. I might have to *match up* with Jason to see which one of us gets to take that old bastard out."

"Maybe…you need to let Jason handle it, Tori. I know, he forced a lot of hate and anger to build up inside you. Mike Petrovsky has a long list of victims; not just from your life, but from Jason's too. And Scofield has had enough of this idiot getting good people killed for no reason."

"Fair enough; Santana and I will take out his latest puppets."
"And Jason will handle the traitorous Petrovsky!"

We traveled to Houston Friday morning and checked into the Embassy Suites Houston-Downtown. Santana and I called Big Bopper Harris and discovered there was a press conference that afternoon at the neighboring Four Seasons in downtown Houston. And the part that made everyone in our party salivate with extreme drool, Petrovsky was hosting the press conference.

Santana and I met with reporters from the sports, wrestling world, and the local press for the city of Houston. One reporter asked, "Ladies, given you haven't stepped into a wrestling ring in over a year, what type of strategy will you utilize against Caged Women?"

Santana fielded the question. She always knew how to answer questions concerning in-ring tactics. We both wore different shades of blue in our tops and blue jeans as Santana took the mic. "We know we hurt them last week in Corpus Christi. We finish what we started."

Another reporter asked, "That's...pretty vague Santana. Care to elaborate?"

Elaboration was my specialty. "What she means by that is, we plan on working over the body parts we damaged in Corpus Christi. Look, pro wrestlers perform in this business to entertain the fans. But just because we haven't been on any main event shows or house events; doesn't mean we haven't been staying in shape. I believe we proved that in Corpus Christi last week!"

Petrovsky emerged as Caged Women, Twyla Black and Tanya Tate emerged in nice clothes as Petrovsky sported a tan business suit to match his do-rag. Petrovsky sat down. "Since Chi-Chi Gonzales has been barred from ringside, I've...volunteered to stand in her place, in case the match gets...out of hand?" The crowd booed as we stared at him, and then motioned Jason to step forward.

THIRTY-THREE

When Jason stepped up in his dark gray pin-striped two-piece suit, Petrovsky leaped from his seat and screamed, "What the hell are you doing here? You're not in wrestling; get your ass out of here Vaughn!" Petrovsky glared at me specifically, and I smiled like my dark ego...*Rosa del Diavolo*. He pointed at me, "You, you conniving little bitch!"

"Oh temper, temper Mikey-boy; as allegedly weak as your heart is, you might have a massive coronary from all that stress you're allowing to build up." See, sadistic cop worked well in the right places. I stood and faced the old curmudgeon. Santana handed me the mic as I glared into this old, Navy SEAL's eyes. "I didn't ask Command Master Chief Petrovsky; Commander Vaughn volunteered! Ladies and gentlemen; American Angels secured ringside management for this match. We signed a contract with former Navy SEAL Commander Jason Vaughn." Photojournalist snapped pictures of Jason as he faced a wave of reporters. "We were informed by Big Bopper Harris, this morning; Mr. Petrovsky volunteered to stand-in for Chi-Chi Gonzales at ringside for our match tomorrow night. So, he offered us the option to have him banned from ringside or secure a corner manager for tomorrow night. Mr. Vaughn...is our answer."

Jason walked over and stood where I did and...glared into the eyes of his former Navy Chief. "Longtime no see Mike. It's been what...twenty-five years? You know, I caught your spiel about you being some kind of war hero of Desert Storm. But you never saw one minute of action with Alpha Platoon; that was my team. The same team that took my effects and left me to die at the hands of the Iraqis. And I'm afraid the usual suspects to corroborate your story...are all dead; even the alleged traitor I supposedly killed to protect our operations during the war. He was hung for treason." Horror streamed from Petrovsky's eyes as Jason smiled like the devil ready to claim Petrovsky's soul.

I stole a little more mic time. "You get the point...Mike?" Then I sat down as Black and Tate looked at us with fear in their eyes. "You girls pissed off the wrong team; you'll be title-less tomorrow night."

Then Jason glared into Petrovsky's eyes, and we finished our conference/promo. "And after the match; you're real hell begins. Give your soul to Jesus, Satan or whoever you believe will hear your pleas for help. None will answer. See you tomorrow night ladies."

We returned to our hotel as Dillon and Jennifer met us in the lobby. Gracie, the grandparents and other TFCC-related friends and peeps remained up in their rooms. Another body appeared Santana's new boyfriend...Deputy Marshal Jim Slater. "Well, well...how are the ladies Agent Vaughn?" He said it low enough no one in the media could hear. Then he kissed Santana. "How's my wild, Floridian warrior princess today?"

"You would've been proud of me; I didn't break one nail!"

"That's my Santana!" Then he looked at me. "Heard you guys challenged your target?"

"We'll be ready tomorrow night; no fail!"

Jason, Santana, and I arrived at the Toyota Center two hours prior to our match. Zelda, an old female warrior of the seventies women's wrestling era, made sure the star-spangled costumes for our championship match, kept with our sense of style, flexibility, and comfort. What made me jump back in mild shock was who assisted her in the design and assembly. "Good evening Angels!"

"Nikki; what are you doing here?" Of course, I asked, since someone of Dominique Dubois Matthews' caliber of fashion design, mostly revolved around evening gowns, stylish suits, and acrylic athletic wear. Then I looked into Zelda's eyes and saw a flash of brimstone yellow with blood red pupils. "Nikki, how long have you and Zelda...?"

"Known each other; oh since what...1979?" Zelda smiled as I noticed the laugh lines on her face and wrinkles on her cheeks disappear. "Zelda's the one who helped me and my company through a rough patch back during the Carter Administration and all the fuel rationing. And in return, the elders of David's family felt…we owed her a special favor. She's been… like me for the last fifty years."

"And you don't tell a soul, or Bopper will want me back in the ring. And at my age and temperament; that's dangerous!" Zelda winked at us as we smiled. "Okay girls, let's go try on your costumes so we can fix any potential; malfunctions!"

"True, we wouldn't wanting something popping out regardless if this is a pay-per-view event or not!" Santana smiled as we went into a ladies room close to Zelda and Dominique. We walked out and found some minor alterations were needed. "Now I know why you just tucked material out of the way, my bust-line needs a little more breathing room."

"And my ass doesn't need to be hanging out this much!" I looked like a stripper at a topless bar. We remained in costume as Zelda and Dominique fixed our attire.

After our wardrobe adjustments, we found Jason in the common-area of the locker rooms, applying the camo-grease paint for his face. Lightning appeared to make sure Jason looked appropriately menacing. "So, that's what a Comanche death-face looks like with all the camo-war paint. Yep, the boss looks scary!" Jason slightly grimaced a smile as Lightning put on the finishing touches. He wore a black tank-top with blue camo BDU trousers and black combat boots. On his right arm near the shoulder, the tattoo of SEAL Team Three rested as a reminder of his warrior days. On his left arm, Jennifer painted a wash-off tattoo of our faces with the encircled words *Archangel of the American Angels.*

Jennifer looked up and smiled. "Your manager needs some special notation of his purpose. Guardian Angels look after people on earth; Archangels fight the wars between Heaven and Hell. Added to the fact he'll wear his Spec-Warfare beret as well, Petrovsky's about to see a version of Jason he's only seen in his nightmares."

"Which begs the question; if Jason's getting war paint; why not the Angels as well?" Dominique looked at us and smiled. We nodded as Dominique used the old yell from Vaudeville, "Maaake-uuuup!"

Two hours passed with commentators and experts using a brief intermission to relive the history between us and Caged Women. As our manager for the night, Jason spent time helping us stretch and plan our strategy for the event. Earlier in the day, as pro wrestlers, we are required to prepare with our opponents on some level for the event for safety reasons. With trainers and promotion execs in attendance, we went through a typical Texas Tornado match setting. With certain movements, you never want to intentionally hurt anyone. But with our two teams, this workout was designed to remind us not to push things too far. And usually, both managers are present when both teams have such personnel involved in a match. Prior to the workout, Big Bopper, who himself was a wrestling manager, gave Jason the basic break-down for his role in the match. Then Jason informed Bopper of our real intentions. The old man simply smiled with his stogie in his mouth and nodded. Hence, only Petrovsky was present at the workout. Bopper was there in Jason's place while Jason worked out the arrest details with the Marshal's Service. "Where's your manager ladies, he's required to be here!"

Bopper's towering frame with caramel skin and brown eyes bent down into Petrovsky's face. His big nose rested on the old SEAL's and he said in a low bass voice. "Mr. Vaughn was called away by his boss in Chicago. Something involving an old case needed to be reviewed. He sends his regrets. And he will see you tonight. The ladies and I gave him all the required information he needs to entertain the fans tonight."

As the present returned, we gathered around as the other ladies match, Alley-Cat Kitty Lebeau, took on Frieda Martinez for the Women's World title. Santana and I knew Frieda from our time in Japan and she was known for using her Japanese strikes to her advantage. Frieda wore a tan, native-American-like legging costume with a halter top and topped off her ensemble with a big, brown felt sombrero. Kitty wore a black leotard with leggings and black boots. She looked as if she'd claw someone's eyes out in a catfight. But as their match progressed, Kitty ran out of steam and as with many young wrestlers, Frieda smelled blood in the water like a shark. After an *Enzuigiri* kick to the back of Kitty's head, Frieda locked in a Guillotine submission hold and then soon after…Kitty tapped out. Frieda was our new world women's champion. And now, it was our turn to win gold!

Because of our opponent's own arrogance and that of Mike Petrovsky, Bopper allowed the champions to be introduced first. "Ladies and gentlemen, this is your main event for TGCW Gulf Coast War, and it is set for one-fall. Approaching the ring, accompanied by their special match consultant, "Menace" Mike Petrovsky, from the Department of Corrections, your Women's Tag-Team Champions; Tanya Tate and Twyla Black…Caged Women!"

Then our theme music, *Angel's Anthem* blared over the speakers, the ring announcer continued, "And their opponents, accompanied by their Archangel, Jason Vaughn, from the Original Thirteen Colonies, Santana Garvin and Tori Blanton…American Angels!" On heavy down-beat, all three of us rushed the ring. We slid under the bottom rope and began pummeling our opponents. I could see out of the corner of my eye, Jason nailed Petrovsky in the mush.

When we Irish-whipped them against the stage-set of ropes, Santana and I landed drop-kicks on Black and Tate while Petrovsky grabbed the top ring rope. He looked into the closest camera and pointed to his right temple, and indicated he was smarter than Jason. When he turned, Jason landed a bone-crushing sidekick to the man's head and he fell out of the ring.

The crowd went wild as we stood tall and our opponents realized, we weren't taking a dive. We were here to win, and the Texas Tornado match was in full swing! Jason popped out of the ring by the announce table as Tate and I ended up in the ring with Black and Santana in our respective corners. Both felt the full effect of our attack and neither woman was on a steady vertical base. We were three minutes into the match and Santana, and I decided to not prolong the suffering. I twisted Tate's right arm with an arm-wringer and brought it between my legs as I jumped up and brought my full weight to her right elbow. Then I brought her up screaming in pain as I tagged in Santana.

After a double ax-handle to the elbow, Black jumped in…big mistake!

THIRTY-FOUR

Instead of a Shining Press Moon sault, Santana chose a sit-out Fujiwara armbar and I nailed Black with a superkick and put her in a straitjacket cross-face submission hold. When Petrovsky tried to interject, Jason hit him with spear and knocked the old Navy Chief on his ass. Finally, after a few seconds, Tate tapped out and the bell rang! "Ladies and gentlemen, the winners of the bout, and new...TGCW Women's World Tag-Team Champions, the American Angels!"

Our star-spangled mask makeup hadn't even melted, and we held our shiny new hardware above our heads. We handed the belts to Jason as we rolled Caged Women out of the ring and into undercover US Marshals posing a security for the event. Another set appeared as Jason handed our titles back to us and tossed a groggy and angry Mike Petrovsky to Jim Slater and his arresting team. Ringside commentator Marty Calder entered the ring and interviewed us. "American Angels, congratulations on a long overdue and certainly, well-earned victory!" The crowd cheered as Dillon, Teddy and all of those we called family and friends, clapped the proudest. "Tori, Santana, this has been called by some...a long-awaited journey come to an end. What are you feeling at this moment?" Calder held the mic to Santana.

"You know Marty; I've been around this business since I was a kid. I started at age sixteen learning from my father Kenny Garvin and never looked back. Then two years ago in Duluth, GA; I met a little hell-cat from Charlotte, North Carolina named Victoria Blanton and she goes by the name Tori. And for us to return to our home country and win a championship on American soil, can you think of a better homecoming Legion?"

She yelled as the crowd yelled along with her. Marty Calder then held the mic to me. "Tori, how does it feel to return home and become a world tag-team champion?"

I couldn't find the words. And then Jason put his right arm around my shoulders and whispered, "Speak from your heart."

I wiped the tears from my eyes as I held on to my half of the title. "Marty, this particular journey, for me, began the night my mother died at the hands of some extremely brutal people. My stepfather and their two youngest children also died in that attack, so no need to review all that. But suffice to say, next to receiving a Medal of Valor from the Secretary of Defense, this is the best feeling in the world!" As the crowd reacted to my exclamation, I looked over to see Dillon smiling at me and standing next to him, my father Teddy. "I know I did this last week, but could you wonderful folks in security, help those first two rows of friends and family up here please?" The crowd roared as Security opened the barricade and let Jason's family, Teddy and TFCC's agents into the ring.

When everyone stood around us, I continued, "You see Marty Calder, these people gathered in this ring; they are my family. They became my family when Teddy and I needed such a family the most, and...I love them for what they've done. From Jason, hiring me to be on his federal task force in Corpus Christi; to the agents who challenged me to be more than I saw in myself, to Jason's son Dillon, who thought I was...pretty special he wanted to date me." The crowd cheered and gave disappointed 'awe' as I spoke further. "I know, I know guys; some of you wanted to tape up my broken heart over the years and be my guy, but Dillon...I needed him for some reason and...he's a good fit for me." Applause rang out as I motioned Leah and Boop to step forward. "But these two ladies, along with Corpus Christi Police Chief Jennifer Vaughn; are the ones who have gone from loving me to hating me, back to loving me in the span of two weeks. And the one aspect they have taught me in that amount of time; my team...my family expanded the day I walked into their office. I love you both for that and I can't thank you enough!"

Santana and I, to show our appreciation for the welcome Leah and Boop extended, we placed our title belts on their shoulders. And then Marty approached Jason. "Jason, this was your first time in a professional wrestling ring, first time to manage talent in this setting. But you already knew these women from your law enforcement endeavors. Tell me, what was it like to ride to war with American Angels?"

Jason held his head close as he hugged us both. "It feels…like victory Marty!" The crowd cheered as Jason continued. "I could spout off about what Tori and I particularly suffered at the Menace, Mike Petrovsky's hands, but why spoil it? Suffice to say, Karma finally frowned on Petrovsky and he'll get his!" The crowd roared again. Man, these fans can't get enough! "Two days ago, Tori and Santana came to me and said, 'Big Papa; we have a little problem. Menace Mike Petrovsky's trying to…thwart our victorious return, by intruding on our match. Would you care to give us…a little backup Saturday night?' And how did I respond you ask? This is the first time in my life, I was in a bar fight, and my wife didn't threaten to divorce me or arrest me. It felt pretty damned good!" The crowd roared as Marty Calder signed off from Houston and the pay-per-view…ended.

As September ended and October loomed on the horizon, Santana and I settled into our usual law enforcement routine. Sadly, we vacated our world tag-team titles to pursue those who would continue the criminal activity or be threats to our country. As a result of our closing twenty-five years of mystery and illegal activity, CIA Director Martin Scofield awarded Santana and I distinguished service plaques for the arrest of Michael Petrovsky. That chapter of Jason's embattled life closed with little fanfare.

Now we dealt with the every-day activity: drug busts, busting up bar fights, illegal gambling operations, deterring homegrown terrorist threats, and the occasional team cookouts at Jason's place. As I finished up some long-overdue paperwork on the Malta case, I caught Jason at the window as he gazed out on Corpus Christi Bay. He knew he had a similar view from his office, but it occurred to me, maybe he had a reason for coming downstairs. So, I got up from my desk and joined him. "Penny for your thoughts…boss?"

"Sailor's lament Tori; things I should've done and things I couldn't do. But as I see the twilight of my career, I find myself looking forward to possibly retiring…and becoming a grandfather."

"Maybe Dillon and I can work that out…after Valentine's Day?" I smiled as he smiled at me. "Yep, I found a home here, and I want to stay."

"Thank you, for giving us a chance to be that family for you, Tori." Jason smiled again as Danny joined us. "Danny?"

"Dispatch, Col. Jessup received a call about a dead Marine mechanic at the Army's maintenance depot here on station. Army CID wants us to handle it." Jason nodded as I went back to my desk. "Grab your gear, dead body at the Army Depot on station!" And away we go!

Then out of the blue, Dominique appeared. "The dead body is a false alarm. Trust me."

"Okay, how did we get a dispatch about a dead Marine?" Then David walked up and smiled. "Of course," Jason shook his head. "So, I didn't invite you two here...who did?"

I looked over and Santana stood. "I did, and before you get mad Jason, I cleared it with Vale and Director Darrow. We still have one piece of unfinished business with all this adventure...the chest?"

Jason nodded; then he glared at Santana. "Next time...Angel, clear it with your Archangel before you do something like this again?"

Santana answered sheepishly, "Yes sir." Then she reached into her bottom right desk drawer and removed the small eighteenth-century, antique iron chest. "David, I believe this belongs to your family and that...of Alexander's?"

David accepted the old chest with the Russian S over the keyhole. "Either a Sardovsky or Sartinsky could have opened this and won the clan wars centuries ago. For the evil enemy...eternal darkness, for the light, salvation for all." Then David looked at all of us and smiled. "Cardinal Arthur Devane doesn't need to know this chest ever existed. Or...that it still exists. We'll keep it in the secure archive vault at DMD Security."

"Dad took steps to secure the information years ago." Santana smiled. "And only Jason and this team know what we know...but not everyone."

Then David smiled. "Thank you, American Angels. You've done our peoples...a great service."

I walked up and hugged both David and Dominique Matthews. "You've watched over my family, helped my father out with a job so can be productive, and we have a solid friendship. As far as I am concerned, all debts are square!" I waved my arms in front of me and called it safe.

The Jason Vaughn Case Files
Black Widow Murders
Master Sleuth
Sailor's Blues

Vaughn: NCIS
First Test
Tigers Forever
Law of the Road
Savannah on My Mind
Deadly Force
Operation Night Wolf: Man Hunt
Operation Night Wolf: End Game
The Aunt Boop Mob
The Daughter's James

Task Force Corpus Christi
Gulf Coast Wraith
Storm Rider and the Specter

The Joseph Hampton Mysteries
Foreman's Fortune
Suicide Warrior

Christmas Shorts
Savannah Christmas
Christmas I Do's

For more by author Jim E. Johnson; please visit https://www.johnsonmedia. biz

ABOUT THE AUTHOR

Growing up in West Texas with only a reading interest in comic books, Jim E. Johnson never cultivated much an interest in reading much less writing. But when TV series such as *Kindred: the Embraced*, and *Buffy the Vampire Slayer*, Johnson looked at writing his first book *Soldier and the Lady*.

After some methodical research led to this first novel published in 2005, he added other writing credits. Which include the novel series lists: *The Jason Vaughn Case Files, Vaughn: NCIS, and the Joseph Hampton Mysteries.* And articles such as: *A Whole New Game* for the Abilene Reporter News, *Market Research Tips and Publishing* for both the Abilene Writers Guild Newsletter and Writing.Com.

Johnson is a former Executive Board Member of the Abilene Writers Guild and a current member of The Authors Marketing Guild. He lives in Abilene, Texas with his wife Wilma.

PREVIEW OF A NEW BOOK BLACK OUT

ONE

The previous months in Corpus Christi have flown by as I settled into my life here as part of Task Force Corpus Christi. As October closes and November draws near, I kept a close eye on my new boyfriend, NCIS SAC Jason Vaughn's son Dillon. Today my partner Santana Garvin and I worked on the Texas A&M-Corpus Christi campus near the Dugan Wellness Center. NCIS received a dispatch that concerned a Navy ROTC midshipman who appeared drunk and disorderly at the gymnasium. Part of the special interdiction mandate requested by the campus administration; our job was to investigate anything unusual that transpired.

In the case of the midshipman, a young woman named Jessica Dorn, she began to strip naked in the middle of the NROTC unit's physical training or PT session. We re-dressed her and escorted her to NCIS as a precaution. I rode in the back of our G-ride with Midshipman Dorn as Santana drove. She started coming out of her trance as we drove through NAS Corpus Christi's Ocean Drive entrance. "Are you feeling better Midshipman Dorn?" I took a visual inventory of this young lady: dark hair, blank hazel eyes, pouty lips and a gray tank-top with matching shorts. Whatever put her in such a strange mood had also done this to another female Navy midshipman.

Santana reminded me of this girl a bunch. She also had the dark hair, hazel brown eyes due to her contact lenses, and a very fit figure. And that's because we once roamed the highways and by-ways as professional wrestlers. But due to our last case, Santana and I have put our secondary career on hold until the heat from all the issues with the Dixie Mafia blew over. Of course, being Victoria Dominique Blanton or Tori Blanton for short; my father Teddy lived in Dallas these days and worked as the chef of DMD International's president Dominique Dubois Matthews.

But, back to the business at hand. I decided to try again with my young midshipman named Dorn. "Are you currently taking any medications that might cause you to behave strangely?"

"No, I'm not taking any medications and no, I feel sick to my stomach."

"San, pull over please?" Santana stopped the car as Dorn dove out and started retching on the shoulder of the road. When she finished puking her guts out, I handed her a breath mint and let her return to the car's back seat. I carefully used a small pocketknife I kept in case I needed it and scooped up as much of the vomit as I could. I sealed the evidence bag, logged it and made myself a mental note to drop it by Chip Meeker's lab when we returned to the office.

We resumed our trek back to TFCC/NCIS as Dorn apologized. "Sorry about that; must've been something I ate at the campus cafeteria. I hardly ever get sick like that."

"That's why I scooped up some of the vomit. I want to know if someone put something in your food, or if the cooks served a bad batch of something. Do you know another midshipman named Taylor Morgan?"

"Taylor? Taylor's my roommate Agent Blanton. What happened to her?"

Santana and I have another piece of this puzzle. Both Dorn and Morgan were either poisoned or drugged and both had the same reaction to it. I set out to calm and sooth the young midshipman. "Taylor's at the Poison Unit at Christus-Spohn Hospital. Whatever you two ingested, it affected you both in a similar manner. Both of you acted strangely after you had lunch or dinner at the campus cafeteria. We obtained a sample of blood from Taylor and ran a toxicology screen; she had Scopolamine or Devil's Breath in her bloodstream. Someone programmed her to strip during PT and dance around like she was in a rainstorm."

Dorn shook her head. "Why would someone do that to us? We're just scholarship students from the Rio Grande Valley.

"We're not a threat to anyone!" When she started to sob on my shoulder, Santana looked at me in the rear-view mirror. *Someone is either targeting female NROTC midshipmen, or someone targeted these two ladies for a reason.*

Once we arrived at NCIS, all three of us ended up in the fourth-floor conference room where our boss, NCIS SAC Jason Vaughn, sat waiting for us. "Agent Blanton; give me a sit-rep."

Now Jason was a man of five-foot-eight-inches tall and weighed approximately a trim two-hundred pounds. He wore suits made by Dominique Dubois Matthews' businessmen's fashion line. Jason kept his green eyes focused on me as he waited for my preliminary report.

I nod to Santana as she escorts our young guest to get some water. "We could've done this in your office."

"I wanted Midshipman Dorn to see how serious this might get. According to Captain Woodman, who is in charge of the entire NROTC unit at TAMU-CC, both of these midshipmen exhibited the same odd behavior after lunch at the campus dining hall. So where are we on this?"

"I called over to Col. Jessup's office and spoke to Quid. We asked if they could send an undercover over to the dining hall and covertly ask around about any new chefs or ingredients. Unfortunately, they're in the middle of an MP-Readiness Deployment Exercise. So, I'll get on the dining hall angle first thing after we get Midshipman Dorn calmed down." Jason knew due to other case concerns; Santana and I were working this as quickly as possible while the campus interdiction program was still in effect. "Anyway, I have some...regurgitation to run down to Chip."

"She threw up on the way here? That's one difference between them. It may not be Devil's Breath."

"The thing with Devil's Breath; both had short-term memory loss...a block of memory wiped clean."

"GHB or other roofies can cause the same kind of memory loss. Okay, go run the puke down to Chip and see what turns up." As I turned to leave, Jason called back, "How's San doing?"

I shook my head. "You mean after Jim Slater decided to return to Houston to work in the Marshal's office there? She's still mad as hell. He just broke up with her; no warning and no goodbye." I simply grimaced and shook my head. "He'd better not come back anytime soon, or Lydia will need to pack him up in a cast iron suit with a Kevlar interior."

"He might need to invest in a Miguel Caballero line of suits...as well as a new Kevlar vest." Jason smiled as Santana walked into the conference room. "How are you San?"

"Getting better every day Jace. But Jim Slater won't be in serviceable condition if I ever see him again; really, I'm fine."

"I'll...let you two talk while I run down to the lab." I left quickly as possible and went to visit Meeker.

Chip Meeker wasn't your average lab rat. He was one of those gamers who loved conspiracy theories and went down every investigative rabbit hole we needed to find the truth. The cute-as-a-button red-haired lab chief smiled as I walked in. "Well, we finally meet NCIS Special Agent Tori Blanton. Chip Meeker; it's a pleasure." I looked Chip over and his freckles complimented his red hair. His red t-shirt had a Halo Five design on the front and made a wicked contrast to his navy trousers and white sneakers. "I would hug you, but Jason warned me about your pro wrestling background."

I smiled as he chuckled nervously, "Aw don't worry about that Chip. If you start to bear-hug me, I might flip you around in a belly-to-belly suplex; but I will restrain myself if you can tell me what's in this puke."

"Ah, lovely puke; where did you get it?"

"From our most recent and possible victim, TAMU-CC NROTC Midshipman Jessica Dorn. She up-chucked on the way here." I gave Chip a sideways glance as he smiled. "You know, Jason told me you really get off on the forensics side of this job."

"Yeah, I tend to freak people out for the first time they meet me. You should've seen your partner Sgt. Garvin's reaction to me." Santana gave me the play-by-play on her first encounter with Chip. Apparently, he was wearing a pair of yoga pants and orange high-top tennis shoes. Yes, Chip's a real character. Santana spent too many months as DEA and in the ring to deal with Chip's brand of weirdness. Lucky for Chip, I'm immune. "I'll get on it!"

"Thanks, Chip; you're a prince!"

"By the way Tori, I met someone a couple of days ago at the federal courthouse when I went to give a deposition. He's a Justice Department agent named Trevor." I turned and glared at Chip Meeker. I hope he didn't meet who I think he met. "I believe he said his full name was Trevor Martin." Oh damn; anyone but Trevor Martin! "I told him I knew of you but hadn't met you yet."

"Well, if you happen to run into him again; tell him our introduction was brief...and that I am seeing someone new!"

I return to the squad room as everyone's gathered near my desk. "What in the world's going on here?" As I approached my desk, he rose from my chair. The same old dark bristled hair; same chocolate brown eyes and a thin mustache that drove all the women crazy. His father was black, and his mother was Navajo, and I wished Santana had warned me he would appear.

"Look who popped into town Tori?" Santana smiled nervously as I came face-to-face with my ex-boyfriend...Trevor Martin!